Play It Down

Gregory Payette

8 Flags Publishing

Copyright © 2022 by Gregory Payette

All rights reserved. 8 Flags Publishing

This book is licensed for your personal enjoyment only. All rights reserved. This is a work of fiction. All characters and events portrayed in this book are fictional, and any resemblance to real people or incidents is purely coincidental. This book, or parts thereof, may not be reproduced in any form without permission in writing from the publisher.

Print ISBN: 979-8-9858460-5-8

Ebook ISBN: 979-8-9858460-4-1

Chapter 1

JOE WALKED UP THE open stairway, with a slight breeze at his back, stepping off the top step onto the third floor at the Oaks Apartments in North Miami. He glanced out at the orange sky over the parking lot, the sun just starting to rise, then looked at the paper in his hand. He'd already checked it three times, making sure he had the number right.

As he walked past each apartment's green door, he looked at the brass numbers on the wall to the right of the doors until he got to apartment number 309.

He checked the paper in his hand one more time, then knocked.

Joe waited, his ear turned toward the door trying to listen. But it seemed to be quiet on the other side. He looked over toward the stairs, looked at his watch, and glanced over his shoulder at the door on the other side of the hall.

A car with a loud muffler drove along the street on the other side of the parking lot.

Nobody came to the door.

He waited another thirty seconds, looked at his watch again, and knocked once more.

This time, he heard the slide of the chain on the other side, followed by the *click-clack* of two separate locks, one after the other.

The door opened. On the other side stood a woman with messy, dirty-blonde hair, wearing a white terry-cloth robe like the ones seen in hotels. A sweet, fruity smell came out from the apartment. Joe thought maybe it was one of those artificial air fresheners you plug in the wall, the kind he always assumed was poison.

"Are you Suzanne?"

She stared out at him with her blue eyes, somewhat bloodshot, one opened more than the other, like she'd taken a shot to one eye. The woman pushed her hair down on her head with her flattened hand. "Who the hell are *you*?" She pulled the robe's tie around her waist tighter.

"I'm Joe. I'm looking for your husband, Craig."

The woman, in her late thirties, kept her eyes on his and shook her head. "He's not around here anymore."

He tried to look into the apartment, but she pulled the door closed, up against her body. "But he *is* your husband, correct?"

She gave Joe a sly smile and shrugged one shoulder. "On paper, he is. But I don't refer to him as such any longer."

Joe took a quick glance at her bare feet, toenails painted red. "If he's really not here, can you tell me where I can find him?"

"I'm telling you the truth. He's *not* here. I have no idea where he is. And other than the fact he took three grand from my account before he disappeared... I'm not sure I care where he is." She stepped back and started to close the door, but Joe put his arm straight out, putting his hand against the door to stop her from closing it. He used his foot to block the opening.

"Hey! What the hell do you think you're doing?" She tried to push the door closed. "I have a gun in here, you know."

Joe didn't move or take his hand from the door. "I'm not here to cause trouble. I just need to find your husband."

"Stop calling him that, okay? It makes me sick to my stomach just thinking I married such a piece of shit."

"But you *are* still married to him, correct?"

She tried to push the door closed, but Joe had his foot wedged into the opening.

He wondered if she really did have a gun. "Please, listen. What if I told you I could get you your money back? The money he owes you?"

She eased up the pressure on the other side of the door and poked her head out. "I doubt he has any of it left."

Not only did Craig owe Dickie the money he lost, but he also owed the money he was fronted to place the bets in the first place. "He owes a friend—an associate—twenty-five grand. I'm sure I can get my friend to make it worth your while, get you back some of what your husband took from you. But you have to tell me where he is."

She shook her head. "If I *knew* where he was, I'd get it back myself. He left me with nothing."

Joe thought for a moment. "Do you think he's still around here? In Miami?"

She looked out into the open-air hallway, toward the stairs. "He's too dumb to leave the area. I'm sure he's shacked up with some slut he conned into thinking he's not a piece of shit."

"Does he work?" Joe said.

She took a moment before answering. "He was driving a truck, working for a food wholesaler. But that was a while ago. He's not one for holding on to a job."

"What about... does he hang out anywhere?"

Suzanne was quiet, thinking. "He was delivering to the National Pancake House, over on Northwest Forty-Second. Friend of mine who goes there said he saw him hanging around more than once, flirting with the waitresses." She narrowed her eyes. "You're not a cop, are you? You're a dead giveaway, if you are. I mean, the unshaved face, your hair is a little long, and..."

"I'm not a cop."

"I guess you're too cute to be a cop." She looked him over. "So, then, what are you?" Her eyes opened a little wider, clearer than they were when she first opened the door, but still a little bloodshot. "You're not a hit man, *are* you?"

"I'm just looking for your husband."

She held her gaze on him, sizing him up. "So, are you going to tell me your name, or *what?*"

Joe looked past her, into the dark apartment. "It's Joe."

"Joe?" She smiled, like she didn't believe him. "You couldn't come up with something better than *Joe?*"

He didn't respond.

"You have a last name?" she said.

He looked into her eyes and could tell maybe she was all right just by looking at her. But he knew it wasn't necessary for him to tell her much else. "How about we just stick with 'Joe' for now. And I'll assume it's all right to call you Suzanne?"

She smiled. And right there Joe realized she was more attractive than he'd noticed at first, even with her bed head hair and bloodshot eyes, her skin a little pale for someone in Florida.

He couldn't help but wonder what kind of body was attached to the long legs coming out from under her white robe.

"Would you like to come in?" she said, pointing with her thumb over her shoulder. "I can make some coffee."

Joe couldn't help but think there was a chance Craig was inside that apartment. Maybe she was going to set Joe up, get him inside...

He looked at his watch. "You know, how about I take a rain check, let you get back to whatever it is you were doing."

She stepped over the threshold, leaning against the frame of the door. "I was just sleeping," she said with a sly smile. "Isn't that what most people do this early in the morning?"

Joe heard a door open behind him and looked over his shoulder.

A good-looking young man walked out of the apartment across the hall, dressed in khaki pants, with a blue blazer over his shirt and tie: hair slicked back, clean shaven, if he even shaved at all. He looked like a kid straight out of college.

He gave Joe a nod and looked at Suzanne, a crooked smile on his face. "Good morning, Mrs. Peters." He stood still for a moment, staring back at her.

She watched him head down the stairs. "Have a nice day at work," she said.

Joe found it a little odd the way this woman, twice the kid's age, stared at him like he was a piece of meat. But then he thought maybe he should go catch the kid in the parking lot, ask if he'd seen anything. Or anyone.

"I'm going to give you my number," he said. "Maybe you can give me a call if you hear from your husband?"

"Sure, I guess I can do that," she said. "But I doubt I will."

"You doubt you'll call me? Or you doubt you'll hear from him?"

She smiled, her hand out, holding it open. "Just give me your number."

He pulled a pen and piece of paper from his pocket, leaning with the paper against the wall as he wrote the number down and handed it to her.

She looked it over, backed away from the door, and closed it without another word.

Joe stood there, hands in his jacket pockets like he wasn't sure she'd open it again. But then he heard the chain slide across the top of the door, followed by two locks clicking.

He went down the stairs to the parking lot. The sun had risen and brightened up since he first got there. He looked around the lot for the kid from across the hall, but the only cars he heard were the ones out on Northeast Third.

He unlocked the driver's side door of his Mercedes, a 1986 convertible with the original forest-green paint. His friend Dickie Caldwell had picked it up for him at a steal, knowing how much Joe liked those German luxury cars. Not the new ones. He didn't like much of anything that was new.

Joe put down the windows but left the top up. The car had a smell to it he hadn't been able to get rid of, embedded somewhere in the air system or buried in the foam under the cracked leather seats. He hadn't planned to dump any money into it, figuring he'd just live with the smells and sounds that came with just about anything that was vintage.

He turned the key in the ignition and pushed in a Joe Cocker cassette he'd picked up from his friend Juan's pawnshop, south of Little Havana. Joe hadn't been in to see Juan in a few weeks, usually dropping in whenever he could to see what vinyl albums had come in. But ever since he got the Mercedes, he had Juan keep his eye out for cassettes. He listened to just about anything—rock, country, jazz, R&B—but preferred the older stuff. With the last cassette produced sometime around 2002, it wasn't like there was any other option.

He opened the center console and took out his phone, tapped Dickie's name, and put it on speaker.

It rang five times before Dickie finally picked it up. "How'd you make out?" he said, the first thing out of his mouth.

Joe said, "Good morning to you too, Sunshine."

Dickie didn't respond. There was a ruffling sound on the other end and the phone got muffled.

"Dickie?" Joe said. "You there?"

After a brief pause, Dickie said, "Yeah, I'm here. I'm still in bed. I was just hoping to wake up to some good news for once."

"Oh," Joe said. "I get it. You're *all business* today." He looked in the rearview mirror toward the apartment building on the far side of the parking lot from where he'd parked. "Sorry to inform you: no luck. Craig wasn't there. I spoke to his wife, though."

"The wife, huh? She's a hottie, isn't she?"

Joe adjusted the rearview mirror so he could look at himself and the bags under his eyes. He was tired. "She said she hasn't seen him."

"And?"

"And *what*?"

"She's probably full of shit?" Dickie said. "Did you go inside?"

Joe slipped on his sunglasses and turned the mirror back so he could see across the parking lot behind him. "No, I didn't go inside. She was sleeping when I first got there."

"So what, she was sleeping? You couldn't have gone inside, had a cup of coffee? Take a look around?"

Joe turned up the volume on the stereo when "You Can Leave Your Hat On" came on. He kept it low enough, he could still hear Dickie but didn't like the way the conversation was going. "Why are you giving me shit?" he said. "All of a sudden, you don't trust what I'm doing?"

"Of course I trust you, Joey. But, I mean, for a tough kid, sometimes you let these good-looking broads push you around more than you should. I don't know what it is, you get weak in the knees or..."

Joe laughed. "You're kidding, right? What women do I let push me around?"

"I'm just saying, she tells you he's not there; you just walk away without even suspecting she's lying to you?"

"Of course I thought about it. I'm still here, watching the place." He didn't tell Dickie she invited him in for coffee. But he could tell she was being straight with him. He was almost certain Craig Peters wasn't there. But even the slightest bit of doubt... "What am I supposed to do?" he said. "Bust down the door? Crash around the place and rip everything apart? You know that's not my gig, Dickie."

Crashing through doors wasn't part of their deal. Joe was paid to track people down. Find out where they were, give a fair warning, then let Dickie do what he had to do. He had a couple of heavies Joe hadn't even met. He didn't want to know what happened once he located his target. He was just the first step: the part that took someone with half a brain.

"Then maybe it's time you take on more of a role," Dickie said. "I don't know why you wouldn't. I told you, it'd be worth it. Maybe you don't want to get your hands dirty?"

"Jesus Christ, Dickie. I've barely started looking for the guy. Why don't you..." He bit his tongue, looked at the arms ticking on the dashboard clock. He watched the second hand tick, almost to the exact beat of the drum coming from the cassette. "What happened to giving me a week to find him?"

Dickie said, "You're the one who said it would be an easy one."

Joe let out a sigh, rolling his eyes. He looked up in the rearview and saw a woman walking down the stairs. He turned and looked over his shoulder to get a better look.

It was Suzanne Peters, dressed, wearing sunglasses, her hair pulled back tight on her head.

She continued into the parking lot, but Joe lost sight of her behind some palm trees and shrubs in the center of the space.

Dickie started to say something into the phone, but Joe didn't listen.

"Let me call you back," he said. He hung up and tossed the phone on the passenger seat, turned, looked back and spotted Suzanne getting into a black Ford Mustang convertible.

Joe grabbed the plaid wool fedora he'd gotten from Juan as nothing more than a disguise for a job he did for Dickie. It reminded him of Gene Palmer, one of the old writers at the *Post* who taught Joe the ropes when he was just a dumb kid out of college. It was a little warm for the Miami heat, but Joe liked wearing it.

He noticed the music had gotten lower, and he wasn't sure why. He turned up the volume a notch, then turned the key in the ignition to start the engine.

But nothing happened. The ignition just clicked...

Click-click-click-click-click-click-click.

"Shit," he said, under his breath. He looked out the open passenger window, toward the entrance to the parking lot and saw Suzanne in the black Mustang driving onto Northeast Third. As soon as she hit the street, the car took off, the engine loud but fading as she turned the corner and disappeared.

Chapter 2

Joe leaned back against the front fender on the passenger side of the Mercedes, his arms crossed, watching the blue tow truck with *Ray's Auto Repair* painted on the door pull into the parking lot and drive toward him.

Dickie's mechanic, Colt, was behind the wheel, a cigarette hanging from his mouth. He turned the wheel, pulled forward, and parked across four empty spaces to the right of Joe's car. He stepped down from the truck, took a drag from his cigarette and walked toward the hood of the car. "What happened?"

Joe shrugged. "I don't know. It won't start."

Colt stood at the front of the car, his back up against the shrubs. "Pop the hood, will you?"

Joe opened the driver's side door and pulled the latch under the seat.

Colt lifted the hood, tucked the support rod under it, and leaned with both hands resting on the steel frame between him and the engine. He reached his hand in and wiggled a wire running from the battery as Joe stood to the side, watching.

"It was running fine," Joe said. "Perfect."

Colt glanced at him, nodding. "Yeah, this cable's bad. Honestly, it looks like someone messed with it."

"You think so?" Joe ducked his head under the hood from the side, watching Colt play with the red cable and pull a wrench from his pocket, tightening the nut on the battery post.

Colt straightened up from over the engine. "Go ahead, see if she'll start."

Joe slid into the driver's side and turned the key. The engine started, first try.

Colt slammed down the hood and wiped his hands on a red rag he pulled from his back pocket. He came around to Joe's door. "You got time, come by the shop and I'll replace the cable. It's all right now, but the bolt's stripped. It'll only take a few minutes."

Joe looked at the clock on the dashboard, then toward Colt. "But how come the clock worked? And the radio?"

Colt removed his John Deere baseball cap and scratched his sweat-soaked head. "Still had contact with the battery post. Just not enough juice to turn over your engine."

Joe shifted into reverse and threw his right arm over the passenger seat, backing out from the parking space. "I'll bring it over to the shop now, get it taken care of, if that's all right?"

. . . .

Dickie was in his office at the shop, phone to his ear, leaning back in his oversized desk chair with his feet in faded brown leather boat shoes up on the desk. He had his free hand resting on top of his bald head, rubbing it back and forth like he was making a wish.

Dickie's shop was called Ray's Auto Repair, a business Dickie told most people he bought from the original owner, Ray Madison. But the truth was, Ray had gone deep into gambling debt with Dickie and couldn't pay him all what he'd owed. Dickie liked the guy, so gave him a long leash knowing if he had to, he could always take the shop.

So when Ray's debt went up instead of down, that's just what Dickie did: he took the shop. Even though he didn't know the first thing about fixing cars, he hired Colt, then got into selling cars here and there and sold them mostly to people he knew.

Joe remembered the place when it was Ray's, even as far back as when he was a kid. His mother took her car there once or twice after his father, who knew a thing or two about fixing cars, left her high and dry for another woman.

Joe sat down in the green faux-leather chair across from Dickie. The office hadn't changed at all since Ray owned the place: the same brown paneling on the walls, the same tiles on the floor. Even the gray metal desk Dickie sat behind was the same.

He looked behind him out the doorway toward the customer service area, trying not to listen to Dickie's phone call. One of the fluorescent lights over the service counter flickered so much Joe thought it would give someone a seizure.

"Listen," Dickie said, talking loud enough on the phone he didn't seem to care if Joe heard him or not. "This is the last time." His eyes were raised toward the ceiling, his head leaned back with his hand resting on the back of his neck. "Yeah, I know you made good last time. But you can't always depend on someone else like that." He paused, listening. "Carlo, how long have I known you?" Dickie straightened up, leaning forward with his elbows on his desk, his head now resting in his hand. "That's right. I've known you ten years. And I consider you a friend. So I'm just telling you, these bets you've been placing..." Dickie was quiet, rolling his eyes and again shaking his head, listening. "Yeah, I know. You think you're smarter than the rest of us?" Quiet again. "There's a reason guys like me drive the nice cars. You know what I'm saying?" He picked up a pen and scribbled something down on the yellow legal pad in front of him. "All right. But I'm not going to be able to do it again, this don't work out." Dickie was still, switching the phone to the other ear. "All right?" He nodded. "You'd better be, Carlos."

He hung up the phone and ran both hands over his face, his high school class ring still on his left ring finger where his handful of wedding bands used to go. He kept his eyes down on the pad and let out a sigh, still shaking his head. "You know, Joey? I go out of my way to stop people from doing stupid things, but nobody wants to listen. You know what I mean?"

Joe nodded, but didn't ask for details. He didn't need them.

Dickie placed his reading glasses on, started to type onto the keyboard in front of his computer. He looked at the pad, read whatever was written there to himself, his lips moving like he was making sure he'd remember what he just read, and pecked the keyboard with one finger from each hand. "You know what?" he said, his eyes not leaving the keyboard. "Screw 'im. More money for me, the bum loses."

He finished whatever it was he typed and tore the piece of paper from the pad, ripped it in half a couple of times and crumpled it into a ball. He tossed it into the trash can next to his desk and took off his glasses, flinging them across the desk. "So," he said, looking at Joe. "No idea where she went, huh?"

Joe shook his head. "It wasn't ten minutes after I left her apartment. Kind of odd, seeing it looked to me I woke her up out of bed. She certainly didn't look like she was going anywhere when I left."

"No sign of the husband, either, huh?" Dickie said.

"He wasn't there."

Dickie held his gaze on Joe for a moment. "How long were you there, waiting for Colt?"

"About an hour," Joe said.

"And she never came back?"

"I didn't see her. No."

Dickie rubbed his eyes with both hands curled up, like a little boy ready for bed. He leaned back in the chair. "You ever think maybe she wanted you to follow her?"

"For what?" Joe said.

"Well, you said you didn't go inside, right? So you don't know for a fact whether or not he was there. Maybe she knew you were out there, tried to get you away, so he could get out of there."

Joe didn't like Dickie's tone, like for some reason he'd lost his faith in him. "We already went over this."

Ever since Joe had started doing more work for Dickie—almost full-time at that point, doing forty, fifty hours a week—their relationship had changed. And Joe wasn't too excited about where it was going. He had other things he wanted to do. But the money Dickie was paying him was decent and hard to pass up.

Dickie picked up his phone and looked at the screen, before placing it back down on the desk. "So, what's next?" he said. "I'd suggest you get cracking, before Craig Peters gets too far."

"You're assuming he's still in the area," Joe said, thinking about what Craig's wife had told him. "I told you he owed her three grand, didn't I?"

"Who owes *who* three grand?"

"Craig owes Suzanne. His wife. She said he wrote a check, cashed it for three grand... emptied out her checking account."

Dickie shrugged. "What's that got to do with me?"

Joe was hesitant to continue with Dickie who seemed somewhat more irritated than usual. Joe liked to brush it off as Dickie got older, closer to becoming just another crotchety old man.

"Well," Joe said, "I kind of told her if she helped me track him down, maybe I could talk to you... cut her a little something off the top of whatever money we recover."

Dickie's eyes bugged out, his eyebrows shooting up high on his forehead. "You told her I'd give her three grand for helping you find him? Was this before you thought about the fact she probably made the whole thing up... likely knows exactly where he's hiding?" Dickie picked up the pen and tapped with it on top of the desk. "Joey, why would you promise something like that without talking to me first?"

Joe just stared back at him. "I don't know. I just thought... she didn't seem to show much love for him. I thought maybe a little extra incentive would get her to give him up, if there was something she wasn't telling me."

"You mean, something like that the bastard was probably on the other side of the door, listening to every word you said?" Dickie shook his head. "I know you're a nice guy, Joey. Maybe *too* nice, sometimes. But you just... You want to be in this business, you can't be so goddamn naïve all the time. You know what I'm saying?"

Joe was ready to get up and walk out, tell Dickie what he could do with that pen in his hand. "I don't know how you can say I'm being naïve, when you're doing nothing more than *speculating* he was there."

He got up from the chair and stepped to the window, looking out toward the parking lot. He kept his back to Dickie. "You pay me to find people, not kick down doors. You want me to do that?" He turned around, folded his arms across his chest. "Then I'm not doing it for what you're paying me now. You'll have to pony up."

"Pony up?" Dickie said, smiling. "I already told you—I don't know how many times—you want to take more on, put those muscles of yours to work... I'll throw in another ten percent, on top of the cut you already get."

"Ten percent?" Joe shook his head. "Are you serious?"

"Come on, Joe. I pay you well already, don't I?"

"Not enough where I'm going to put my life on the line. Not any more than I already do."

Dickie sighed. "I know you could handle more, though. I've seen you in action. I think you'd get a kick out of it."

"A *kick* out of it?" Joe laughed, shaking his head. "You think I do this for fun? I already told you, once I get my book finished, I'm out. Done."

Dickie grinned. "I know you see yourself hanging out in some café in Paris, writing the next great novel. You think you're going to make from a book what you could with me? I know ten percent don't sound like a lot. But when you think about it..."

Joe sat quiet, not feeling he needed to explain to Dickie where he could go if he could only get the book done. It had been over a year since he'd found an agent, and he struggled like he never had before, just getting the damn words down on paper.

"I'm not telling you to give up on your boyhood dreams," Dickie said, a bit of sarcasm in his voice. "I'm just saying, like I've told you all along, you put enough money in your pocket working for me, maybe take on a little more of the work, you won't have to worry about paying your bills. Take a little pressure off." He squinted his eyes, like he was thinking. "Isn't it true, authors don't really make much money until they're dead?"

Joe stared back at Dickie, shaking his head. "What are you talking about? Famous painters, maybe, but, I mean, the thing is..."

He wasn't going to bother getting into it.

"Anybody even *read* books anymore?" Dickie said. "I don't ever see anyone with a book. Do *you*? They come in here, everybody's on their goddamn phones, looking at what their friend from high school had for dinner."

Joe slouched in the chair, feeling a bit dejected.

Dickie held a pen, twisting it between both hands. "If I could find someone else to do the work I could trust, I wouldn't be asking you. I know it's not something you ever thought you'd be doing. But I've seen you in action, Joey. You're not afraid to throw someone around when they have something you need. And, the truth is, most of these idiots don't put up much of a fight anyway. You've seen these losers. They're all small-time. They cave easy as it is. If you gotta rough them up a little..." He turned, looked out his office window toward the parking lot. "All I'm asking, you take on a little more of the job until I can find another guy. I promise, you'll be well compensated."

Joe hated the fact he was even having the discussion, like he thought he'd be in a better position by that point in his life. But Dickie was right: money was a necessity. And having more of it wouldn't be such a bad thing. "So, what you're saying is all I do, like I've been doing, is locate someone? But I bring 'em to your doorstep, I get another ten percent?"

Dickie shook his head. "No, you don't bring anyone to my doorstep. You get the money out of 'em. That's all I'm really after. I mean, you don't get the money out of them, there's another course of action you may need to take. That's the part you haven't had to deal with. But we'll worry about that when the time comes."

"You're making it sound easy," Joe said. "And I'm not convinced it is."

Dickie cleared his throat. "It's easier than you'd think. These guys... you put a gun to their heads, suddenly they're able to come up with the money they owe."

"A gun?" Joe said.

Dickie got up from the desk, straightened out the tail of his black, silk button-down shirt, pulling it tight over his khaki shorts. "I know you don't like guns, but—"

"It's not that I don't *like* them. I just prefer not to use them."

"I know, I know. And I've seen you shoot." He laughed. "Not a pretty sight." He looked out the window. "What happened to your friend, the cop? Didn't he say he'd take you out to the range, show you how to shoot?"

Joe nodded. "He did. But I kind of let it slip out one night I was working for you again, and—"

"You told a cop you chase down welshers for me?"

Joe cleared his throat, shaking his head. "Bart's not stupid," he said. "And he's not a cop anymore. He's retired."

Chapter 3

JOE TURNED INTO THE National Pancake House parking lot, up in North Miami, and had to park around the back because the place was so busy. He turned off the engine and sat thinking about what Dickie had asked him to do. He couldn't get his head wrapped around how he'd ended up where he was, going from a fairly successful crime writer to no job at all, then working for a bookmaker, tracking down lowlife gamblers who couldn't pay their debts.

He watched an elderly couple get out of their gold Lincoln Town Car—one with Maine plates—and walk around the corner toward the front of the building.

Maybe he could pull off whatever Dickie needed without the violence, he thought. Maybe just negotiate, persuade the deadbeat to pay Dickie what he owed, be done with it.

But all he heard in his head was Dickie's voice:

Don't be so naïve, Joey.

He got out of the car and walked around to the front of the building, stepping around another older couple taking their sweet time on the walkway. The two weren't far enough from the door when Joe got to it so he held it for them, waiting for what seemed like five minutes before they made it all the way inside ahead of him.

"Thank you, young man," the woman said.

Joe couldn't remember the last time someone had called him that.

The place was full, although somewhat quiet considering all the people who were in there: lots of clanking of dishes and mostly white and gray heads of hair sticking up from over the booths.

He found a single seat at the counter between two men eating, and sat down. He grabbed the menu tucked into the metal condiment holder and looked it over.

A waitress, maybe about Joe's age, came up to him and stood on the other side with a big smile. "Good morning, sweetie," she said. Her pen was in her hand, poised over the pad. "Are you ready to order?"

Joe just stared back at her, shaking his head. "Uh... not really. I just sat down."

"Oh," she said, looking somewhat confused. She glanced toward the vestibule. "I guess someone else must've just been here, right there in your seat." She looked along the counter and toward the entrance to the restrooms. "I guess he left."

Joe looked at the older man to his right, minding his own business. He looked left at a younger man dressed in some kind of blue-collar uniform. He asked the waitress if he should move, in case whoever was sitting there before him came back.

She scratched her head with the end of her pen. "No. I'm sure he just left. We're kind of busy today, so maybe he thought I was too slow." She tucked the pen and pad in her brown smock. "Can I get you a coffee?"

Joe nodded. "Please."

The waitress turned and grabbed a mug and carafe from the counter behind her and poured him a coffee. She placed it down in front of him. "I'll come back in a few minutes for your order."

Joe watched her walk away, then looked down into his cup. He couldn't remember the last time he'd been in a National Pancake House, and was somewhat hesitant to sip the coffee. He sniffed it and glanced at the men on either side of him. Neither paid him any attention, both just eating their breakfast. Joe looked toward the dining area behind him, with all the tables full. Not one empty table.

Was the place even that good?

He opened the menu and looked it over. Of course, the restaurant, as the name indicated, specialized in pancakes. Joe had changed his mind about eating pancakes, thought maybe he'd get something else instead. There was a long time he couldn't eat pancakes, going back to when he was a kid in junior high school, and slept over at his friend's house. In the morning his friend's father blamed Joe for stealing his cigarettes, got good and mean about it. But then the mother forced him to stay and eat pancakes as the father kept chirping about how foolish they were. The mother just served the pancakes and kept quiet.

He pulled out his phone and flipped through his contacts, stopping at his friend Bart's number. Joe thought maybe he should send him a text, just to check in. They hadn't spoken in a while, and the last time they did, Bart acted like a real ass, giving Joe shit for the work he was doing for Dickie.

Bart was a retired cop who didn't like Dickie very much. With over thirty years as a member of the Miami Police Department, going back to when it was the Metro-Dade PD, he told Joe he couldn't understand why he'd want to be associated with a man like Dickie.

Joe started to write a text, but the waitress showed up again and stood in front of him, the pen and pad in her hand.

She smiled, although it looked a bit forced. "Are you ready to order, darlin'?"

Joe hadn't decided, but picked up the menu and quickly glanced over it. "How about, uh, I'll have the scrambled eggs..." He ran his finger over the items. "Wheat toast. And a glass of orange juice."

"What size?"

"Large." He scanned the menu one more time before closing it, wanting to make sure he ordered enough. He was hungry. "I'll take a side of those hash browns." He closed the menu and handed it to the waitress.

"Is that it?" she said.

Joe thought for a moment. "Do you have anything somewhat healthy I can get? On the side?"

She gave him a look, like her lids were heavy. "We sell pancakes, sweetie."

Joe took the menu back from her and gave it a quick look. "Bring me a fruit cup. Please."

She wrote it down on the pad and walked away, stepping through the swinging door into the kitchen.

Joe sipped his coffee. It wasn't bad, although it had gotten cold because he'd let it sit for too long.

The door swung open from the kitchen and the waitress walked out, balancing a handful of dishes in her hands. She started past him, but Joe put up his hand for her to stop. He said, "Can I ask you a question when you're done with that?"

She nodded but continued around the counter before he could ask. She delivered food to a table with four women, said something Joe couldn't hear, but all four women laughed as she walked away from the table and stepped around the counter. She wiped her hands on the side of her brown skirt and said to Joe, "You had a question?"

He leaned forward on the counter and kept his voice low. "Any chance you know who delivers here for Siskey Foods?"

She looked up at the clock on the wall. "I think they've already come today. He was here early, but there may be another delivery this afternoon."

"Actually, I'm looking for someone; a man who delivers for them. At least, he used to. Name is Craig Peters."

She shook her head and started to walk away. "Sorry, I haven't seen him."

"Hold on," Joe said. "But, you know who he is? I understand there was a woman who works here he might've been hanging around."

"Oh," she said. "Wendy?"

"Was she a waitress?"

"She was one of the managers."

Joe sipped his coffee. "Any chance she's here right now?"

She shook her head. "Wendy doesn't work here anymore. And, honestly, I don't remember the last time I saw Craig. It's been a few weeks."

Joe watched the man to his left get up and leave. "Any chance you know how to get in touch with her? Or, if you or anyone else knows where I might be able to find Craig?"

She stared back at Joe, a look on her face like she was wondering what he was up to. "All the girls around here found him kind of creepy. He'd try to flirt, but he was so gross, the way he'd keep his shirt open at the top, show off the hair on his chest." She snorted out a slight laugh.

"What about Wendy?" Joe said. "Did these two have something going on?"

The waitress shrugged. "I don't know. You can go ask her. Last I heard she was running a bar up in Miami Gardens."

"You know the name of it?"

She shook her head. "No, but I can go in back, see if one of the cooks know. One of 'em lives up that way."

Joe shifted on the uncomfortable stool. "I'd appreciate it, if anyone knows..."

The waitress started to walk toward the swinging door but stopped. She turned back to Joe. "Are you a cop?"

"Nah, I'm just trying to help a friend." He picked up his coffee, took a sip and watched her go through to the kitchen. He pulled out his phone and flipped through the recent calls. He'd missed one of them from Lauren.

Lauren was a friend of his; actually more than a friend, but he didn't quite know what to call it. He'd known her for as long as he could remember, going back to their time working together at the *Miami Post*. She'd moved out of Miami for a job with a newspaper up in Daytona, and the two had what some would call a long-distance relationship, even though neither saw themselves as a couple. And the most they'd see each other was once or twice a month—sometimes more, sometimes less.

But Joe missed Lauren when she wasn't around. Whatever they had together, for the most part, seemed to work out all right.

He used his phone and punched *Craig Peters* into the search bar.

The waitress came back through the swinging door, plates balanced in both hands, walking right past Joe toward the dining area. He turned and watched her deliver the plates to a table with two older couples, then stepped over to the table with the older couple who had walked in when Joe had.

She rushed past Joe and back into the kitchen without a word, acting like Joe wasn't there. He could tell she was busy, but wondered if she'd spoken to anyone about the bar where this Wendy lady supposedly worked.

He had searched online for Craig Peters a handful of times before and had always come up empty. He didn't find the man anywhere on social media, which wasn't that odd considering he was running from a debt owed to someone who'd whack more than just his credit if he didn't pay it back. The one thing Joe *did* come across was a business, Peters Construction, listing Craig Peters as the owner. But Joe found nothing else about the business, and wasn't sure it even existed or maybe had gone out of business.

Made sense, since the guy was delivering pancake batter for a living.

Joe did a quick search on his phone for Craig's wife, Suzanne. Unlike her husband, there was plenty about her online. He couldn't quite figure out what she did for work. He thought, at first, maybe she was an artist. She had paintings posted on different sites. *They weren't bad*, he thought. She also had a so-called blog, although it looked like every other blog out there, with the last post from four years ago.

When he had first looked her up, the night before he showed up at her apartment, he found her on a couple of dating sites, which is part of the reason he believed her when she'd said Craig wasn't there, at the apartment.

The kitchen door swung open and Joe slipped his phone into his pocket. He looked up as the waitress walked toward him with plates and a bowl in her hands, placing them down in front of him. He looked down at the eggs and the hash browns and the fruit bowl. She turned from him, grabbed a tall glass, and poured orange juice from the big brown plastic box-like machine behind her with a Minute Maid sign on the front.

"Is that fresh squeezed?" he said, smiling as she turned to him.

"At some point, I'm sure it was," she said with a grin, placing the glass in front of him on the counter. She looked to her left and right and over her shoulder toward the kitchen. Leaning down, her hands on the counter, she kept her voice low and said, "Wendy runs the Village Lounge, up in Miami Gardens. One of the guys back there said she owns the place. I don't know if that's true or not."

• • • • • • • • • •

Joe drove down Biscayne Avenue and turned into the parking lot at Mickey Cho's, the restaurant overlooking Biscayne Bay. Even though Dickie had asked him to meet him there for lunch, Joe was already full from breakfast.

Besides, he didn't like sushi, and that's what Dickie almost always ordered for both of them every time they met there.

Joe parked his car near the entrance and walked through the double glass doors into the restaurant.

Dickie was already at the bar, eating. He turned as Joe sat on the stool next to him. "Where've you been?"

"Didn't you get my text?" Joe said.

Dickie picked up his phone off the bar, pulled his reading glasses from his shirt pocket and slipped them on his face. He read Joe's text:

Running late. Be there asap.

Dickie wiped his mouth with the cloth napkin from his lap. "Oh, okay. I didn't see that." He put his hand on Joe's forearm. "I'm sorry, Joey. I was being a bit of a hard ass earlier." He leaned forward on the bar and sipped from his martini glass. "I haven't been sleeping well lately, you know. If I don't get my beauty rest, I get a little crotchety." He took another sip from his glass.

Joe brushed it off with a shrug. "I hadn't noticed," he said. But of *course* he had noticed the way Dickie had been acting like a jerk for at least the past few weeks.

"You know what I need?" Dickie dipped a piece of sushi into a small glass dipping bowl with the soy sauce and wasabi, before he finished. "I need a pretty lady to tuck me in at night." He wiped his hands with the napkin, fixing it again on his lap. He cleared his throat, leaned with his elbows on the bar and turned to Joe. "Scarlett's out, you know."

"Scarlett?" Joe said. "She's out of prison?"

Scarlett was Dickie's last girlfriend. And he still talked about her, even though she was the one who had schemed him into giving up a few hundred grand to get her back after a kidnapping that never actually happened. Joe was the one who, at the time, had smelled something fishy when he'd first met her. And in the end, he was the one who got Dickie his money back.

That's when Dickie realized Joe had talents that went far beyond being able to write a good column about local crime. He knew Joe had talents they could both benefit from.

But Joe couldn't figure out why Dickie would even give Scarlett a second thought. The woman purposely tried to clean him out. She *did* clean him out. And now it was as if he'd blocked out what she'd done. Or chose to ignore it for some reason.

Although it wasn't often that a short, balding man in his late sixties, with a belly you could rest a drink on, woke up next to a beautiful woman in her twenties.

Joe swiveled on the stool to face Dickie. "I hope you're not talking to her again, *are you?*"

Dickie didn't exactly answer. "Well, Joey, you get to be my age... the seas with all those fish start to dry up. You know what I mean?" He sipped his martini and looked straight ahead toward the bay through the windowed wall at the back of the bar.

"By the way," Joe said, "I have a lead: a woman who may know where I can find Craig Peters. She runs a bar, up in Miami Gardens."

Dickie stuck another piece of sushi in his mouth and followed it with a sip of his martini, then wiped his hands with his napkin. "You think she'll know where he is?"

Joe didn't want to be overly optimistic, have Dickie up his ass if it turned out to be a dead end. "I'm taking a drive up there when I leave here. I'll find out what she knows."

Dickie nodded, pushed the plate of sushi toward Joe. "You gonna have some?" He reached for a small empty cocktail dish he had in front of him and slid it in front of Joe. "You can't go out there on an empty stomach."

Chapter 4

Joe headed north on Third Street, turned left, drove another mile, and jumped on 95, heading north. After a couple of miles, he took the exit for Route 441 and turned right at the Taco Bell onto Northwest Second Avenue, drove another block and into the parking lot of a place called the Village Lounge.

The property, including the building and the parking lot and just about everything around it, appeared to be run-down and in disrepair. The pavement was cracked with chunks of asphalt missing. The sign, the Village Lounge, was missing one of the L's in Village.

It was hard to tell from the outside exactly what kind of place it was. Joe thought at first maybe it was a strip club, or just some kind of trashy nightclub.

He parked the Mercedes out front, put the roof up, and stepped out. The lot was empty, the only noise outside coming from some kind of construction machinery off in the distance.

A car drove by as he walked up a concrete ramp. He grabbed the rusty handrail but yanked his hand away when the sharp edge of chipped paint poked into his palm. He stood in front of the plate-glass door at the entrance and tried to look inside, but the glass was taped over with faded, homemade-looking signs promoting what appeared to be nightly events at the Village Lounge: *Karaoke night on Wednesdays, Trivia Night Thursdays, Milk Drink Mondays*. That last one caught Joe's eye, made him gag just thinking about it. He'd never heard of *Milk Drink Mondays* and wondered what it could possibly mean. A White Russian, perhaps? He didn't have much use for milk as it was, but mixing it with liquor was a whole different ball game he wasn't interested in playing.

Joe assumed the place was closed, but was surprised when he yanked on the handle and the door pulled open. He walked inside to a place much brighter than he'd expected, mostly from the hot lights on the ceiling. He looked up at the large fans turning hanging from the ceiling and almost tripped on the push broom leaning up against a black lectern.

He heard a voice—maybe two—from somewhere toward the back. But only for a second.

The place stank of stale beer and damp cigarettes. The walls, ceilings, and doors were all colored black, like someone had gone around with a big power paint sprayer and hit everything in sight. A stage to his right looked like it was made out of scrap wood, thrown together in a couple of hours. Like everything else, it was also painted black, although you could see some of the bare wood underneath.

Four doors blended into the walls, making them easy to miss. He thought about how hard it'd be to find them at night, when the lights weren't so bright. Although one of the doors on the wall to Joe's left, just beyond the bar, had the illuminated emergency EXIT sign over the top of it. The two doors to the left of the stage were for the bathrooms. One for the boys, the other for the girls. The only other door had an EMPLOYEES ONLY sign on it.

There were at least a dozen or so small round tables with two chairs each, plus another five larger tables with four chairs. The long bar to the left had roughly twenty stools, all pulled away from the bar.

He still couldn't quite figure out what kind of place it was. It reminded him of the old bars he'd gone to in his early twenties, when he'd go out almost every night to see live music, wherever he could find it. Some of the bars were seedy, like the one he was in.

The door toward the back with the EMPLOYEES ONLY sign opened, and a woman walked through. She carried a large cardboard box between her arms, big enough it covered her face, so she might not have noticed Joe. But she didn't appear startled when she stuck her head out from behind it and looked right at him.

"Who the hell are you?" she said. "How'd you get in here?"

Joe pointed with his thumb over his shoulder. "The door was open."

The woman wore a white tank top, showing off her sagging breasts through the opening in her shirt, with the way she was holding the box. Her skin was tan, but looked like cracked leather from too much of that Florida sun, and long, skinny legs with raisin-like skin hanging from her bones coming out from under a pair of orange gym shorts. In fact, the way she was dressed made Joe think she was at one time a waitress at Hooters.

"Goddamn Eddie," the woman said, dropping the box down on the floor. "I don't know how many times I tell him to lock the goddamn door when he leaves." She pulled a stack of napkins out from the box and started stuffing them into the black metal napkin holders on each table. "Well, we don't open until four, so if you're looking for a drink, you'll have to come back later." She started toward the door. "I'll lock it behind you."

Joe didn't move. "I'm not here for a drink." He paused and looked her over. "Any chance your name's Wendy?"

She squinted her eyes and held her gaze on him for a moment. "Who's asking?"

Joe was set to give it back to her, if that's the way she wanted to play. He looked around the place. "Well, since I'm the only one here, I'd have to say *I'm* the one asking." He smirked.

She pulled a stack of napkins from the box. "Are you going to tell me what you want? Or do I have to call the police?"

"You don't have to call the police. But I'll go ahead and assume you're Wendy if you're not going to tell me?"

She stopped what she was doing. "If I tell you I am, you gonna leave me alone so I can get this place cleaned up?" She looked him up and down. "You look like a normal guy. But, to be honest, you're making me a little nervous." She looked toward the bar. "And, just so you don't try anything crazy... I *do* have a gun."

Joe shook his head. "I'm looking for someone. And I heard you might know where he is."

She narrowed her eyes, staring back at him. "Well, if you'd stop beating around the bush and just tell me who the hell it is you're looking for... maybe I can tell you. But I don't have all day."

Joe glanced over his shoulder toward the front door. "I'm looking for Craig Peters."

She reached into the box and pulled out another stack of napkins, continued loading the holders on the table as if she hadn't heard what he'd said. She had her back to him now, leaning over a table. When she finally straightened up and turned toward him, she was shaking her head. "Never heard the name before."

Joe had a slight grin on his face. He was almost certain she was lying. "How about you tell me the last time you saw him?"

She grabbed more napkins from the box and filled another holder at a table closer to the bar. "I don't know if you're hard of hearing or what. But I just told you, I don't know anyone by that name." She nodded toward the door. "Now, if we're done here, I'd like you to leave. Or, as I've already told you, I'm going to call the cops." She stared him in the eye and gripped the box at the top with both hands, tore it in half, then dropped it on the floor. She crushed it flat with her white Reeboks. She picked up the flattened box and walked through the door at the back.

Joe walked after her. He wondered if she was serious about the gun. "Wendy?" he said, standing just outside the door. He tried to peek inside, but she came right back out, closing the door behind her.

She walked toward the bar. "Why are you still here?" she said. "I can't help you."

He followed her over, watching her go around the other side of the bar.

She reached down and Joe braced himself for the possibility she'd be reaching for a gun.

But instead she pulled out a pack of Newport Lights, stuck one of the cigarettes in her mouth and gave it a light. She took a deep drag, closing her eyes, and leaned on the bar, raising her chin and blowing a stream of smoke toward the ceiling. "So why're you looking for, uh... what's this guy's name? Gary?"

Joe leaned on the bar, a few spaces down from where Wendy stood on the other side. "Why don't you just tell me where I can find him, so I can let you get back to work?"

She took another drag and stared back at him, sucking her bony cheeks in as she inhaled. She held the smoke in, like she was smoking a joint, finally blowing it out in Joe's direction. "You want a drink?" she said.

Joe wasn't sure why she'd suddenly offered him one. He glanced at the glasses not far from where he stood, a few dozen turned upside down on top of the red mat next to the beer tap. He noticed the stains inside the glasses and shook his head. "I'm good," he said. "So, are you trying to tell me you don't know Craig? Because that's not what I've heard."

She shrugged. "I don't know what to tell you, buddy. I've never heard the name." She held her cigarette with one hand but reached the other behind the bar.

Joe didn't like that. "You know what?" he said. "Why don't you do me a favor. If you decide you've suddenly heard the name Craig Peters, then—"

There was a crash in the back, like something had been smashed or tipped over. Joe looked toward the EMPLOYEES ONLY door, then back at Wendy.

She hadn't moved.

Joe said, "Aren't you going to see what that was?"

"What *what* was?" She acted as if she hadn't heard a thing.

Joe turned from the bar and started toward the door at the back.

"Hey, where do you think you're going?" she said.

He had a bad feeling, turned to look back, and saw the woman had put her cigarette down in an ashtray and replaced it in the same hand with a .38 pistol. She had it pointed right at Joe.

He ran for the EMPLOYEES ONLY door and crashed through it right as a shot was fired. The wood frame on the door shattered right behind him as he rolled on the floor and back up on his feet. He stood in the back room, looking at dozens of boxes stacked up against the wall and all around him. There was a walk-in cooler with the door left wide open.

He looked to his left toward an open exterior door with sunlight coming in from outside. Hurrying toward it, he glanced back as Wendy entered the area and fired another shot. Joe ducked and ran for the door, slamming it closed behind him.

He squinted as the bright sunlight blasted him in the face but started after a man running full speed across the parking lot.

The man climbed up a tall chain-link fence and over it, landing on his feet on the other side. He kept running away from Joe without looking back and put quite a bit of distance between the two of them before Joe even made it to the fence.

But Joe ran as fast, grabbed the fence high up and tried to climb it. But another shot was fired, and he had no choice but to jump down without making it over and run away to find cover.

Wendy was coming at him, her gun raised as she fired another shot.

Joe covered his head with his arms and stayed low as he ran along the fence trying to avoid getting shot as Wendy moved closer.

He wasn't paying enough attention to know how many shots she'd already fired. But he guessed she only had one or two left.

She yelled, "You'd better keep running, you son of a bitch. Cops are already on their way!"

Joe looked back at her and saw she'd lowered the gun and was looking it over.

Maybe she'd run out of bullets.

He took his chance and ran toward the front of the building for his car, staying low as he opened the driver's side door. He slid behind the wheel, started the engine and drove out into the street, slouching in the seat with his head low and barely seeing over the steering wheel until he knew he was in the clear. The car skidded out of the parking lot and he took a quick right toward the brick commercial building next door. It looked empty, just like the bar, and had a FOR LEASE sign on the entrance.

He drove slowly around it, looking back and forth for the man he had no doubt was Craig Peters. He made a full lap around the building and came out on the other end, at the front, shaking his head. He turned off the engine and stepped out from his car, looking around the area behind the building, then out toward the street.

A Miami Gardens Police vehicle showed up out of nowhere, blue lights flashing. The officer driving cut the wheel and turned his vehicle, blocking Joe from driving away.

Two officers stepped out, guns raised toward Joe.

One of the officers, gun aimed, yelled for Joe to get down on the ground.

Joe had his hands up, shaking his head. "Whoa, whoa..." he said. "This is a big mistake! I didn't—"

"Get on the goddamn ground!" the officer yelled.

Both cops moved in closer toward Joe, one on either side of him.

"Get on the ground!" he yelled again.

This time, Joe listened and did as he was told, getting on his hands and knees, then onto his chest on top of the hot asphalt.

"Hands on your head!" the other office yelled, moving closer, standing over Joe with his gun pointed at him.

"What did I do?" Joe said from the ground. He turned his head, trying to get a look at the two officers.

The officer closest held Joe down, the other slapped the cuffs on his wrists and read him his rights. The two officers lifted Joe to his feet by the crux of each arm and dragged him to the vehicle.

Joe felt a hand on his head, pushing it down, as he ducked into the back seat, hands cuffed behind his back. He started to say something else, but the car door slammed shut in his face.

Chapter 5

Joe was alone on a bench in a small holding cell at the Miami Gardens Police headquarters when an officer came through another door with a set of keys dangling from his hand. He unlocked the cell door and gave Joe a nod. "Someone's here for you."

Joe stood up from the bench and followed the officer. He kept his mouth shut, as he had when the officers asked him what he was doing at the Village Lounge and why he'd broken into the place.

This was the problem working for Dickie. When something went down the way it did, and someone called the cops and made up a story, Joe had no choice but to bite his tongue. Or make something up. Whatever Wendy had told the police was a lie. But Joe wasn't in a position to deny it.

He signed the papers and got his wallet, his phone, and his keys back, in a large envelope the officer passed under the glass.

Dickie was out in the lobby waiting when Joe walked through the door and turned the corner. He gave Joe a pat on the back. "Don't worry, Joey. Stanley'll get this cleaned up for you."

Stanley, Dickie's lawyer, was the man Dickie liked to call The Fixer because, more often than not, he could make just about any legal problem Dickie had go away. It didn't hurt that Stanley had friends in the US Attorney's Office in Florida and a handful of police officers in greater Miami in his pocket. Dickie was smart enough not to ask too many questions. He just let Stanley do his thing.

Joe and Dickie stepped outside and walked under the yellow glow from the streetlamps on Northwest Twenty-Seventh Avenue, Joe looking back at the station as they headed for Dickie's car.

"How could they just arrest me like that?" Joe said. "Take the word of some crazy lady, looks like she just crawled out of a rat hole. She was the one firing the shots."

"Stand your ground," Dickie said. "We're in one of the few states you can pull out a gun and pop somebody when you feel threatened."

"The only thing she felt threatened about was me finding her boyfriend."

Dickie shrugged. "I still don't know exactly what happened. How about we go get a drink; you can tell me all about it." He walked ahead of Joe and pointed his key fob toward the white Lexus, the handicapped sign hanging from his mirror.

Joe looked up and down the street at all the empty parking spaces. "You really don't see anything wrong with using that?"

"Using what?"

"The handicapped sign, hanging from your mirror?"

Dickie shrugged, gave Joe a look across the roof as he opened the driver's side door. "There's no handicapped people coming to the police station this time of night."

Joe rolled his eyes and opened the passenger door, sliding into the black leather seat.

Dickie said, "You know, I got tickets to the Dolphins next Sunday; you want to go?"

"What? I just got out of jail. I have no idea what I'm doing next Sunday. Probably not going to a football game." Joe looked back over his shoulder toward the police station. "I have to get my car."

"You know where it is?" Dickie said. "I passed the impound lot, around the back of the building."

Joe shook his head. "No. They left it there, in the lot where I was arrested."

"They left it there? You kidding me?" Dickie pulled out onto the street and drove another block to the red light. He turned to Joe. "Which way am I going?"

Joe looked around at the streets. But he didn't know Miami Gardens very well. "It's off Northwest Second Avenue. Place is called the Village Lounge."

Dickie tapped the GPS on the dashboard over the stereo and said, "Village Lounge." It came up on the GPS right away and he turned the wheel, jumped on

Northwest 199th. "So," he said, "this broad called the cops on you and here you are... charged with burglary? But all they're going by is whatever shit came out of her mouth?" He sighed, shaking his head. "And you saw it was Peters? Running away?"

"I didn't exactly see him. But whoever it was took off from the back room of the bar. It had to've been him." He looked ahead as they came up on Hardrock Stadium, on the left.

Dickie said, "So if you didn't tell the cops why you were there, what'd you tell them?"

"I was looking to get a drink. Told them the front door was open, I walked in and she pulled the gun on me."

"They buy it?"

"Did they *buy* it? Does it look like they bought it?"

Dickie grabbed his phone from the center console and looked at the screen. "Stanley was supposed to call me back, while they had you in there." He placed it back down. "So what kind of place is it?"

"Honestly, I'm not even sure. It was closed, but looks like a dive bar. Had a stage, looked like it would collapse, anyone got up on it. I thought maybe it's a strip joint, or some kind of adult entertainment."

Dickie raised his eyebrows. "Yeah? Is it open? Maybe we should get a drink?"

Joe looked out the window along the dark streets as Dickie followed the voice on his GPS, telling him to turn left. "I don't think that would be very smart."

"No? Why not? We go in, grab a quick drink. Who knows, maybe the moron Peters will show up."

Joe thought for a moment, shaking his head. "I don't think so."

Dickie reached for the glove box, pulled out a 9mm and handed it to Joe. "Here. You're going to be taking on a little more of the work, you'll need to protect yourself a little better. You know? Sometimes this is all it takes, get someone to start flapping their gums. *Nobody* likes getting shot."

Joe looked at the gun in Dickie's hand but didn't take it from him.

"You don't want it?" Dickie said. He leaned over and stuck it back in the glove box.

Joe was tired. It'd been a long day. A long *night.* And he wasn't in the mood for Dickie at this point. He just wanted to get his car and go home, put on some music and have a drink. Maybe sit out on the balcony and stare out over downtown, give his friend Lauren a call.

Dickie seemed to be in somewhat of an odd mood, not as agitated as he'd been the past few days. Of course, he knew all Dickie wanted was to get his money, especially with how things had changed since online legalized gambling could end up throwing a wrench in Dickie's business. More than ever, he had to depend on the schmucks who didn't have the cash up front, needed a loan just to place a decent bet. Otherwise, they'd just go online and wouldn't need Dickie at all.

When someone didn't pay Dickie, it hit him in the pocket more than it had in the past.

"I was thinking," Joe said. "I should have listened to you."

Dickie laughed. "That usually goes without saying." He gave Joe a friendly nod. "You talking about something specific?"

"Well, maybe I *have* been a little naïve. Maybe instead of walking in the front door, I could've gone in the back way, started tearing things apart."

Dickie looked confused, pointing with his finger into his chest. "*I* told you that's how you should do it?"

"Not exactly," Joe said. "But you asked why I didn't go in that apartment. And you were right. It was foolish of me to just turn and walk away. I was just thinking, the way Craig's wife took off after I left." He paused, thinking. "Something's up with her."

"I'm not following," Dickie said. "If you think he was up there at that bar, then that broad who shot at you's gonna know where he is."

Joe nodded. "Of course. But going in there, we'd be asking for trouble. All she has to do is call the cops; you know how that'd look? I get out of jail, go right back in there? I need to be smart, at least until these charges are dropped."

Dickie said, "But I told you Stanley'll take care of it, didn't I?"

Joe and Dickie both looked straight ahead as they pulled into the parking lot of the Village Lounge.

"My car's not in here," Joe said. "It's in the parking lot next door."

Dickie reached past Joe's legs and grabbed the gun from the glove box, lifting himself from the seat so he could tuck it in his pants. "How about I just go inside, have a look around?"

Joe grabbed Dickie's arm. "How about you just drive around to that building next door so I can get my car? And we can get the hell out of here."

Dickie pushed open the door. Right away you could hear loud music booming from the bar. He left the car running as he stepped out, turning to Joe before he closed the door. "Just give me a minute. I'll poke my head in there, see what's going on." He slammed the door closed, and with it, the loud music coming from the bar was muffled.

Joe looked straight ahead through the windshield, watching Dickie walk toward the bar's entrance. He couldn't imagine Craig Peters would be in there, although he wondered if Dickie just wanted to go in because Joe mentioned it might've been a strip club, Dickie hoping to catch a glimpse of some girl's boobs.

Dickie was almost at the door when Joe saw him duck, almost dropping to the ground, covering his head with his arms. It was as if something went by Dickie's head, but Joe had no idea what it was.

Joe jumped out from the passenger seat as Dickie ran toward the car and slipped into the driver's seat.

"Holy shit!" Dickie said, breathing heavy. "You hear that?" He slammed the door closed and slouched in the seat, getting low behind the wheel.

Joe got back in the car, shaking his head. "I saw you duck, but—"

"A gunshot. Someone fired a gun."

"What? At *you?*"

Dickie was breathing heavy, shaking his head. "I... I don't know. I don't think so. But someone definitely fired one."

Joe pushed open the door and stood outside behind it, looking. He poked his head inside the car. "You sure you heard a gunshot?"

"I know a goddamn gunshot when I hear one," Dickie said, still trying to catch his breath. "Might've come from somewhere behind the place."

Joe looked toward the back of the building and toward the fence between the bar and the building next door. But it was mostly dark, other than the dim lights over the lot and a streetlamp. He couldn't see what was going on inside, most of the windows covered up. There were quite a few cars, but nobody had gone in or out since they got there. He stuck his head inside the car again. "You didn't see anyone?"

Dickie looked at him, looking somewhat frazzled. "Come on; maybe you were right about coming to this place. Let's get the hell out of here."

Joe got in and closed the door. He tried to think, watching Dickie pull his gun from his pants and rest it on his lap.

"Give me that," Joe said, reaching for the gun. He took it from Dickie's hand and pushed open the passenger door.

"Where're you going?" Dickie said.

"Wait here." Joe got out and closed the door behind him, walking toward the building. He glanced back at Dickie but couldn't see in the car through the windshield, the way the lights reflected off it.

Joe started toward the back of the building, let the gun hang down by his side. He stopped at the corner of the building and looked toward the door—the same one he'd run out of earlier in the day after Craig Peters. He saw it was cracked open as he walked toward it.

He stopped when something on the ground caught his eye, just to the side of the door. He moved closer and saw what looked like a person sitting on the ground, leaned up against the building.

Joe said, "Hello?" slowly edging closer. He held the gun up in front of him and stopped. "Hello?"

Whoever it was didn't answer him.

Joe pulled out his phone and used its flashlight, shining it in the direction of whoever was there.

He shined it on the person's face and recognized it right away.

It was Wendy Johnson, her face covered in blood. Her eyes were open, staring straight at him.

"Hello?" he said, nudging her with the toe of his shoe.

Wendy tipped over and fell to the ground.

Joe looked around, then crouched down and felt her wrist for a pulse.

There wasn't one.

Chapter 6

THE PARKING LOT WAS filled with more than half a dozen Miami Gardens Police cruisers, two rescue vehicles, a fire truck, the coroner's van, and whatever cars were still left after the police had cleared most of the people out from inside the Village Lounge.

An officer, older than Joe, his head buzzed tight under his hat, stood by the Lexus, asking Joe and Dickie questions. Most he'd repeated more than once as he took notes on a small flip pad with a wire spiral. The car was parked in the same spot it had been in when Dickie first got out and heard the gunshot, and where Joe had gotten out and around the back of the building and found Wendy Johnson dead, with at least two holes in her chest.

The cop, who had introduced himself as Officer Dwight Feeley, stood facing Joe and Dickie, the Village Lounge behind him. The three turned at the same time to look as the coroner and his assistant wheeled the gurney around the corner, carrying Wendy's body in the bag, pushing it over toward the back of the van.

Officer Feeley said, "Mr. Sheldon, will you tell me one more time: Did you say you *didn't* hear the gunshot?" He glanced at Dickie. "But Mr. Caldwell, you *did* hear the shots fired?"

Dickie nodded. "I heard just the one. But, like I already told you, I got out of the car. Joey stayed put."

Joe pointed with his thumb over his shoulder. "I don't know if you've ever been in a Lexus like this one, but it's pretty much airtight in there. You can't hear a thing outside."

The officer stared at Joe, his eyes somewhat squinted, nodding. He wrote something on his pad, turned and glanced back toward the bar, shaking his head. "Makes no sense, if I'm being honest. Nobody else in this place heard a thing. Not one person." He looked from Joe to Dickie, like he was waiting for a response.

Dickie said, "The music in there was pretty loud. But so was the gunshot. I mean, I think I told you, when I first heard it, I *swore* someone took a shot at me." He ran his hands flat down his shirt, like he was feeling around to make sure he *hadn't* been shot.

Feeley had a look, like he had real doubts about what they were telling him.

Joe said. "Why would I call nine-one-one if one of us had anything to do with this?"

Feeley narrowed his eyes. "Why don't you tell me this: Who gets arrested for burglary, comes back to the same place not even twelve hours later?"

Joe looked across the parking lot through the chain-link fence, toward the building next door. He could see his Mercedes. "Didn't you write down any of what I already told you? I came here to get my car."

The officer licked his finger and flipped the paper on his pad. "You said you came back for your car? But neither of you had much of an answer when I asked you why you came here, to this bar. You come to pick up your car, someone with half a brain gets in it and gets the hell out of here." He looked from Joe to Dickie.

Joe rubbed his face with both hands, taking a deep breath. "I'm sorry. It's just... I've done nothing wrong here. I had nothing to do with this woman being shot. And whatever she tried to say I did earlier today wasn't true, either. I never broke in the place."

Feeley said, "Sounds to me you were looking for trouble to begin with."

Joe shook his head, looking away. He knew it wasn't worth trying to defend himself or explain much more to an officer who seemed to have potatoes stuffed in his ears. Joe couldn't figure out if the man was dense or simply refused to believe there was an ounce of truth behind the words coming out of Joe's mouth.

Dickie said, "Joe's a straight-up guy, you know. To be honest, I was the one, told him let's get out of here, let someone else call you. I mean, the lady was already dead. It wasn't like there was any urgency. And here we are, getting our balls kicked for doing the right thing."

The cop gave Dickie a look, like he couldn't believe what he'd just said. "Are you telling me you were going to leave the scene of a crime? Without—"

"No, no, no," Joe said. "Don't listen to him. He just likes to say things." He grabbed Dickie by the arm and tried to pull him away.

Dickie pulled his arm from Joe. "No, listen," he said, looking the cop in the eye. "We didn't do anything to that woman. That's the truth. Now either you're going to press charges and arrest us, or I believe we should be free to go at this time." He held his gaze on Officer Feeley, waiting. "So what's it going to be?"

The officer shifted his stance and stepped forward, standing tall over Dickie. He had at least six inches on him, looking down over his nose as he tucked his pad in the breast pocket of his shirt. "How about you watch your mouth, or we'll go for a little ride. *I'll* show you what it's going to be."

Joe pulled Dickie away. "Listen, Officer Feeley, sir," I said, trying to butter the guy up. "I think my friend here's a little tired. He gets like this when he hasn't had his beauty rest. He means nothing by it."

Dickie opened his mouth, about to say something else but Joe put his hand over it.

"So if there aren't any more questions..." Joe had Dickie's arm, pulling him toward the driver's side door.

The officer glared at Joe and Dickie until they both got in the Lexus, then walked away, over toward a group of four or five officers standing before the front entrance, the door wide open with bright lights pouring out into the darkness.

The officers all turned and looked toward Dickie and Joe, one of them nodding as he said something to Officer Feeley.

Joe couldn't make out what they were saying.

Feeley walked back to Joe and Dickie and knocked on the passenger side window. Joe put it down and Feeley said, "Don't plan on going too far. This isn't over. For either of you."

"What does that mean?" Joe said. "Are we suspects?"

The officer looked at Joe but didn't answer, walking away and back over toward the other officers. But he went right past them and into the bar.

"What a prick," Dickie said, turning the key in the ignition.

Joe looked straight ahead through the entrance with the door wide open, seeing the other officers talking to some of the bar patrons and employees that remained behind. One of the women being spoken to looked like a stripper, but Joe didn't know if she was or not. He turned to Dickie. "Maybe I should've just told him about Craig Peters."

Dickie shook his head. "Uh-uh. No way. We can't give the police any more than we have to, to save our own asses. That's just part of the gig. We tell them something like that—we're after this guy Craig Peters—all it does is crack the door open to where they start sticking their dicks in my business. And I promise you, Joey... it's the last thing I need right now." He put the car in park. "I'll talk to Stanley in the morning. He'll take care of it."

Joe said, "Don't forget I still have this BS burglary charge hanging over my head. You sure Stanley's going to—"

"You gotta stop worrying so much," Dickie said, looking at his watch. "I gotta get some sleep." He nodded to Joe. "You ready?"

"I gotta get my car."

"Yeah, no shit. I'm driving you over."

Joe wished Dickie had just given him a ride over there in the first place, not even pulled in the parking lot of the Village Lounge. He looked toward the other building and could see the front end of his car sticking out. But it was hard to see through the chain-link fence and the darkness surrounding the other building. He pushed open the passenger door and stepped outside. "You know what? I think I'll just walk over there."

Dickie shrugged. "Yeah? Suit yourself." He leaned over the passenger seat before Joe closed the door. "Hey, Joey, before you go, uh, listen: I know this's all been kind of a shit show so far, but I promise it'll get easier. Let's just get this son of a bitch so we can get my money, all right? We got other fish to fry."

Joe didn't respond. The truth was, he wasn't sure he wanted to do *anything* with Dickie anymore. He knew all along it wasn't his bag, but the money was tough to pass up, even though he always swore he'd never do something just for the money.

But on the other hand, Joe wondered why he couldn't just tell Dickie he was done and walk away. Maybe it wasn't just about the money. Maybe there was more to it. He did like the action, and sometimes even enjoyed acting like a tough guy. It made him feel like a kid again, the way he rarely ever passed up a good fight back then.

He put his hand on the top of Dickie's roof and leaned in to look at Dickie. "We'll talk in the morning." He slammed the door closed and started walking toward the street and over to the building next door. He watched Dickie drive past him, blow his horn, and continue down Northwest Second until he turned right at the light and disappeared.

Joe walked across the empty parking lot to where his car was still parked. He was somewhat surprised it was still there; a 1986 Mercedes convertible would bring someone a few bucks. He looked back toward the Village Lounge through the chain-link fence, watched as some of the Miami Gardens police vehicles left the parking lot. A couple remained.

The coroner drove away, followed by the two rescue vehicles.

Joe got to his car and unlocked the door without paying much attention until he looked to his right, at the passenger seat, and saw it was covered in broken glass.

The passenger window had been smashed. "Shit," he said, hoping it was nothing more than a couple of kids causing trouble.

The stereo was still there, although he couldn't imagine who would go through the trouble of stealing an AM/FM cassette stereo from a thirty-something-year-old car. He unlocked the glove box, checked inside, and saw his cassette tapes. All still there.

He didn't have anything in the car to clean up the glass but pulled out his phone and searched for a twenty-four-hour car wash with coin-operated vacuums. He thought he remembered passing one in the car with Dickie on the ride there but didn't remember where it was.

It crossed his mind for a split second to go over and tell whatever officers were still at the bar what had happened. But what good would that do? It wasn't like they'd drop what they were doing to go find whoever might've tossed a rock through his window.

He slid the key in the ignition and sat for a moment, thinking. He started the engine and took off toward the street. When he took a hard right turn onto Northwest Second, the glass slid on the leather seat and fell between the seat and the console. "Goddamnit," he said, the glass glistening in the streetlights. The fragments were all over the floor.

He hadn't thought to look in the back seat, but when he raised his eyes to the rearview, he saw a man sitting behind him.

A gun came up, and Joe felt the muzzle press up against the back of his head.

The man said, "Keep your eyes ahead and keep driving."

Joe knew, as soon as he got a better look of the man's face, it was Craig Peters.

He did as he was told and kept quiet. But after about a minute, he turned and looked at Craig over his shoulder. "So why'd you kill her? Were you afraid she was going to tell me where you were?"

"Wendy? Who said I *killed* her?"

"I guess I just assumed you did. But, if you didn't, then who did?" Joe took a quick left onto Northwest 193rd and headed south on 441.

"I might know," Peters said. "But I can't say for sure. I'm just glad it wasn't me."

"You don't seem too broken up about her being killed," Joe said, looking at Craig in the rearview.

Craig shook his head, turned and looked out the rear window. "So you work for Dickie Caldwell?" he said. "Are you one of his goons?"

"Nah, I'm not a goon," Joe said, and left it at that. He was calm, even with the cold steel pressed against his neck. "You really think it makes a difference if you push that muzzle into my skin or hold it a couple inches from my neck? You pull that trigger, it'll make quite a mess of both of us."

Craig Peters didn't seem to want to listen, pushing the muzzle with even more pressure now.

Joe glanced in the rearview mirror and saw Craig turn, looking toward the rear window again. "Are you looking for someone?" he said.

Craig locked eyes with Joe through the mirror. "Just shut your mouth and drive."

"I'm driving," Joe said. "But you gotta tell me where I'm going. You want me to just drive in circles all night?" He looked at his gas gauge, down to a quarter of a tank. "I'm going to need gas if that's the plan."

"Just keep driving."

Joe saw the car wash he was looking for, driving right past it without a word. "If you're planning on killing me," he said, "Dickie will know it was you. And he's got a lot of men working for him now. A whole army of guys, a lot tougher than me." Other than the muzzle pressed into his neck, he actually felt all right. Maybe it was just adrenaline, getting him all jacked up so he didn't notice whether or not he was freaking out.

"I want you to listen to me," Craig said, turning again to look behind him. "This money you're after... I can't give it to you. I mean, I don't have time to get into it now. But the money I owe Dickie... he's not on the top of the list, okay? So what I'm going to ask you to do is back off. Stop looking for me. Because, I got someone else after me. And if they find out you're after the same thing they're after, I promise you they won't hesitate to kill you and everyone you know. They'll kill your family, your friends, or whoever else you give two shits about."

Joe said, "Just so I get this straight, you're telling me you don't have Dickie's money because you owe it to somebody else?" He looked at Craig in the rearview.

"Yeah, that's it. Not much more to it than that."

Joe thought about it, not exactly sure what to say.

Craig said, "Stop the car."

"Stop the car?" Joe looked at the speedometer, doing about fifty-five in a thirty. He gave it a little more gas, got it up to sixty-five.

"What the hell are you doing? I told you to stop the car."

Joe nodded. "Okay, where, *here?*" He slammed his foot on the brakes. The tires squealed, the rear end fishtailing, Craig Peters flying to the front, smashing his head on the stereo as the car came to a sudden and complete stop.

Joe grabbed him by the back of his head and slammed his face down on the center console. He pushed open the driver's side door and dragged Peters out and onto the pavement, the man's hair clumped up in Joe's hand.

But Craig hadn't dropped the gun and pointed it at Joe, firing off a shot.

Joe ducked and put his hand up in front of his face as if to block the bullet. He felt the sting, his arm whipping back, as the bullet got him. He fell back against his car, grasping his hand. He checked to make sure he still had all five fingers. He did, but there was still plenty of blood dripping down his wrist.

Luckily, Peters didn't fire a second shot. He instead ran away to the other side of the street toward a small brick strip mall. He disappeared between two buildings: a tire shop and a dry cleaner.

Joe held his hand, trying to stop the bleeding, and started to run toward the direction Peters was heading. But it was no use.

Craig Peters had disappeared.

Chapter 7

Joe sat forward on the couch in his apartment with a vodka cranberry next to a box of gauze pads and white surgical tape on the coffee table in front of him. The bullet had only grazed the side of his hand, the fat part under his pinkie. Although it took quite a while for the bleeding to stop, he didn't think he needed to go to the ER and waste half the night.

He admired the tape job he did to his hand. Maybe he could've used a stitch or two, but the bleeding seemed to stop, at least for the most part. He got up with his drink and walked to his record collection that took up a full wall, from the left side of the room by the balcony to the other, almost to the kitchen. Twelve feet of wooden shelves he built himself when he'd first moved in the place ten years earlier.

He wasn't sure what kind of music he was in the mood for but decided on Stan Getz and Bill Evans, one of his favorite jazz albums from '73.

It was already past midnight when he dropped the needle on the first song, "Night and Day," keeping the volume somewhat low.

Although the garage beneath the apartment building was generally safe, he worried about his car being left open the way it was, with the window missing on the passenger side. Joe was more upset about his Mercedes than the chunk of flesh missing from his hand, courtesy of the bullet.

He didn't need to deal with having to get the damn glass replaced.

His phone buzzed, but he wasn't even sure where he'd left it. He looked around the couch, walked into the adjacent kitchen, and looked all over the counters. It wasn't on the table, either. The phone buzzed again, but it was faint. He walked down the hall toward his bedroom and stopped to look in the bathroom. Before he flipped the light, he saw the glow from the phone's screen.

He picked it up, saw he had a couple of texts from Lauren. The last one said *Are you awake?*

He wasn't sure why she'd ask. Joe rarely went to bed before one or sometimes two in the morning. But he still woke up before sunrise on most days.

He didn't reply to her by text but instead dialed her number as he walked down the hall to the living room. He picked up his drink off the coffee table and took a sip, lowering the music, holding the phone up to his ear.

"Hey," Lauren said, her voice quiet.

"Is everything all right?" Joe said. He looked at his watch, even though he knew what time it was. "Isn't this a little late for you?"

"I fell asleep on the couch after work and woke up hungry. Now I'm wide awake."

"You don't sound like you're wide awake," Joe said.

Lauren didn't respond. She paused on the other end. "I had a dream while I was asleep," she said. "Something happened to you."

Joe walked to the sliding glass doors and looked out over downtown. "Was I shot?"

"Shot?" She laughed. "No. You were in an accident."

"Car accident?"

"Yeah. I mean, I think so. It seemed so real... but it was like I showed up and you were already being taken away in the rescue. I... I'm not sure what happened. You were driving your old Mercedes."

"Which one?"

"The yellow one."

Joe thought for a moment. "That's a little creepy. Was I *dead*?"

"I don't know. I woke up. I hate dreams like that, wake up... your heart's racing. You don't even know where you are."

"Drool coming down your chin, all over the cushion," Joe said, laughing.

But Lauren didn't laugh. "So, I'm glad to hear you're okay?" she said.

Joe looked at his bandaged hand. A spot of blood had already come through the gauze. "Never been better."

But Lauren knew him too well. She was smart. And she could read people, especially Joe. She said, "Why'd you say it like that?"

"Like *what?*"

"'Never been better.' You're being facetious."

"*Am* I?" Joe said. "Well, I didn't die in a car wreck. So, we can both rest well tonight."

Lauren was quiet on the other end. "I called you earlier today; you didn't answer. I thought maybe you'd call me back, but—"

Joe said, "Oh, yeah. Sorry. But you didn't leave a message. I just thought it was one of those calls, by the time you call back, the person's not in the mood to talk anymore."

"What if the person still wanted to talk?"

"Usually not the case. You call back, they're home eating dinner, don't even answer your call."

That time, Lauren laughed.

"So is that why you had the dream about me being dead? Because I didn't call back?"

"I told you, I'm not sure you were dead."

Joe had wanted to talk to Lauren all week. But he didn't call. She was one of the few people he liked to talk to.

"So, how's work?" he said. Lauren had been living up in Daytona after leaving Miami for a job with a newspaper.

She said, "Actually, I have some news I wanted to tell you about."

"Good or bad?"

"I think it's good. I got a promotion."

Joe sipped his drink and walked over to the couch. "Last time we talked, you said you wanted to quit?"

"I did want to quit. But then I was offered the promotion."

"Oh," is all Joe said.

"Aren't you going to congratulate me?"

"Oh, yeah, of course. Congratulations." He forced a smile into the phone, as if she could see it.

"Don't sound so excited for me," she said.

"I'm sorry," he said. "Last time we talked, it sounded like you might be moving back here to Miami."

Lauren was quiet on the other end.

"But, really," Joe said. "It's great. I mean, if you're happy about it, then I'm happy for you."

"It was an offer too good to pass up, Joe. More money. But it's a lot more pressure too. I have people working under me now. I have a different boss, someone I don't even see most days."

Joe felt like a jerk for not being genuinely excited for her. But he couldn't hide the fact he missed having her around. He said, "Seriously. Congratulations. It sounds great."

"Now you're just saying it," Lauren said. "And, we talked about this last time we saw each other. It works like this, right? I just... I don't think it'd be the same if I was down there again. I really don't."

"You mean we'd get sick of each other?"

She laughed. "I'm not sure you have to put it that way, but..."

The line went quiet again.

"Are you dating anyone?" he said, wishing he hadn't said it, as soon as the words left his mouth.

"No, not really."

Not really? Joe thought. *What kind of answer was that?*

She said, "What about you?"

Joe sipped his drink, shaking his head into the phone. "I've been too busy. I'm writing again, although not as much as I should."

"Did you have any luck finding another agent?" Lauren said.

Joe walked toward the kitchen. "I haven't really looked."

Joe had an agent who got him a deal, but he missed too many deadlines and the publisher canceled the contract. His agent stopped taking his calls, and Joe realized he didn't like her much anyway.

But he was determined to get back on track with his novel, even though his mind was never clear enough to get more than a few sentences down here and there.

He put his glass down on the counter and used his good hand to get some ice out of the freezer. He dropped it in the glass and poured Grey Goose vodka and cranberry juice over it.

Lauren said something about an agent she knew, but Joe had zoned out while he was making his drink.

"Sorry, who is this again?"

"The agent?"

"Yeah, I didn't catch the name."

"She's in Miami. Friend of mine works with her. She has a lot of contacts, and I thought maybe you could talk to her about your book."

Joe sipped his drink and walked over to the turntable. He turned up the volume just a bit, starting to feel the vodka going to his head. He felt good talking to Lauren and started to forget about the hellish last couple of days.

He wanted to tell her all about it but knew she'd only tell him the same thing she always did: he should stop doing work for Dickie, or he was going to get himself killed.

• • • • • • • • • • •

Six thirty the next morning, the sun barely up, Joe drove over to Winnie's twenty-four-hour car wash on Second Avenue to vacuum the broken glass. From there he headed to Dickie's auto repair shop, Ray's Auto Repair, to see how soon Colt could replace the broken window.

Joe was surprised when he pulled in and saw Dickie's white Lexus parked out front. It was early, especially for Dickie. He usually didn't get in until after eight.

Joe parked next to the Lexus, walked up to the service entrance, and yanked on the glass door's handle. But it was locked. He looked at his watch—five after seven—and started knocking. Dickie didn't come to the door, so Joe pulled out his phone to call him.

"Yeah?" Dickie said, answering on the first ring.

"It's me," Joe said, knowing if Dickie didn't have his reading glasses on, he couldn't see who it was.

Unlike Joe, Dickie answered just about every call, even when he didn't know who it was. He said it'd cost him money if he missed one.

Joe had his face up close to the glass, trying to see if he could spot Dickie inside. "Can you let me in?"

"Let you in? Where *are* you?"

"Where do you think I am? I'm outside."

"The shop?"

"Yes, Dickie. The shop. At the service entrance. Can you please let me in?"

Joe waited a couple of minutes until Dickie finally showed up on the other side of the door reaching in his pockets, phone up to his ear, staring out at Joe through the glass.

Dickie put up his finger and said, "I can't find the keys," then walked away from the door. Joe watched him walk behind the service counter and duck behind it, coming up dangling the keys so Joe could see them. He finally unlocked the door. "What are you doing here so early?" he said, holding it open for Joe.

"I was going to ask you the same thing." He turned and pointed with his thumb toward the Mercedes. "Can Colt replace my window?"

Dickie closed the door and turned the lock, looking out through the glass. "What window?"

"The passenger side. Craig Peters smashed it."

Dickie had a smile on his face. "You found him?"

"Not exactly," Joe said. "He found *me*." He walked to the coffee maker and took a Styrofoam cup from the stack. "Is this coffee from today?"

Dickie nodded, staring back at Joe, his eyes narrowed. "Did you get my money?"

Joe poured coffee into the cup, then held up his bandaged hand. "No. But I did get shot."

Dickie's eyes bugged out of his head, his eyebrows up high. "He shot you? What do you mean *he shot you*? Where did—"

"Right after you left, he was waiting for me in my back seat."

Dickie stared at Joe, like he was waiting for more but not sure what to say.

Joe told him how it all went down, and the warning Craig gave him.

Dickie shook his head. "No, that makes no sense. What do *I* care if he owes someone else money? He owes me. And I want it back." Dickie walked toward his office, waved his hand in the air. "It was probably just some bullshit story to get you off his back."

"I thought of that," Joe said. "The thing is..."

"Listen, Joey. Sometimes these guys, guys like Peters... they hang around with some bad players who might try to get in your way. But you can't let that intimidate you." He walked around his desk and sat in the oversized leather desk chair. "Did he say anything about his girlfriend? The one who was killed?"

Joe leaned in the doorway, shaking his head. "He said she wasn't his girlfriend. And he didn't seem to care that she was dead."

"It wasn't him?"

"That killed her?"

Dickie nodded. "Not that he'd admit to it, but..." He leaned back in the chair, his feet up on his desk. "So what's the story?"

"The story is that Peters claimed someone else is after him. He said if I get in the way, they'll come after me."

"Nah," Dickie said. "He's just trying to scare you."

"I'm not sure about that," Joe said. "He seemed pretty nervous, like he thought we were being followed."

Dickie rolled his eyes, folding his arms across his chest. "Hey, so I spoke to Stanley. He said with the broad being dead, he's sure he'll have no problem getting your burglary case dismissed, no trouble at all."

"Okay, well that's only half the problem. Cops still seem to think you and I had something to do with it," Joe said. "And, on top of it, if Peters was telling the truth, I'm not sure I want to be the one to get in their way."

"You don't even know who they are," Dickie said. He put his foot down and leaned forward, elbows on his desk, hands folded in front of him. He had a squint to his eyes, like he was thinking it through. "Well," he said. "Then it'd probably be smart you put aside this anti-gun stance you have."

"I'm not anti-gun," Joe said. "I just don't want to deal with shooting someone." He looked to his right, out the window toward the parking lot. He walked over to it and stared outside. "I'm not sure I want to be involved in any of this anymore." He turned to Dickie.

Dickie laughed. "You don't want to be involved any-more? What the hell's that supposed to mean? You are *already* involved." He stared back, his gaze on Joe. The smile dropped from his face. "Are you serious? Are you saying... Do you mean you're not going to finish the job?"

Joe had been holding his breath without even re-alizing it, exhaled, nodding his head. "This whole gig has turned into more than it was supposed to," he said. "This isn't something I want to be a part of, Dickie. I'm not a bad guy. I'm not some thug..."

Dickie leaned back in his chair and ran his hands over his face. "What, you want to go back to eating rice and beans? 'Cause I know what your situation was like before you started helping me out, Joe. And you're kidding yourself, you ever think that so-called book of yours is ever going to put you on easy street. Speaking of not finishing something."

Joe didn't appreciate the dig at all. He started to walk away, out of Dickie's office.

"Where you going?" Dickie said, coming to his feet.

Joe didn't answer, walked past the service desk and out the door into the parking lot.

Dickie came out behind him. "Joey? Come on, man. Why're you acting like this? You can't just walk away, leave me hanging. I got no one else to turn to right now." He stood just outside the door. "Joey?"

Joe looked back at Dickie as he opened his door and slipped inside behind the steering wheel.

Dickie walked up to the passenger window and picked a piece of broken glass from the rubber gasket. "I thought you wanted the window repaired?"

Joe started the engine and looked straight ahead, shifting into gear. "I do. But I'll worry about it some other time."

Chapter 8

JOE DROVE OUT TO South Beach to grab a drink, trying to think clearly about what the hell he was going to do. He hadn't slept much, and maybe overreacted without thinking things through when he'd said what he did to Dickie.

But the fact was, what he'd been doing for at least the past year made him feel like he'd become a completely different person. He had a feeling it might've been one of the reasons Lauren decided against moving back to Miami, and why he'd pretty much lost touch with his friend Bart.

It felt like Dickie was his only friend. And to say he was a friend might've been a stretch, considering Dickie had, for the most part, become his boss more than anything. Joe didn't like the way their relationship had taken a turn away from what it had been. The two went back to the old days, when Joe was writing for the *Post*, and Dickie would turn him on to information he could only get from someone on Dickie's side of the law.

Pete was behind the bar when he walked into Jack's Hideaway. And, although he technically considered Pete a friend, they never hung together outside of the bar. Maybe once or twice, but Joe couldn't really remember what they did. And it wasn't like Pete knew anything about the work Joe had been doing for Dickie, so he wasn't about to sit at the bar, see if Pete could talk him out of his predicament.

Being it was barely noon, the place was mostly empty. Joe sat in a stool, his back to the door.

Pete gave Joe a nod when he saw him, pouring a vodka cranberry before Joe had even asked, then brought it over, and placed it on the bar.

Joe lifted it for a toast. "Thanks."

"Been a minute," Pete said.

"Been a minute" was what people had been saying when it had been a while, and Joe didn't really like it. The first time he heard it was when he went to the coffee shop, the one near his apartment. The young barista said it to him, and he looked at her funny, not having the slightest clue what she meant.

Jack's normally had a crowd that seemed to Joe, to be getting younger. It just meant that Pete was hip to all the new lingo and the way the younger people talked.

Although, Joe knew the truth: it wasn't as much the *crowd* getting younger. He was getting older.

Before Pete and Joe got into any kind of conversation, Joe pulled his phone from his pocket when it rang. He looked at the screen but didn't recognize the number, a local 954 area code. He didn't really want to answer it, but for whatever reason, he did. "Hello?"

"Is this Joe?"

"Who's this?"

"It's Suzanne. Suzanne Peters."

Joe had to think for a second until it registered who she was. He got up from his stool and walked toward the door. "Yeah, this is Joe."

"I hope it's okay I'm calling you. I know it's kind of out of the blue like this, but—"

Joe stood, facing the door, but he didn't leave the bar. "Well, the thing is, if it's got to do with your husband, right now I'm not actually—"

"No," she said. "I still haven't seen Craig. But, well, I just thought I'd call, since I had your number... I know this is a little out of left field, but I was wondering if maybe you'd be interested in getting a drink?"

Joe walked back to the bar and grabbed his vodka cranberry. "A drink? Uh..." He sat back on the stool, looking toward Pete down the other end serving a group of women who had walked in a few minutes after him. "I'm actually, coincidentally, at a bar right now. So I don't know what you had in mind, but— "

"Where are you?" she said.

"South Beach. "

She laughed. "I didn't know it would be this easy. I usually wouldn't call someone like this, but, you know, I'm actually just across the bay. I can jump on the tollway, be there in ten minutes, if you're up for some company." She paused. "I assume you're alone?"

Joe nodded. "Just me. My friend Pete's behind the bar. You know where Jack's Hideaway is?"

"Jack's? Of course. Yeah. But, you're sure it's all right if I come by? I don't want to interrupt anything."

"No, of course. Yeah. I'm right at the bar. There's nobody else here, except for a handful of people. You'll see me as soon as you walk in. I'm ten feet from the door." Joe had a slight smile on his face, caught completely off guard by the call.

"I'll see you in ten minutes," she said, and hung up without another word.

Joe sat and wondered if he'd even recognize her when she walked in. It was early and barely light out when he first saw her. She said she'd just woken up out of bed when he showed up at her apartment and looked like she was still half asleep. But he wondered if there was something more to her call. Even if he wasn't going to keep working with Dickie, he couldn't help thinking how she took off as soon as he left her apartment, when he was outside in his car. And, of course, she was legally married, no matter what she said about her relationship with her so-called husband.

He thought, *Could she have known what happened at the Village Lounge?* He looked at his phone and tapped the screen, saving the number for Suzanne Peters into his contacts.

He took a drink and started to think about Lauren. It wasn't like he couldn't have a drink or even date other women if he wanted to. It was something they had both agreed to. No commitment. But Joe knew if he had his choice, Lauren would be in Miami. Whether or not they'd be together was a different story.

Pete walked over and leaned with both hands on the bar. "Everything all right, Joe?"

Joe nodded. "I think so. Yeah." He didn't tell him at first about the surprise guest he was expecting.

"You haven't been here in a while," he said. He cracked a slight grin. "I wasn't sure if maybe you'd moved up to Daytona, with Lauren."

Joe shook his head, picking up his glass. "No, I'm not going anywhere. Lauren's staying up in Daytona for the foreseeable future. She actually just got a promotion, so..."

"Things cooled off between the two of you?"

"You could say that." He finished what was left in his glass. "I'm actually meeting someone else. She's coming here." He turned and looked toward the door. "She's on her way now."

Pete folded his arms, took a quick glance over his shoulders at his customers down the other end of the bar. "Are you going to tell me anything about her? Before she shows up?"

"I'm not sure I know enough to tell," he said. It wasn't like he could tell Pete how he actually met her.

Pete looked down at the bandage on Joe's hand. "What happened there?"

Joe lifted his hand, looking it over. "I slipped, cutting a bagel." He also wasn't going to tell Pete he was shot by the woman's husband.

Pete shook his head. "You gotta be careful, man. I remember some ER doctor used to come in here, saying there are like a couple thousand people who end up in the ER, sliced their hands open trying to cut a bagel. But that was a few years ago."

Their conversation was cut short when sunlight filled the bar where Joe was seated. He turned to look and, for a second, wasn't 100 percent certain the woman who had just walked in was Suzanne Peters, with the way the sun was bright all around her as if she glowed.

She walked toward him, looking like a different person from the one standing in the doorway of her apartment with the white robe, her hair sticking up in all directions.

Suzanne Peters had dirty-blonde hair, straight and down past her shoulders. She removed her sunglasses and held on to them, smiling at Joe as she approached the bar. She was dressed nice, too, with heels and a tight skirt with a top cut low at her chest.

Joe, on the other hand, was dressed in his usual khaki shorts and a T-shirt with canvas slip-ons on his feet.

"Joe?" she said, asking in a way he could tell she wasn't sure it was him.

"Hi," is all he said at first. He could smell her perfume, and stood up, facing her. He wasn't sure if he should shake her hand or help her sit. The whole thing felt weird and uncomfortable.

She reached out and shook his hand. "Nice to meet you, again." She laughed.

"Can I get you a drink?" he said, turning the stool next to him for her.

Pete walked over and smiled, giving Joe a side-eye as he looked Suzanne over. He introduced himself to her. "What would you like to drink?"

She leaned with her elbow on the bar, her chin in her hand, tapping the polyurethane top with her long nails. She narrowed her eyes, like she was in deep contemplation. She looked at Joe's drink, like she was considering the same, but turned back to Pete. "How about a dirty vodka martini?"

"You got it," he said with a nod. "Any preference on the brand?"

She shook her head. "As long as it's top shelf."

Pete walked away to make her drink.

Joe felt a little nervous. It wasn't normal for him, the way his adrenaline seemed to be boiling. Not many things got him off kilter, but a beautiful woman sitting next to him seemed to be doing it. And he still wasn't sure this sudden meet-up was as spur of the moment as she wanted him to believe.

"I'm not sure I would have recognized you," he said. He looked down at his own outfit. "If I'd known you were going to be dressed up..."

"What would you have done? Gone and bought a new outfit?" She looked him over. "You're fine. I'd much rather be wearing something a little more com-fortable myself. I just came from a meeting..."

Joe wanted to ask what her meeting was about, but didn't. She would have told him if she wanted him to know. At least that's what he assumed.

He turned his stool to face her. "I'm going to be up front," he said. "I'm having a hard time believing you called me just to have a drink. Is there something more to this?"

"Would you have a hard time believing me if I told you I called because I thought you were cute? And I wanted to have a drink with you?" She smiled and turned the stool, her knee rubbing up against his leg. "If I had information about Craig, I'd tell you. But I don't. If that's what you were hoping for."

Pete dropped off Suzanne's martini and placed another vodka cranberry in front of Joe. "Let me know if you kids need anything else." He gave Joe a somewhat cheesy wink and walked away toward the other end of the bar.

"Well, the thing is," Joe said, picking up his glass, "I'm not sure I'm going to be looking for Craig anymore."

"No?" she said, almost like she was disappointed. "Why not? Your friend doesn't want his money?"

"It's not that at all," he said. "The truth is..." He hesitated, knowing he probably didn't need to be getting into the details with this woman he wasn't sure he could trust. "It's a long story."

She picked up her martini and looked at Joe over the rim of the glass. "I have all day, if you want to tell me." She gave him a sly smile and took a sip, placing her glass gently down on the bar. "I was kind of hoping you'd found him."

"Craig?" Joe shook his head, his elbow on the bar. "I don't know where he is."

Of course, even though he left out some important details, he *was* telling her the truth. He *didn't* know where Craig Peters was. And he wasn't sure he cared at that point, either. As long as it was far away from where Joe sat with this attractive woman next to him.

Chapter 9

Joe pushed open the door to his apartment, putting a gentle touch with his hand on Suzanne's back, guiding her ahead of him. He watched her stop once she was past the threshold and looked around.

"Nice place," she said, going right past the kitchen and into the living room. She walked over to the long shelves holding his collection of vinyl records. It's what most people did the first time they'd gone into his apartment. "I guess you like vinyl records, huh?" She held her phone up toward him. "I like music too. But I can keep it in my purse."

Joe grinned, not about to come off like some snobby record guy and go into why he preferred the sound of vinyl over the tin-sounding garbage you got from a compressed digital file. Of course, the real reason he enjoyed collecting records—and a lot of other vintage items he had around the apartment—was because he appreciated life from a different time, when life was different. But when it came to albums, he felt the recording was closer to what the musicians were playing in the studio. "Pick out a song, if you want."

He walked into the kitchen and pulled a bottle of Ketel One from the freezer, placed it on the counter, and reached up for the only martini glass he owned. The other three had broken at one time or another, and he'd never gotten around to replacing them. He would have if he drank martinis himself. He looked at Suzanne, flipping through his albums. "You like it dirty, right?"

She looked at him and smiled but didn't exactly answer.

Joe held up the martini glass. "I'm talking about the martini."

She nodded and walked toward the far end of the room, stopped in front of the sliding glass door before the balcony. "Quite the view," she said. She stepped over to the glass-enclosed fireplace built into the wall a few feet off the floor. "Do you ever actually use this?"

Joe had poured the martini and found a half jar of olives, but he didn't have vermouth. She'd already had a few, and he had a feeling she wouldn't know the difference anyway. Most people wouldn't. He carried the glass over to her, keeping his eyes off it so it didn't spill—a tip he learned when he waited tables when he was first out of college.

"It's just for ambiance," he said, flipping the switch as the fireplace came on. "It doesn't throw off any heat. In the ten years I've lived here, I've probably only turned it on five times." He handed her the martini, went back to the kitchen and grabbed his vodka cranberry. "Did you find something to play?"

"An album?" She shook her head and started flipping through his collection again. "Why don't *you* pick something. Surprise me."

Joe brushed against her, walking toward the turntable. He sipped his drink and placed it on the shelf where he normally wouldn't put one and risk having it spill. "What kind of music do you listen to?"

"I don't know. Pop, I guess. But I'll listen to anything."

Joe had to think. He wasn't a fan of pop, although appreciated all musicians. He listened to most music, but most of what he owned was produced in prior decades. "You listen to jazz?"

"I used to hang out at a place a few years back... it was kind of a jazz club, I guess." Suzanne held up her martini. "That's where I started drinking these. Even if you didn't like them, you'd order a martini just to fit in with the pretentious crowd."

Joe looked through the albums, assumed by the way she said it, she wouldn't be up for jazz. He removed the album, *Songs of Leonard Cohen*, from the shelf and held it up to show her. "Have you ever listened to this?"

She had her martini glass up near her lips, but pulled it back, holding it still below her chin. She gazed at the album for a moment, shaking her head. "Leonard Cohen? I've heard of him, but I couldn't name any of his songs."

"Seriously?" he said. He pulled the record from the jacket, carefully placed it on the turntable and dropped the needle on the first song, "Suzanne."

She stood, nodding, as the song with her name played through the tall, wood-encased speakers on either end of the shelves. Sipping her martini, she looked at him over the glass, then stepped back to the sliding glass door, her back to him, and looked out toward downtown.

Joe grabbed his drink and took a sip, watching her, taking in the words of the song:

For you've touched her perfect body with your mind...

She turned from the door and stared straight into Joe's eyes, then started toward him, slowly. Stepping to the coffee table in front of the couch, she placed her martini down and continued toward him, her gaze held on his. Suzanne stood before him, close enough he could smell the alcohol on her breath, wrapping her arms around his neck. She pulled him toward her, placing her mouth on his.

Joe placed one hand on the small of her back, still holding his drink with his free hand. He pressed into her, turned her so her back was into the shelves. Taking her hand, he led her across the room, put his drink down, and fell with her onto the couch.

• • • • • • • • • •

It was three in the morning when Joe opened his eyes, then turned over in his bed. Suzanne was no longer next to him. He sat up, pulled the sheet up to cover at least the lower part of his body, and looked toward the hall. He thought maybe she was in the bathroom, but the rest of the apartment was dark. "Are you still here?" he said, listening for her voice, somewhat expecting she'd answer from down the hall. He hung down off the bed and grabbed his shorts, pulled them up, and walked out into the living room. He stood just past the hallway and looked from the kitchen to the balcony and toward the front door.

But she was gone.

He went into the kitchen, picked up the empty bottle of vodka and tossed it in the recycling container under the sink. He picked up the jar of olives to put it back in the refrigerator, but there was only one left in the jar. And there was barely enough juice for another martini.

His phone was on the counter on top of his unopened mail. He picked it up and saw he had a call last night from Dickie, but he'd turned the ringer off early so didn't hear it. He also had a couple of texts he hadn't yet seen.

One was from Lauren.

She sent at eleven thirty: *Call me if you're not busy.*

Joe felt bad as soon as he saw her text. He didn't do anything wrong. But he felt like he had. He tried to tell himself she was the one who moved away for the job, that she was the one who didn't want either of them to worry about "having fun" with other people.

The second text was from Suzanne:

Thanks for the fun night. I left my car in your garage. Took a cab home. Call me when you see this. xoxoxo

Joe smiled. He was glad she'd left her car there, considering they'd polished off the whole bottle of vodka. But he wondered how she'd get it back. He'd have to go get her, give her a ride back. Or maybe she'd get a ride over. *Who knows.*

He looked at the Elvis clock on the wall over the shelves in the living room, thinking of a reply he could text back to her. He felt like a little kid, scared to say the wrong thing. But, also, she was likely asleep. He thought he'd at least wait for the sun to come up before he texted back.

He dialed to listen to Dickie's voicemail:

Joey? It's Dickie. Listen, we need to talk. So call me when you get this. It's important. I know you've got your panties all twisted, but... I need to fill you in on something. It's kind of important. So if we can talk as soon as you get this, uh... Just give me a call. Okay, pal?

Joe let out a sigh and deleted the message, leaving the phone on the counter. He walked to the refrigerator, poured himself a water and went over to the turntable with the power still on. He put away the Leonard Cohen album.

He was tired. Maybe still a little bit drunk, feeling it as he went out onto the balcony and stared out toward downtown Miami. He sat on one of the lounge chairs he had out there but hardly used, leaned his head back, and closed his eyes.

• • • • • • • • • •

Joe was in the kitchen making coffee after a four-hour nap on the balcony. Luckily, an alarm of some sort blasted a high-pitched sound from one of the buildings below, or he might've still been asleep out on the lounge chair.

He poured himself a cup and picked up his phone, saw he had a couple of texts he'd missed from Suzanne. The first one asked him if he was awake yet. Since he never responded, a second came over ten minutes after it:

I can either take a cab back to your place to pick up my car. Or maybe you want to come over for coffee when you wake up?

She put a smiley face at the end of her text.

Joe texted back:

Sorry, I took a nap, fell into a coma. Too bad you didn't leave your keys, I'd drive your car over.

He sent his text but followed it up right away:

Coffee?

Joe sipped the coffee he already had, holding the phone up in front of him waiting for her reply. He wasn't even sure why he questioned coffee. He was hungry. He had a crooked smile on his face, sending another text:

No breakfast?

He waited, staring at the screen. She hadn't replied, and he realized he went from not replying to her first text to shooting one after the other. The last, he thought, maybe was pushing it. He didn't mind texting. It was easy for basic questions. But when it came down to it, he preferred to just pick up the phone and talk to someone. And he was about to do just that when she replied to his text:

Help

Joe smiled at first, for a split second, and read the text to himself. "Help?" He was about to text right back but thought it was a good time to just pick up the phone. *She must've meant something else,* he thought.

He tapped her number and the phone rang. He put his phone on speaker and listened to it ring once... twice... three times. It rang six times before the voice-mail came on:

Hey, this is Suzanne. You know what to do.

The line beeped, then Joe hung up without leaving a message but texted her back:

You all right?

He stared at the screen, waiting for a reply. His heart started to race. "What the hell's going on?" he said. He put the cup down in the sink, tapped Suzanne's number again and hit the speaker button. He waited until it rang.

But, once again, six rings and her voicemail greeting came on.

This time, he left a message. "Hey, I'm sorry for being weird about this. You sent that text, kind of, I don't know. Just making sure you're... You're not answering, so, uh, call me right back?" He looked at the screen again for a moment before he tapped the red button and ended the call.

Something wasn't right.

He took the phone in his bedroom and threw on a shirt, didn't even bother to brush his teeth, hurrying past the bathroom. He grabbed his keys from the hook by the door and took a quick look at his phone, hoping she'd texted back.

Nothing.

No text, no call.

He locked his door behind him and hurried for the elevator, pushing the button a bunch of times, waiting, watching the digital numbers over the door.

The elevator opened and his phone rang—without looking to see who it was, he answered it. His voice was panicked. "Suzanne?"

"Joey? Huh? Who the hell's Suzanne? It's me, Dickie."

Joe stepped onto the elevator. "I can't talk right now," he said. "I'm going to lose you going down the elevator."

The door slid closed, and Joe watched the digital screen up over the door, each floor's number flashing as he descended.

He could hear Dickie talking on the other end of the phone, but his voice was all broken up. The call dropped.

The elevator door slid open, and Joe stepped out into the parking garage and ran to his car. As he unlocked the door, he looked over at Suzanne's Mustang GT, parked in one of the guest parking spaces on the far side of the lot.

He jumped in the Mercedes and backed out of his space, tires squealing. His phone rang again, and when he saw it was Dickie, he tapped ignore as he turned onto Northwest Sixth and slammed the pedal to the floor.

Chapter 10

JOE PARKED THE MERCEDES in the fire zone in front of Suzanne's apartment in North Miami, jumped out with the top still down and ran for the stairs. He turned sideways and stepped past a woman and three children on his way, skipping every other step on the stairs.

He was out of breath when he got to the third floor, turned toward Suzanne's door and stopped when he saw it was open by no more than a few inches. He put his hand flat against it and eased it open, being careful, not knowing who was waiting for him on the other side.

"Suzanne?" he said, stepping into the apartment's kitchen. The rectangular fluorescent light above was on. The place smelled of coffee, and Joe saw a full pot on the counter. The only noise came from the air-conditioning. He felt the cool air blowing down from the vent on the ceiling. "Hello?" He walked slowly from the kitchen and into the living room area, the two rooms divided by a four-foot-high wall with a laminate countertop. There were plants in the two far corners on either side of the sliding glass door, with a patio on the other side overlooking a pond at the rear of the building.

He looked down the short hall at a door slightly ajar at the end of it. "Suzanne? Are you here?"

His mouth was dry and his heart pounded so hard he thought it was going to bust through his ribs. He went past a bathroom on the right where the light was on, continuing toward the door. He eased it open. "Hello?"

The bedroom appeared empty. The queen-sized bed was unmade, although it was apparent only one side had been slept in. Joe's eyes moved to a door that was closed, but a light glowed from underneath it.

He turned the knob and pulled open the door. His pounding heart stopped.

Suzanne was on the floor, clothes piled on top of her as if pulled from the empty hangers on the rod above her head.

He rushed to her, clearing the clothes that covered her face. "Suzanne!"

Her white face was bloodied, as was her shirt.

Joe put his hand under her neck to feel for a pulse. But he already knew there wouldn't be one.

And he was right.

•·•·•·•·•·•·•·•·•·

The police arrived while Joe sat on the bottom step of the apartment building. He had his phone out and looked at the last text he'd received from Suzanne:

Help

Sirens screamed as police and rescue vehicles arrived, taking up any available space in the parking lot at the front of the building.

Joe had called Sgt. Woody Thomas directly as soon as he realized Suzanne was dead and looked up when he heard his name.

"Joe?" Woody stood over him, then started up the stairs.

Joe stood up and followed him.

Woody looked back at Joe. "Can you at least tell me how you know the victim?"

"I... uh..." He paused, thinking. "Her name's Suzanne. Suzanne Peters. I've only known her for a couple of days. That's why I called you directly. I was worried how something like this could look."

"Considering your recent history," he said, turning the corner toward the final set of stairs. "You didn't say how you know her. Were you dating? Or..."

"Uh, well, like I said, we only met a couple of days ago. But, I mean, I don't know what to tell you. We spent some time together last night, at my apartment."

"She was at your apartment?" Woody stopped at the wide-open door to Suzanne's apartment, with at least six or seven cops and a handful of paramedics. He turned to Joe. "You still live in the same place?"

"Yes, she was over. And, yes, I'm still there. She left; I guess it was pretty late. Or, early morning, really. She took a cab back here, then sent me a couple of texts a little while ago, inviting me over for coffee." Joe pulled his phone from his pocket, tapped the screen and showed her last text to the sergeant.

Woody looked at it, turned his eyes to Joe. "Did you speak with her after she left your apartment?"

Joe shook his head. "No. Just the texts."

"We're probably going to need that phone," Woody said. "I'll have someone take your statement. Or, better yet, it'd be good if you'd come down—voluntarily—to the station when we're all done here?"

Joe wasn't sure he'd really have to or wanted to. But with the way the sergeant put it, he made it sound like no big deal. "Yeah, I can come down, if you need me to?"

One of the officers called for Woody from Suzanne's bedroom. "Sarge? You want to come back here?"

Woody said to Joe, "You should probably wait out here." He continued into the apartment and disappeared around the corner.

Joe leaned against the exterior wall outside the apartment at the door across the hall, then looked at that last text one more time. He wondered who he could call or who would even understand. He knew he'd have to call Dickie back sooner or later and thought about Dickie's attorney, Stanley, hoping he'd taken care of everything the way Dickie said he would. Because he knew he might need him once again. The BS burglary charge was dropped; he knew that much. But there was still a chance he and Dickie could be suspects in Wendy Johnson's murder.

He started to think the best thing he could do, with the situation only getting worse, was to cooperate with the police and tell them whatever they needed to know. He didn't care what kind of trouble it got him in, although there was a chance he could cause trouble for Dickie if he said too much.

But hiding information wasn't something he was willing to do. Not if it got in the way of finding whoever killed Suzanne.

•••••••••••

Joe turned the corner onto Northwest Sixth and saw his friend Bart standing in front of his building, leaning up against his green Buick LeSabre. Joe stopped in the street, the top and windows already down. "Are you looking for me?"

Bart took a drag from his cigarette and nodded. "Why don't you park your car; we'll go grab a drink."

Joe looked at Bart and knew he was up to something but wasn't quite sure what it was. "I have to go down the station in a couple of hours. I'm not sure I need to show up with booze on my breath."

Bart shrugged, dropped his cigarette on the ground and crushed it with his foot. "Then we'll get a coffee. I don't give a shit. I'm just telling you, we need to talk."

"You want to come up?" Joe said.

"Not really," Bart said.

"Well, I gotta go up first."

Bart said, "Why don't you go do what you gotta do. I'll wait here."

Joe was hesitant, staring out at Bart, nodding. "Yeah, okay. Give me a few."

Bart pulled another cigarette from his pack and stuck it in his mouth. "All right, but I don't have all day."

Joe rolled his eyes and drove off, turned around the building and into his parking garage. He thought about Bart, wondering why he was acting a little odd. But he also knew sometimes that was just how Bart was.

He parked the Mercedes in the empty space, right in front of the elevator, stepped out and pressed the button. He still couldn't believe Suzanne was dead. The night they spent together, not more than a few hours earlier, was still clear in his mind. Nothing felt real.

He stepped onto the elevator and pushed the button for the twenty-third floor, leaned against the rail at the rear and watched the numbers jump. He hoped nobody else got on with him, although most tenants never went up unless they'd gotten on in the garage.

The bell dinged and Joe got off. He stood still for a moment, alone in the hallway looking toward his apartment ten doors down on the right. Past his door, where the hall turned, was Joe's friend Gopal's apartment. Gopal had been out of the country on a three-week trip to India.

Joe pulled the key from his pocket, slipped it in the lock, and opened his apartment door.

He stepped in and locked the door behind him, picking up a hint of Suzanne's perfume like she was still there. He walked into the kitchen, and his eyes immediately went to the empty bottle of vodka on the counter. The empty martini glass Suzanne had used was still in the sink. Joe picked it up and looked at her fingerprints on the sides. Her lipstick stained the rim. He thought, for a second, he should just throw it out. He knew any other time, going forward, when someone drank out of it... he'd think of her. But then he thought if the police decided to take a look around his apartment, they'd find it suspicious if he'd tossed out the glass.

His phone rang, and he pulled it from his pocket; looking at the screen, he saw it was Bart.

Joe answered, "I just walked in my apartment. Can you just give me a minute?"

"Take it easy, will you? I gotta use your bathroom. Drank too much coffee, is that all right with you?"

Joe nodded into the phone. "Yeah, I'll unlock the door. But don't park on the street; you'll get a ticket."

"What about your garage?"

"You know where the guest spaces are, right? On the other side, from the elevators?"

"Yeah, of course. I'll be right up." Bart ended the call.

Joe walked past the door and unlocked it, continued down the hall and into his bedroom. He walked toward his unmade bed and looked down at it. The smell of Suzanne's perfume was even stronger in his room. He reached down and picked up the pillow on the right side, where she'd slept before she left while he was still sleeping. He put it up to his face and smelled what was left of her scent.

He heard the door to his apartment creak, and wondered how Bart could've possibly gotten up so fast.

There was no way.

He reached for the Miami Marlins baseball bat he'd had leaned up in the corner of his bedroom. It was the bat his friend Will had gotten signed back in the nineties when Andre Dawson was still playing. He could hear someone coming down the hall toward his bedroom.

Joe raised the bat up, like he was at the plate and ready to take a swing. He took a step closer to the door, knowing someone was about to turn the corner.

There was a shadow on the wall. Joe wished he had a gun, even if it was one that didn't work. But all he had was the bat, which wouldn't do much if whoever was walking toward him was armed.

But he realized, whoever it was, wouldn't know if he was armed or not. He said, "Whoever's out there, I have a loaded gun in my hand. Don't take another step," he said.

The footsteps stopped.

"You hear me?" Joe said. He got to the door and leaned back against the wall. He wanted to poke his head out to see who it was but didn't want to take the chance.

"Joe Sheldon?" the voice said. "Is that you?"

"Who is it?"

There was a pause. "Craig Peters. Come on out. We need to talk."

Joe stayed where he was. "Talk about *what?*" he said. He stuck his head out just enough to get a look and Craig Peters was facing the other way, as if the guy didn't know where Joe's voice was coming from.

Joe jumped out with the bat but had it turned around, taking a swing at Craig Peters. He hit him hard, with the thin part of the bat, and knocked him to the floor. "What the hell are you doing here?" He stood over him, the bat raised with both hands, the thick part over his head now.

"Please! Don't!" Craig had a gun in one hand, shielding his head with both arms covering his face, his eyes closed. "Please..."

"Drop the goddamn gun," Joe said, his heart racing, blood pumping in his neck.

Craig dropped the gun without hesitation.

Joe kicked it away, out of Craig's reach. He looked up toward the front door when he heard it open.

"Joe?"

"I'm over here," Joe said, knowing it was Bart. "Down the hall." He picked up Craig's gun, held it in one hand and kept the bat in the other. "I have a guest who just showed up uninvited."

Peters sat up, rubbing the back of his neck where Joe had hit him. "You broke my skull."

"You're fine," Joe said. "I didn't even take a good cut."

Bart stepped from around the corner and immediately went into the Weaver stance, his gun out in front, pointed at Craig Peters.

"Whoa, whoa, whoa," Joe said. "Easy, Bart." He held up Craig's gun for Bart to see it. "I took his gun."

"Who the hell is this?" Bart said, the gun still pointed at Craig.

Joe heard Suzanne's voice in his head, asking him not to refer to Craig as her husband. "Craig Peters. Suzanne Peters' husband."

Bart looked surprised. "No shit?" He nodded toward Craig. "This is what I wanted to talk to you about. The police are looking for this guy."

"Who's looking for *me*?" Craig stared at the muzzle on Bart's gun. "For *what*?"

"For murdering your wife."

Craig shook his head. "I didn't kill Suzanne." He looked at Joe. "*He* did."

Chapter 11

BART AND JOE STOOD next to each other on the other side of the coffee table with Craig Peters in front of them on the couch. Bart had his gun in his hand, hanging by his side.

"I didn't kill her," Joe said. "So get that thought out of your head."

"Why should I believe you?" Craig said.

Joe held up his bandaged hand to show Bart. "This guy busted the window on my car and threatened to shoot me. Next thing you know, he's firing his gun at me."

"This guy shot you?" Bart said.

Craig shook his head, his eyes on Joe. "It was your fault."

"My fault?" Joe said. "How the hell could you say—"

"All right, all right," Bart said. He had his eyes on Craig. "The police are looking for you. You're a suspect. So, you came here because you think Joe killed your wife?"

"That's right."

"Christ," Joe said. "I didn't kill her."

"Then why were you there? I saw you."

"You saw me *where*?" Joe said.

"At the apartment."

Joe paused, thinking. "If *you* were at the apartment, and I know I didn't kill her, then—"

"I was there to get some of my things," Craig said. "I pulled up and saw you get out of your car, going up the stairs. I stayed outside and waited. Next thing I know, the cops are showing up."

"Who do you think called them?" Joe poked himself in the chest. "*I* did. The cops know I'm the one who called, which kind of, at least for the most part, keeps me off the hook."

Craig sat, quiet for a moment. "I thought... I thought maybe Suzanne called them, when you showed up at the apartment. She was probably scared when she saw you, some stranger showing up looking for her husband."

Joe shook his head. "I'm sorry, buddy. But I wasn't there to hurt her. I was there because I knew she was in trouble."

Bart looked at him, like he had no idea what he meant.

Craig had a dumb expression on his face, looking confused. "What do you mean, 'you knew she was in trouble'? How would you—"

"That's not important right now," Joe said. "The point is, she was dead when I got there. But if you didn't kill her... then I have a feeling you probably know who did. And, if I haven't made myself clear, I did *not* kill Suzanne."

Craig shrugged, shaking his head. "I have no idea. How would *I* know?"

"Don't play stupid," Joe said. "When you were in the back seat of my car, you told me someone else was after you. Wouldn't you think whoever it is that's after you must've killed her?"

Bart waved his gun's muzzle at Craig. "Why don't you just tell us who's after you?"

Craig ignored the question and stood up between the couch and the coffee table.

"Sit your ass down," Bart said, holding the gun steady, pointed at Craig.

Craig froze, swallowed hard, and sat back down on the couch.

Joe wasn't about to tell Craig Peters the truth of how he knew Suzanne was in trouble. Joe thought maybe he'd find out eventually, especially once the cops told him the whole story. But, at least for the time being, he knew it was best to keep his mouth shut.

Craig's eyes were narrowed, looking up at Joe. "You work for Dickie Caldwell. I know how his goons like you operate."

"I'm not one of his goons," Joe said. "And that's not how Dickie operates. He's not going to kill an innocent woman just because she was foolish enough to marry some deadbeat who can't pay up the money he owes." Joe glanced at Bart staring back at him.

He was hoping Bart wouldn't have figured out he was still working for Dickie. "Don't worry," he said, giving Bart a nod. "I told Dickie I was done. That I quit. I'm not working for him anymore."

Craig said, "If you don't work for Dickie, then why have you been looking for me?"

"I *was* working for him," Joe said. "But not anymore." He rubbed the back of his neck and glanced through the sliding glass door out past the balcony, toward downtown. He turned back to Craig. "You'd better start talking, tell us who's after you. I guarantee, if *you* didn't kill her, then whoever's after you *did*."

Craig held his gaze on Joe for a moment before answering. "Why don't you tell me, first, why you even give a shit? This has nothing to do with Dickie."

Joe swallowed, trying to come up with a good enough reason that wouldn't sound like total BS. "Don't you want to know who killed your wife? If you're telling the truth, and you didn't do it?"

Craig nodded. "Yeah, of course I want to know. But, I'm asking... why do *you* want to know. What's any of this got to do with *you*?"

Bart watched Joe, like he was waiting to hear his answer.

But Joe didn't respond. He instead walked away, stepped into the kitchen, and leaned on the sink with his hands. He stared at the empty martini glass and realized the smell of Suzanne's perfume no longer lingered in the air.

He turned and looked at the 9mm he took from Craig and left on the table, then picked it up and walked back over to Craig. Without a word or warning, he grabbed a clump of hair on the back of Craig's head and yanked it back, sticking the 9mm's muzzle into Craig's mouth. He clenched his teeth, anger coming through his voice but, at the same time, remained calm. "Tell me who the hell is after you. Who could've done this to her."

"Take it easy, Joe," Bart said, stepping up behind him and reaching out for his arm, at the same time the gun pulled out from Craig's mouth.

But Joe yanked his arm free from Bart's grasp and pushed the muzzle into Craig's cheek. "Start talking, you son of a bitch. Or I swear... I'll pull this goddamn trigger."

Craig tried to shake his head, but it wouldn't move, the way Joe held on to the hair on the back of his head. "Please. Don't. I... I don't know who killed her. If I did, why would I come here looking for you?"

Joe pushed the gun harder into Craig's cheek. "I didn't ask you who killed her. I want you to tell me who the hell is after you."

"Okay, okay," Craig said, fear in his eyes, looking up at Joe. "I'll tell you. I'll tell you what I know."

Joe finally eased up on his grasp and let go of Craig's hair. He slowly eased the gun down by his side. "Start talking."

Craig rubbed the back of his head with his hand, looking up at Joe. "What are you, some kind of psycho?"

Joe didn't think he was. He was normally calm. Cool. But this man rubbed him the wrong way, for more reasons than one.

"All right," Bart said. "I've seen enough. I can't, in good conscience, stand here and watch this. If I don't let Woody know this guy's here..." He pulled his phone from his pocket.

Joe turned and grabbed it from Bart's hand. "Wait. Let's just see what he has to say, okay? You can call Woody when I'm done. But this might be my only chance."

Bart held his gaze on Joe, giving him a look like he might've been thinking he'd lost his mind. He grabbed the phone back from Joe. "You have five minutes, and then I'm calling Woody."

Joe turned back to Craig. "I want names."

Craig held his stare for a couple of seconds. "First I want you to tell me why you give a shit who killed Suzanne. I'm not telling you shit until you tell me what the hell's actually going on here."

Joe cleared his throat and glanced at Bart standing behind him. "All right," he said, turning back to Craig. "You want to know the truth?" He hesitated but didn't really care whether this deadbeat knew the truth or not. "I was with Suzanne yesterday. She spent most of the evening right here with me, in this apartment. And it's very likely I was the last person to see her alive."

He glanced back at Bart to see his reaction, and sure enough, it was about what he expected.

Bart's eyes were wide open, his jaw like it was about to hit the floor.

Craig started to stand from the couch. "You were 'with' my *wife*? What the fuck's that supposed to mean? You *slept* with her?"

Bart had his gun up again. "You'd better sit your ass down, buddy. I'm not going to tell you again."

Craig waited a moment or two, staring back at Joe, before he finally sat.

Joe shrugged. "I don't know what you're getting all upset for. She told me your marriage was over."

"She's my wife," Craig said through his teeth.

"I'm sorry. She's the one who called me, came looking for me. She showed up on South Beach, I thought at first because she had something to tell me about you, but..."

Craig had his eyes on the floor, shaking his head. "Jesus Christ. How could she?"

"Give me a break," Joe said. "You weren't even living there. She knows you were screwing around with that beauty queen up there."

"Beauty queen up *where*?"

"Wendy Johnson. She knew all about it."

Craig had a face on like he'd eaten something spoiled. "I told you there was nothing between us. Not like that." He made a face, like he gagged. "Christ, are you *kidding* me? Wendy?" His body shook as if he had a chill. "I'll admit I wasn't the most faithful husband around. But, Jesus... she really thought I was screwing Wendy?"

Joe tucked the gun in the back of his pants. "Then what's the story between the two of you?"

Craig shrugged. "What, me and Wendy? It was just business."

Bart nodded with his chin toward Craig. "You've got that look, like a drug dealer."

Craig stared back at him, looking him over. "You a cop?"

"Retired," Bart said like he always did, always proud to have worn the badge.

"What kind of business?" Joe said. "What were you and Wendy wrapped up in?"

"Well..." Craig seemed like he was hesitant to talk.

Bart had his phone out again. "Joe, I can't sit here and listen to all this. The cops need to be... I gotta call Woody. I have an obligation."

"You don't have an obligation to anyone," Joe said, turning to Bart, his back to Craig. "Come on, Bart. Just give me two more minutes, get this guy to talk."

With Joe's back turned, Craig came to his feet and reached for the gun tucked in the back of his pants.

Before Joe realized what had happened, Craig had the 9mm pointed at his head.

"Put the gun down," Bart said, pointing *his* weapon at Craig, lifting his phone up with the other. He tapped the screen.

Craig shook his head. "Put that phone down, or Joe here's going to get one in the head."

"He's not calling the cops," Joe said. "Bart, put the phone down. Please."

Bart put the phone up to his ear, listening.

Craig walked away from the couch, going backward, pulling Joe with him toward the kitchen. He had the gun up and pointed at Joe's head, using Joe to shield himself from Bart. "Tell him to put the phone *and* his gun down. I will shoot you, Joe. I kind of want to, if for no other reason than you slept with my wife." He continued past the kitchen and toward the door of Joe's apartment.

"Don't make another move!" Bart said.

But Craig didn't listen, taking his gun from Joe and pointing it at Bart. A gunshot exploded next to Joe's ear, and Craig pushed him out of the way, turning for the door, and disappearing into the hall.

Joe started to run after him but quickly glanced back at Bart, lying on the floor holding his leg.

"Bart!" he said, running over to him, crouching by his side. "You're shot."

Bart nodded. "Yeah, no shit," he said, grasping his leg with both hands. His gun was on the floor, and Joe could see the pain in his face. Bart nodded toward the door. "Don't worry about me, go get that piece of shit."

Blood dripped through Bart's fingers from his leg onto the hardwood floor beneath him.

Joe grabbed his phone and dialed 9-1-1. "We need to get you to a hospital," he said.

Bart looked like he tried to hide the pain. "It's... it's nothing."

Joe got up and ran down the hall toward his bathroom with the phone up to his ear. The 9-1-1 operator answered, and Joe quickly described what happened, then hung up and grabbed whatever towels he could, went into his bedroom and grabbed a T-shirt off the chair.

He ran back out into the other room and kneeled next to Bart, reaching for his waist and undoing his belt.

"What the hell are you doing?" Bart said, pushing Joe's hands away.

Joe knocked Bart's hands back and pulled off the belt, yanking at Bart's pants. They were soaked with blood, but he was able to pull them off without Bart putting up much more of a fight.

He never once cared or wondered if Bart was a boxer-or-briefs guy, but the pink-flowered boxers was a surprise.

Bart's head dropped back to the floor, his face white as milk.

Joe grabbed a pillow from the couch and tucked it under Bart's head. "We gotta stop the bleeding," Joe said, his voice shaking. He tried to remain calm, telling himself there was nothing to worry about. It was just a shot to the leg. *How bad could it be?*

But there was so much damn blood.

He continued with the tourniquet, tying the T-shirt tight around Bart's thigh above the wound, a towel wrapped over it. He did whatever he could to stop the bleeding.

Bart was losing a lot of blood, but Joe hoped he did enough.

Chapter 12

Joe was behind the wheel and had the top up on the Mercedes with a little rain coming down. He stared in a slight daze, thinking of maybe calling Lauren, when the phone rang. He looked at the screen and saw it was Dickie but decided not to ignore him. "Hey Dickie," he said, as if everything were normal.

"Joey? Where the hell've you been? I must've called you a dozen times."

"I know. I'm sorry."

"You hear the news?"

"It depends what news you're referring to." Joe drove ahead and turned into the parking lot at the hospital's emergency entrance and stopped to take a ticket. He waited until the barrier gate lifted, then continued into the parking lot.

"That broad you talked to a couple of days ago? Craig Peters' wife? She's dead. Someone shot her. Shot her twice. Popped her a couple times, right in the chest."

Joe stopped the car and pulled off to the side in a no-parking zone. He left the car running. "I know all about it," he said. "I guess you didn't catch the part I was the one who found her?"

"What? *You* found her? Get outta here. The way you talked... I thought you said you were all done looking for—"

"I am," Joe said. "I mean, I *was*." He had to think, be sure he wanted to tell Dickie the truth. "The thing is... that's not why I was there."

"*What's* not why you were *where*? At her apartment?"

"Yes. I wasn't there because I was looking for Craig Peters."

The line went quiet for five or ten seconds until Dickie said, "You shittin' me?"

Joe went on to tell Dickie everything that had happened. Most of it, at least, going all the way back to the moment Suzanne showed up at Jack's Hideaway on South Beach. "Now Bart's got a bullet lodged in his leg."

"Holy shit," Dickie said. "And Peters got away?"

"I couldn't leave Bart, the way he was bleeding. It was pretty bad, probably stained the hardwoods."

"Christ," Dickie said. "But I gotta tell you. If you'd called me back..."

"I told you why I didn't answer."

"Yeah, I heard that part. You were busy. I get it. But the reason I called you was to let you know you were right."

"Right about *what*?"

"Walking away from this Craig Peters' thing. I mean, before you got yourself involved with the wife."

Joe opened the window and leaned with his elbow out the window, his head resting in his hand. The light rain had already stopped. "What are you saying?" he said. He looked into the side-view mirror toward the hospital.

"What I'm saying is I got a call from a friend who knew Craig Peters owed me money. Tells me Peters got himself in real hot water with people you and me and anyone with half a brain won't mess with."

"I thought we already discussed this? I *told* you what Craig said to me."

"Yeah, no, but what I'm saying is we gotta watch out."

Joe said, "That's what Peters said." He straightened out in the seat, looking up in the rearview at the building. "And now I'm thinking this could be who killed Suzanne."

"Who the hell's Suzanne?"

Joe took a deep breath and exhaled, rolling his eyes. "Craig's wife."

"Oh yeah. Right. I forgot you'd gotten to know her on a first-name basis." He let out a laugh. "I gotta give it to you, Joey. The way you move with these women..."

Joe didn't find it funny. "So who are these people?"

"The people who're after him? It's not exactly concrete information just yet. But, a friend of mine, the one I talked to, is one of those people, may not always have the facts straight. So, for now, I'll take what I'm being told with a grain of salt. But if the information is correct, which it can be once in a while..."

"Dickie, just tell me their goddamn names, will you?"

"Jesus, Joey. Take it easy. I'm getting to it. It's just, well... Craig Peters stole from the company he was working for."

"Siskey Foods?"

"Yeah, you knew that? Well, it sounds like he was involved with that broad up there, the one who was shot up in Miami Gardens."

"Wendy Johnson," Joe said.

"Yeah, apparently she had some kind of scheme going while she was working at the Pancake House."

"A *scheme*? Like what?"

"I don't know all the details. But sounds like they were stealing money from both ends. The pancake place paid for the full delivery, but only half of it got delivered. Maybe the rest of it went to that bar she was running."

"No shit?" Joe said.

"Yeah, shit," Dickie said. "But wait'll I tell you... You know the name, Nick Juliano?"

Joe thought for a second. "You mean *Michael* Juliano?"

"No, *Nick*. Michael's the grandfather. But he's dead. I don't know, been dead maybe ten, fifteen years now?"

"You mean the grandfather? The grandfather's dead?"

"Yeah, Michal Juliano. Old bastard lived to be ninety-nine. Died in prison, three days before his hundredth birthday."

"So what about Nick? He's the grandson?"

"Nick Juliano is the president of Siskey Foods."

Joe said, "Oh, okay, so when you said grandson, I guess I assumed you meant some little kid. But that wouldn't make much sense."

"No. He's not a kid," Dickie said. "He's, I don't know. Middle-aged. Or whatever..."

"So, Peters and Wendy Johnson were, for the most part, stealing from Siskey Foods?"

"Well, indirectly, I guess. I mean, you know, the pancake place paid the bills up until someone finally figured it out."

Joe was thinking it through, trying to make sense of how they'd pull it off, assuming Wendy wasn't just some waitress at the restaurant.

"Is this guy Nick, the grandson... does he have the same criminal ties as the grandfather did?"

"You mean, is he *connected*?" Dickie cleared his throat. "Well, let's just say the grandfather wasn't just connected. He was an actual mob guy. Being connected and being an actual mob guy are two entirely different things. You know what I'm saying?"

"I understand that. Regardless..."

Joe was thinking about Suzanne, visions in his mind jumping from the way she looked when they were together at Joe's apartment, the smell of her perfume... her smile... to the image burned in his brain with the last time he saw her dead under those clothes on the floor of her closet.

Joe said, "You think Nick Juliano killed Suzanne?"

Dickie paused on the other end. "Now, first of all, it's not our place to decide who killed who. That's up to the cops to figure out. I just thought... I knew you'd want to know. And I wanted to tell you—just to say—you were right. So I think we should probably just move on from this Craig Peters' fiasco. Whatever happens to him happens. That money's not worth it, we get in the way of something like this. I mean, Peters ends up dead like his wife, so be it."

Joe leaned forward, resting his forehead on top of the steering wheel with his eyes closed. He had the phone up to his ear but didn't much feel like talking to Dickie any longer.

"Joey, I don't know what you've got in that thick head of yours. But I think you're smart enough to not get involved in any of this. Just because you spent the night with this broad..."

Joe straightened up in the seat. "Listen, I gotta get into the hospital, see how Bart's making out. I'll talk to you later." Joe thought he heard Dickie say something as he was ending the call but wasn't interested enough in calling him back to see what it was. He turned the ringer on silent and tossed the phone onto the passenger seat, shifting the car and turning the wheel. He drove away from the no-parking area where he'd stopped and continued slowly through the lot, driving up and down each row looking for an empty space.

. . . • . • . • . . .

Joe was surprised to see the empty bed when he walked into Bart's hospital room. It appeared to be untouched. He couldn't imagine Bart had already gotten out of there, and tried not to think the worst. But something made him nervous. He had a strange feeling, although he was pretty sure you couldn't die from being shot in the leg.

He walked from the room and down the hall, stopping a nurse coming out from another patient's room. "Excuse me," he said, pointing behind him with his thumb toward what he *thought* was Bart's room. "My friend... he's supposed to be in room three-oh-nine, but the room's empty. He was brought in here with a gunshot wound."

"The former police officer?" she said. "I believe he was assigned to three-oh-nine, but he was rushed into surgery." She pointed toward the desk. "If you go to the nurses' station over there, someone will be able to help you."

"The woman at the desk downstairs gave me his room number. She said he was up here."

The nurse shook her head. "Well, situations often change from the time a patient arrives to when a doctor examines the patient." She nodded toward the desk. "Like I said, they'll be able to help you. If by chance he's in surgery, he'd be in recovery once he was done. Of course, it's also possible, depending on the extent of the injury, he could be in the ICU."

"Oh," Joe said, nodding and not feeling any better about any of it. "Thank you." He continued toward the nurses' station.

A short woman and a younger man were laughing with each other while the other one spoke on the phone, staring at the screen in front of her. Joe cleared his throat, but all three acted as if he wasn't there.

"Excuse me," he said, leaning with his arms down on the countertop between them.

The two looked at him without saying a word. They just stared. The other didn't even look.

"Uh, I was told by someone downstairs, at the main desk, that my friend Bart Holden was supposed to be in room three-oh-nine. But that room's empty. And the nurse I just spoke to said it's possible he's in surgery. Or in intensive care. I don't know if anybody knows where he is, so I'm just trying to figure it out."

The woman who was on the phone hung it up but didn't take her eyes off the computer screen. "What's the patient's name?"

"Bart Holden. He's a former police officer with Miami."

The woman tapped the keys on the keyboard in front of her. "Mr. Holden is still in surgery. He could be in there another hour."

"Does it say why?" Joe said. "I mean, what are they doing?"

The nurse shook her head. "I'm afraid I can't answer that." She pointed toward the elevators. "If you're not a member of his immediate family, you'll have to go down and wait in the visitors' waiting area. Is there perhaps someone else you can talk to? A family member?"

Joe shook his head, thinking of Bart's ex-wife, but he hadn't talked to her since before their divorce. He wasn't sure she'd care if Bart was dead or alive at that point. "Is there a way I can talk to someone, at least see if he's all right?"

The nurse shook her head. "They'd answer questions down in the surgical unit. But only if you're immediate family."

"But I'm the only one here. I'm the only one who knows he's here."

The woman shrugged with a slight smirk on her face. "I'm sorry." She pointed down the hall. "The waiting area's down there, past the elevators. As soon as we know something, we'll send someone down to get you."

Joe took a deep breath and exhaled with a loud huff of air, then walked toward the elevators. He stopped in front of the elevator and looked back at the nurses behind the desk, all three back to doing whatever they were doing. Pressing the button, he waited until the door opened and took it down to the main lobby.

He stepped off but wasn't sure what to do or where to go. He wished hospitals had bars, or at least served alcohol. He was sure most people waiting around, anxious and scared, would be up for a drink or two most of the time.

Joe walked past a small seating area with most of the seats full, people watching the TV or looking at their phones. He continued toward the sliding doors and walked outside, standing on the sidewalk, unsure which direction he'd parked.

He looked at his phone again and, without much thought at all, dialed Lauren's number. It rang three times before he looked out toward the street, saw two Miami police cruisers park in the no-parking area.

Two officers stepped out from one, and Sgt. Woody Thomas got out from the other.

Lauren was on the other line. "Joe? Are you there?"

Joe wasn't paying enough attention to the call to notice when Lauren had answered. He kept his head down and hurried away from the hospital's entrance and slipped around the corner of the building and out of sight from Sergeant Thomas. He said into the phone, "Hey, yeah. I'm here. Sorry, I..." He kept walking, making sure he was far enough away.

It wasn't that he needed to hide from the cops. But he didn't want to have to answer any questions. Not right then. He wasn't exactly sure what he'd tell Sergeant Thomas had happened, then wondered what Bart would tell him, and if they'd have their stories straight.

The truth was, Joe was lucky to get away from his own apartment without answering too many questions when the police showed up in the first place.

He insisted on getting to the hospital to make sure his friend was okay, and the young officer at the scene didn't quite know how to stop him.

A rescue vehicle pulled into the parking lot with sirens blaring and drove past Joe toward the ambulatory entrance.

"Is that a siren?" Lauren said. "Where *are* you?"

"I'm at the hospital," he said. "With Bart. He's been shot."

She gasped into the phone. "Is he okay? What… what happened? Who shot him?"

"He's in surgery. At least that's what they're telling me." He looked at his own hand. He'd removed the bandage but stuck a jumbo sized Band-Aid on it to cover the wound. He leaned against the building with one foot up against the concrete exterior behind him. "Listen, I know you're busy with your new position and everything, but I was hoping you could help me with some digging."

"Digging?" she said, a light chuckle in her voice. "I thought maybe you were calling to say hello."

"I'm sorry. I was, I mean… this thing with Bart. It's kind of, well, I'm caught up in something I wish I wasn't, and…" He was hesitant. He knew he should just come right out and tell her everything. But on the other hand, there were details he wanted to keep to himself.

"Are you in trouble?" Lauren said. "Does this have something to do with this so-called work you're doing for Dickie?"

"What? No. No, it's not... I mean, it sort of is, but... I'll explain more later."

"So it has nothing to do with Dickie? But it does?"

"I can't tell you everything right now," he said. "I was just... Can you help me? Can you see what you can dig up on Nick Juliano?"

"Isn't he dead?"

"No. You may be thinking of his grandfather, Michael. They used to call him Mick."

Lauren said, "But this one's name is Nick? With an N?"

"Listen. Someone else was shot and killed. A woman."

"Oh." Lauren was quiet. "Who?"

Joe was thinking. "Her husband is the one who showed up at my apartment. He's the one who shot Bart."

"Is that why he was at your apartment?"

"Uh, well, technically... yes. But, I don't know if—"

"Oh, Joe," she said. "I hope you weren't messing around with someone else's wife, were you?"

"Me? No. It's... well... Like I said, I'll explain more later. Just see what you can find, then maybe you can call me later tonight?"

"I can't promise I can get right to this, Joe. If you could see my desk..."

"Okay. I know. I'm sorry, I didn't mean to be pushy. But, whenever you can get to it. Just give me a call when you do. Or, call me whenever you want."

The line went quiet.

Lauren said, "Am I looking at criminal records? Is that what you're asking me to do?"

"Sure. Or, really, whatever you can find."

Chapter 13

Joe was in the visitors' waiting area on the third floor and within view of the elevators when Sergeant Thomas stepped off and turned toward him, as if he already knew he was there.

It was too late for Joe to slip away, knowing avoiding the sergeant was a short game he would eventually lose. And as Woody Thomas continued toward him, holding a large take-out coffee in his hand, Joe stood and gave him a nod.

Sergeant Thomas said, "I guess you heard what's going on?"

Joe shook his head, feeling a lump in his throat and his heart pounding hard in his chest. "Nobody's telling me a thing."

"You saved Bart's life."

Joe had a twisted look to his face, pointing to himself. "*I* saved his life? Who told you *that*?"

Woody nodded. "I understand you're the one who tied that tourniquet?"

"Yeah, but... there was a lot of blood."

Woody said, "Doctor I just spoke with said if you hadn't done that, Bart wouldn't have survived."

Joe and Woody stood just a few feet apart, Joe looking past him down the hall toward the nurses' station. The three nurses he'd spoken to earlier were gone. "Where is he now?"

"He's in the ICU. Spending the night."

"But he'll be... Is he all right?"

Woody took his time giving an answer, his eyes toward the floor for a couple of seconds. "There's a chance he could lose his leg, but they won't know for a few more hours."

Joe felt the blood rush from his face, the pounding of his heart loud enough he could feel it in his ears. He didn't know what to say.

Woody continued, "He may need another surgery."

Joe let out a sigh and looked toward the big window and the darkness outside. He could just about see his own reflection in the glass. "Jesus, I..."

"You saved his life, Joe."

Joe felt his eyes gloss over, but part of what he felt was rage. He knew, right then, he wouldn't rest until he tracked down Craig Peters.

The sergeant finished what was in his cup and tossed it in a trash can a few feet away, then crossed his arms. He widened his stance and gazed into Joe's eyes. "The officer on the scene at your apartment said you wouldn't talk, tell him what happened. But I assume you're going to tell *me* what happened?"

Joe had cottonmouth, and his throat was sore, like it could crack if he swallowed. "It was Craig Peters."

Woody's eyes opened wide. "Peters? Are you sure?"

"Of course I am. He showed up at my apartment, trying to say I killed his wife."

Woody ran his big hand over his buzzed white hair, then slid it back to his neck, holding it there. "He's the main suspect in his wife's murder investigation. We've been looking for him, and you're trying to tell me he was in your apartment?"

Joe nodded, hesitant at first to tell the sergeant how much he knew. "I'm sure he had something to do with it," he said. "But, the way he was blaming me, I'm not sure he's the killer."

Woody had a surprised look on his face, his eyebrows raised. "We have a witness who placed him at that apartment," he said. "You told the officer the door was open when you arrived; isn't that right?"

"It was, yes."

"And we found no evidence of forced entry, meaning she either let the suspect enter on her own or potentially he used a key."

Joe said, "And who's the witness?"

"Young man, lives across the way," Woody said.

Joe thought about the kid he saw outside Suzanne's apartment the first time he was there: young man looked like a Harvard grad the way he was dressed in his khakis and a blue blazer.

Joe brushed his hair back. "That's the only witness? The young man across the hall?"

Woody gave Joe a look, like he didn't like the tone of his question. "I'm not going to share all the details of this crime with you, Joe. But, if we're both being honest with each other, a couple of the officers who were at the scene think I'm being too easy on you."

Joe said, "What the hell's that supposed to mean?"

"Well, you didn't try to hide the fact you were involved in some kind of relationship with Mrs. Peters. It goes without saying, normally someone in your position might be looked at as a possible suspect."

"Jesus Christ," Joe said. "I'm the one who called it in when I found her in that closet. You think I'd kill her, then call the police on myself?"

Woody shook his head, put his hand up with his palm toward Joe. "I just told you, it's not me who's asking. And I'm not saying you *are* a suspect. But, I just want you to be aware of where things stand. And now we have Bart in surgery, shot by the victim's husband. There's a lot to unravel here."

"Well, I didn't do it. I showed you the text she sent me. She was clearly in trouble." He looked past Woody at the nurses' station at the end of the hall. "And I hope you don't think this is all just about me and Suzanne Peters. I'm not sure our night together has much to do with what happened to her."

The sergeant shifted his stance. "The husband came after you. Bart wouldn't be in here if that were the case."

Joe shook his head. "I told you already, he showed up trying to say *I* killed Suzanne. That's why... my point about him, I guess—why would he show up to kill me for killing his wife if he's the one who killed her in the first place?"

Woody had a confused look on his face. "You just said you weren't sure it had much to do with what happened to her. But now you're saying—"

"Craig Peters may believe that I killed her. Although I thought I'd convinced him I had nothing to do with it before he ran off and fired his gun on his way out the door. But, what I'm saying is, if I didn't kill her, and Craig came after me because he thought I did... then doesn't that mean there's a good chance someone else did it? Someone *besides* me or Craig Peters?"

Woody took a look at the screen on his phone. "Were you aware he wasn't living there? Because the two were legally separated," Woody said.

"Yeah, I know that. And I don't know what 'legally' separated means. Can you be illegally separated?" He cracked a small grin. "I wouldn't have gotten involved with her otherwise," Joe said. "I mean, I wish I hadn't in the first place. For obvious reasons. But shit happens, you know what I mean? She made it clear their marriage was over, that he hadn't been living there for weeks. At least that's what she told *me*."

The sergeant said, "Then the husband shows up at your door with a weapon? Doesn't sound to me like a man who'd moved on from their marriage, does it?"

"Not at all," Joe said. "But I don't think it changes my point: there's a good chance someone else killed her."

The sergeant had a crooked grin on his face. "I know how you like to get involved in crime, in ways you maybe shouldn't, with your background and all... but I'm going to have to ask you to stick to answering the questions. The last thing we need right now is another amateur sleuth in the way. Christ, you know how many calls we get now from these true-crime podcasters?"

Joe stared back at Sergeant Thomas, feeling a bit insulted being compared to a podcaster. Joe had been involved in crimes and digging into investigations for almost twenty years as a journalist. He had more experience than half the Miami Police force. But he'd decided right then he was going to keep his mouth shut, let the police do what they were going to do without offering the sergeant, or anyone else, any more information than he had to.

Woody turned and started for the elevator, but stopped and looked back at Joe. "Do me a favor," Woody said. "You hear a word from Mr. Peters, give me a call ASAP."

Joe cracked a grin. "Didn't you just tell me you didn't want my help?"

"That's not what I meant."

"So you didn't mean to compare me to a podcaster?"

Woody cleared his throat. "You're not a cop, Joe. I've seen how you've gotten involved in the past. It can be dangerous. And now you're pulling Bart in, and—"

"I didn't pull him into anything," Joe said. "And, in case you haven't noticed, I *am* already involved. It sounds to me you haven't even crossed me off your suspect list. Isn't that right?"

Woody didn't answer right away, turning to look toward the elevators. "Once we've apprehended Craig Peters, we'll have some answers." He turned and started again for the elevator.

Joe said, "What makes you so sure you're going to find him?"

Woody Thomas turned again to Joe. "We'll find him. Don't worry." He continued toward the elevator and pressed the button, waiting but not saying anything else to Joe.

Joe watched him, wondering if he should throw Nick Juliano's name out there and see what Woody would say. But he knew once he did that, it'd open up a can of worms. And Woody would want to know where he got the name. It wasn't like he could tell him it was Dickie.

• • • ● • ● • • •

Joe pulled into Dickie's driveway, hungry and tired and wearing the same clothes he'd had on all day, stains of blood from Bart's leg dried into the fabric.

He knew it was past Dickie's bedtime, but they needed to talk. He stepped out from his car and looked at his phone, hoping Lauren would call with some background on Nick Juliano.

Joe rang the doorbell and waited.

Dickie opened it within a minute, wearing a blue robe over his shorts and a white V-neck T-shirt, showing off his white chest hairs. His hair was wet, like he'd just gotten out of the shower. "This couldn't wait until morning?"

Joe stepped inside without answering, getting a whiff of Dickie's aftershave.

"Bart could lose his leg," he said, following Dickie into the kitchen. "If Craig Peters doesn't go down for murdering his wife, he'll go down for shooting an ex-cop."

"I thought you said he didn't kill his wife?" Dickie said.

"He denied he did it."

"He denied it?" Dickie laughed. "What'd you expect? He'd confess to you?" He reached into the refrigerator and pulled out two bottles of Corona beer.

Joe said, "He wouldn't have come looking for me if he killed her."

Dickie nodded, like he agreed, taking the top off his bottle and taking a sip. He handed Joe the opener with the bottle of Corona.

Joe glanced at the label and popped off the cap. "So, what else can you tell me about Nick Juliano? You think he has it in him to kill a woman because her husband's a piece of shit?"

Dickie shrugged, taking a good swig from his bottle. "From what I know, he plays hardball. He doesn't get his way, or someone crosses him, he's just like the grandfather was. He'll take down whoever he feels he needs to." He looked at the clear bottle from the side and put it down on the counter. "You know, Joey, what do you even know about this woman? Just because you banged her doesn't mean—"

"I don't know *anything* about her. But she didn't deserve to be killed."

"How do you know that?"

"How do I know *what*?"

"How do you know she didn't deserve it? How do you know she wasn't fooling around with you for some other reason? Or, I don't know... what if her being killed didn't have as much to do with her loser husband as you think?"

Chapter 14

JOE WALKED INTO HOSPITAL room 309 where Bart was sitting up in bed, covers pulled up to his chest and the TV remote in his hand, clicking through the channels.

"Hey," Joe said, stepping up to the side of the bed, his eyes on Bart's legs tucked under the covers. "I hear they're letting you keep both legs?" He felt guilty about what Bart had gone through.

Bart rolled his eyes, nodding with a slight sigh. "Guess it was close, the way the bullet nicked the artery. Doctor said if you hadn't gotten that tourniquet around my leg, I might've bled to death, right there on your hardwoods."

"I was mostly just worried about the stain," Joe said, finally cracking a smile. "Management'd charge an arm and a leg for a mess like that."

Bart laughed, nodding. But then his expression turned serious. "Why didn't you just go after him?"

"Seriously? Because you'd be dead."

Bart looked over at the TV up on the wall, quiet for a moment. "Well, I can't wait to get my hands on him, break his goddamn neck."

Joe looked up at the TV where Bart had stopped on a black-and-white movie. Some kind of Western, with the sound down. "I spoke to Woody. They're looking for him. Not only for shooting you, but he's the prime suspect. Woody seems certain he killed Suzanne."

Bart coughed into the back of his hand. "Maybe you should stop calling her by her first name like that. You knew her for, what, barely twenty-four hours?"

Joe said, "So I can't use her first name?"

Bart shifted in the bed, and the look on his face showed his pain. "I know how you think," he said. "You make it too personal, and you're going to go do something stupid, get yourself all caught up in something you shouldn't."

"But it's okay for you to say you're going to find him and break his neck?"

Bart yanked the covers off so Joe could see his bandaged leg. The bandage went all the way from under the bottom of the gown and past his knee, almost to the middle of his shin. "The man almost killed me. It *is* personal to me. But, in your case... I think you'd be smart to just let law enforcement handle it. You know what I'm saying? Her homicide shouldn't be any of your business."

Joe looked away, his eyes toward the window. He thought about what Bart was saying but couldn't see how it made any sense.

"The thing is, Woody mentioned he was getting some heat for going easy on me. I guess someone over there isn't ready to take me off their list of suspects. So, maybe it is personal for me, if I'm not in the clear.

"He didn't mention that to me," Bart said.

"Well, the fact she was with me the night before she was killed doesn't look too good. I showed him her text and told him most of what I could."

"*Most* of what you could?" Bart's look was somewhat perplexed. "Why do I have the feeling you're saying you didn't tell him everything?"

Joe gave a slight shrug with one shoulder. "I told him what I knew. But only whatever I was certain of. But I'm looking into a couple of things. I asked Lauren to look into it for me."

"Are you telling me you have a name of someone who could be involved in this, but for some reason decided not to share it with the Miami Police Department? Why would you do that? So you can play the hero?"

"No, I—"

The door opened and a nurse stepped into Bart's room. "Hi," she said, smiling at Joe. "I'm sorry, but we have to change his surgical dressing. If you don't mind stepping out of the room, you can come back in about ten minutes."

Joe looked at Bart staring back at him. He thought Bart was lucky, having an attractive nurse present and not some of the other women and men in uniform he saw roaming the halls. "I'll come back later," he said, turning to leave.

"You'd better not play any games, Joe," Bart said.

Joe heard him but kept heading down the hall for the elevator.

·········

Joe walked across the parking lot outside the hospital and checked his phone, hoping he'd gotten a call from Lauren. But she hadn't. He opened the driver's side door, got in and dialed her number before doing anything else.

He was relieved when she answered on the first ring.

"Hey," she said. "I'm sorry I haven't called you back by now. I've just been—"

"I know you're busy up there," he said. "And I hope I'm not crossing the line, asking you to help me out again, but..."

"You know I don't mind, Joe. I just hope you're not getting yourself involved in something you shouldn't." She was quiet for a brief moment. "Can you at least promise me you're being careful?"

"You want me to promise you that?" He cleared his throat.. "I'll do my best."

The line went quiet.

"Did you happen to find anything yet?" he said. "Because I've had very little luck myself."

She said, "I can tell you what I have so far. But first, can you tell me what this is all about?"

"Do I have to?"

Again, the line went quiet.

"Can you at least tell me who this woman Suzanne Peters is? And how you know her?"

Joe knew Lauren was going to ask. But he still hadn't come up with something good enough to tell her without her figuring out he wasn't telling the truth. "Do you want me to be honest with you?"

"I was hoping you would be," she said.

Joe took a deep breath and exhaled, nodding. "I'm sorry," he said. "We just... she and I, we... we had a *thing*. It was just, I don't know what it was. We had a few drinks, and—"

"Okay, Joe. I get it. I kind of thought that's what you were going to say. And I certainly don't need the specifics. But I don't know why you're acting the way you are about it. I don't know how many times I've told you you're a free man. And I'm a free woman. Right? We both already agreed a long-distance relationship wasn't going to work. So, here we are. I date other men. And you're sleeping with shady women. So how about we move past the high school drama and be straight with each other, all right?"

Joe leaned his head back against the headrest, slouched in the front seat of his car. He put the key in the ignition and turned it so he could put down the roof.

"I looked her up," Lauren said. "She's very pretty. But she's not the most innocent woman you've ever fooled around with."

"What's that supposed to mean?"

"Well, she has a record. Mostly petty theft. She stole a car. She was arrested for breaking into a jewelry store, but that was five years ago. Her most recent run-in with the law was being arrested and tried for grand theft."

"Are you serious?"

"Why would I joke about that?"

Joe heard tapping coming through the phone, pictured Lauren at her desk, on the keyboard.

"But she was never convicted. The man who could have possibly put her behind bars was killed the day before he was supposed to take the stand in her trial."

Joe thought for a moment, realizing what Lauren and Bart and even Dickie had made clear: he didn't know Suzanne outside of a few drinks and a short evening in bed. "What'd she do?"

"Apparently, she was in a romantic relationship with an older gentleman, seventy-eight years old and very wealthy. His children, who he apparently hadn't spoken to for years before his death, claimed Suzanne Bryant—her maiden name before marrying Craig Peters four years ago—stole money from the father. And they convinced him to press charges. But the day before they were supposed to go to court, the old man was killed in a car accident."

"Oh shit," Joe said.

"Oh shit is right. He drove out of his driveway, took a left turn and was hit square on the driver's side. Hit and run. They never found the driver of the other car."

Joe didn't know how to respond. "It's certainly an important piece of information. But five years later, I'm not sure it has anything to do with her death."

"I'm not sure it does, either," Lauren said. "But I'm just wondering what this is all about."

"What *what* is all about?" Joe said.

"Why you're involved in something like this? Do you even know who Nick Juliano is?"

"Yeah, of course. He's Michael Juliano's grandson."

Lauren said, "That's right. And, although I haven't found any direct connection to say he's connected to the Mafia the way his grandfather was, it doesn't mean he's not. Or is any less dangerous."

"I hadn't made any assumptions yet, since I haven't been able to find much about the man. But I knew you could. The master."

Lauren laughed. "The master, huh? Well, can I assume you already know he's the CEO of Siskey Foods?"

"I *do* know that much."

"He's also single, no kids, no significant other, that I've found yet, although I'm still researching. His parents are together, living in a retirement home in Naples."

"Florida?"

"No. Italy. And he's an only child."

"And nothing's come up that shows any kind of mob connections?"

"No record, no nothing. He looks clean as they come. But that's not uncommon, Joe. You should know that. He could just be careful. Or maybe he has some cops in his pocket, make sure he stays clear of any trouble."

"What about his company? Did you happen to come across any kind of theft within his company?"

"What kind of theft?" she said.

"An employee. A delivery guy had something to do with the National Pancake House, which is one of their bigger customers?"

"Why didn't you mention that in the first place?" Lauren said, "I'll keep digging, but I can't get to it until tonight. As long as that's okay, I'll just call you later."

"Do whatever you can. Maybe there were no charges, or maybe it's something that, for some reason, was handled internally. You might not find anything."

Lauren said, "Do you want to give me some specifics? It'd make things a little easier."

Joe leaned his arms out the window, but the exterior was so hot from the sun, it made him jump when his skin hit the metal. "From what I'm being told, Craig Peters was stealing from them. Or he was involved in some kind of scheme. I don't know exactly what happened yet. That's what I need to find out. I'd still assume the company would take some kind of legal action, but maybe not. Especially if Nick Juliano learned how to handle things the way his grandfather used to."

"Can you tell me anything else? Was there anyone else involved with this guy, Craig Peters?"

"He partnered with a woman who ran a bar up in Miami Gardens. But she's dead. Apparently, the two were stealing from Siskey Foods and the National Pancake House. That's where she worked."

"I thought you just said she ran a bar?" Lauren said.

"She did. I don't know what the story was. But it sounds like she held the job at the pancake restaurant but left when someone must've caught on to what she and Craig Peters were doing."

Lauren sighed again into the phone. "I'm sorry, Joe. But this sounds a little crazy. You sure you should be getting wrapped up in it the way you are? Shouldn't you be a little more careful?"

"I'm always careful."

Lauren paused on the other end. "The *old* Joe was careful," she said. "But this person you've become, I don't know who... I don't know what you are now, Joe. It's like... Are you some kind of vigilante?"

Joe laughed. "A vigilante?"

"It seems like it to me," Lauren said. "You haven't given me a good enough reason why you've gotten caught up in this mess. Is it just because you slept with some woman?"

Chapter 15

Joe drove in his Mercedes, going slow as he came up along the long, white chain-link fence in front of the warehouse off Northwest 125th Street. He turned into the entrance, the gate wide open, and drove past the cube trucks and tractor trailers with Siskey Food painted on the sides, then backed up to the loading docks. The white, one-story building looked like it had rust stains from water dripping down the exterior from the flat roof.

He pulled into a parking space marked Visitor on a small sign on the curb in front of him and stepped out from the car. A white BMW was parked in a space to the right of the entrance. As Joe walked toward the vestibule, he saw the small brown sign, Mr. Juliano, at the front of the space where the Beemer was parked.

The cool, air-conditioned air hit Joe as soon as he pulled open the door to enter the lobby. Behind the curved, maple-wood service desk with a high-countered top, sat a pretty, middle-aged woman with dark, curly hair. She smiled at Joe and kept her eyes on him as he walked toward her.

"Good morning," she said. "Welcome to Siskey Foods." The smile still hadn't left her face, as if it were permanent or forced.

Joe looked to his left at a solid gray door with a sign hung on it that read, WAREHOUSE PERSON-NEL ONLY. There was an electronic keypad with buttons on the wall to the right of it, just below eye level.

Joe said, "I'm here for an appointment with Mr. Juliano." He smiled, calm and cool, even though he had a feeling it wouldn't be as easy as he liked.

"What is your name?"

"Robert Berkley," he said, making up the name at the last second without much thought. He toyed around with the idea of using a fake name before he got there and was stuck between the one he'd used, and Mike Algor, but decided against Mike Algor because it was someone he used to know when he'd worked at the *Post*.

She moved her eyes to the computer screen angled at her right, then typed on the keyboard. With her eyes still down, she slowly repeated "Roberrrt Berrrkley," as she typed. The smile left her face as she squinted, pointing at the screen. "You said it was Berkley? B-E-R-K-L-E-Y?"

Joe didn't hesitate, although maybe it could've been spelled a different way. "Yes, that's correct."

She looked up at him, shaking her head. "I'm sorry, then, but I don't see your name anywhere. Are you sure your appointment is today?"

Joe looked to his right toward another door, this one made of glass and leading to a wood-floored hallway. "Yes, I'm sure. How about... would you mind checking with him? Maybe he didn't tell you about it, or—"

"I have his calendar right here," she said, again pointing toward the screen. "Everything Mr. Juliano does is in here." She gave him a small grin. "I'm sorry, but—"

"Could you please check with him?" Joe said, looking right again, down the hall through the plate-glass door.

"He is a very busy man. He won't be able to see you without an appointment." She looked at the computer screen. "In fact, he may not even be available right now."

"Please?" Joe said. "Can't you just ask?" Joe was hesitant to take his lies to another level, to go along with the made-up name, but decided to go with it: "Tell him I'm with the Department of Employment Services. It pertains to an issue with a recent employee."

The woman held her eyes on Joe for a moment, then picked up the phone on her desk. She pressed three buttons. "Hey. There's a Robert Berkley out in the lobby, claiming he has a scheduled appointment with Mr. Juliano. But I don't see his name on his schedule." She nodded into the phone, glancing at Joe. "I looked there. Yes, okay. Right. I will tell him." She hung up the phone. "I'm sorry, I tried. But just as I suspected, Mr. Juliano is not available right now."

"But you didn't say who I was?"

The woman's friendly smile was long gone. She now appeared annoyed. "You didn't hear me say your name?"

Joe nodded. "You did. But you didn't tell him why I was here, and that I'm with the Department of Employment Services. This is an important meeting and—"

"Okay, okay," the woman said, letting out a sigh. She picked up the phone. "Hey, sorry to bother you again, but Mr. Berkley out here... he's with Employment Services and said it has something to do with a recent employee?" Her eyes were on Joe as she spoke, nodding again, then covering the phone's mouthpiece with her hand. She said to Joe, "Are you sure you're not here to meet with Sarah Adams, in HR?"

"Sarah Adams?" He thought about it. "No, but... if she's available, I could meet with her."

The woman spoke into the phone. "I'll check with Sarah," then hung it up on the base. "I don't even know if she's available. But Sarah's the VP of Human Resources. If you want to speak with her, I'll first have to see if she's available."

"That sounds great," Joe said, glancing once again through the glass door and down the hall. A man poked his head out from a doorway on the left at the far end of the hall, staring back at Joe, his black hair slicked back on his head.

But as soon as he saw Joe look at him, he pulled his head back in.

Joe had a feeling whoever it was, was looking to see who wanted to talk to Mr. Juliano. Maybe he was wrong, but it seemed it. In fact, the man looked somewhat familiar, although Joe couldn't quite place him.

The woman behind the desk was on the phone. "Sarah? Hey, it's Eloise. There's a man here from Labor Services and—"

"Employment Services," Joe said.

"Oh, sorry. He's with Employment Services." She paused, listening. "I don't know. He was here to meet with Mr. Juliano. But there's apparently been a mix-up." She paused again, nodding. "Yes, okay. I'll tell him." She hung up the phone and gestured with her hand toward the set of chairs surrounding a short square table covered in magazines, neatly fanned like a hand of cards. "If you'd like to have a seat, Sarah will be up to see you in a few moments."

"Thank you," Joe said, smiling. He stepped over to the seating area, sat down and reached for a magazine from the coffee table in the middle of the space. *Food Industry Today* was the name of the publication. It was dated two years earlier. He flipped through the pages, not finding much of anything he found interesting. He stopped on a page with an advertisement for Siskey Foods and saw a photo of Nick Juliano in a pin-striped suit, posing with his arms crossed, with his signature printed in gold under the photo. The ad said, "We're Serving Restaurants in a New Way."

Joe wasn't sure what that meant but studied the photo of Juliano, showing the same slicked-back hair as the man Joe spotted down the hall. The photo made the man look tall, with the angle of the camera, but Joe knew better. Like his grandfather, Nick was far from tall. Maybe he was five seven with the thick heels short men like him might wear when they got dressed up.

Joe looked up when the glass door opened, and a younger woman, tall and thin, walked toward him. "Hi," she said. "I'm Sarah Adams. I understand you're with State Employment Services?"

Joe stood from the chair and reached out to shake her hand. "Hi." He had to think for a second. "Robert Berkley."

She had a perplexed look on her face. "I don't recall ever having a visit from someone at Employment Services before." She glanced at the woman behind the desk. "Eloise said this pertains to a former employee of ours?"

Joe nodded. "Is there somewhere we can go speak in private?"

Sarah nodded, held the door for Joe, then stepped past him, leading him down the hall.

He peeked in the room on the left, where the man with the slicked-black hair had been looking out at him. But the door was closed. He didn't believe it was Nick Juliano, just someone with the same look like Joe saw in the magazine.

He followed Sarah Adams down the hall, turning right at the end of it and into a conference room with a small round table and six chairs around it. "Please," she said, gesturing toward the chair across the table from where she stood. She brushed a strand of hair from her face, looking Joe over as he sat. "I'm a little surprised you don't have anything with you? Some kind of paperwork, or..."

"Oh, well, like I told the woman at the front desk... I had an appointment with Mr. Juliano."

She nodded, giving Joe a look like she didn't know what that had to do with him not having anything in his hands. "Well, I spoke with Mr. Juliano, and he doesn't recall who you are."

Joe put on a surprised look, his eyebrows high. "What? Seriously?" He laughed. "That doesn't make any sense. We spoke on the phone."

Sarah leaned forward. "All right, well, either way, he asked me to get to the bottom of this and try to understand what this is all about." She squinted her eyes. "You said it's got to do with a past employee?"

"Yes. It's an unemployment claim, and we need to verify some things."

"Couldn't you have just done whatever you needed to do over the phone?" She held her gaze on Joe.

"Yes, of course. But we've been spending more time in the field with employers." He grinned. "Sometimes, a special case such as this one requires a face-to-face meeting. I had explained that to Mr. Juliano when we spoke on the phone."

"But, as I just said, he doesn't know who you are." She leaned back in her chair. "Who is the former employee?"

"His name is Craig Peters. So, if you can just tell me exactly what happened with his employment here, that's really all I need from you for now."

The woman's expression dropped. "Craig Peters?" She tried to hide her swallow, but it wasn't something she seemed able to do. "Craig is... what exactly would this have to do with...?"

"We just need to understand the reasoning behind his termination," Joe said.

"His termination?" She shifted in her chair, her eyes going toward the door she'd left open. "Mr. Peters was not terminated. He stopped showing up to work."

"He stopped showing up? He wasn't, uh, let go?"

"That's what I just said." She stood from the table. "So, if that answers your question... you could have saved yourself a trip by picking up the phone." She stood with her hand on the door.

"Well, there's more to it," Joe said. "What about his job performance?"

She gave Joe a confused look, her eyebrows pinched together over her eyes. "I'm not sure I understand the purpose of your question. I told you already, he stopped showing up to work. We did not terminate him. It had nothing to do with performance, or—"

"Or him stealing from the company? Or from one of your biggest customers?" Joe said.

Sarah Adams poked her head out into the hall and looked back and forth, as if looking for someone. She turned back to Joe. "Mr. Berkley, I'm going to have to ask you to leave this office."

Joe stood from his chair, a smirk on his face. "You seem to've tensed up a bit. And you don't seem the least bit surprised I know he was up to something. It would be my assumption he'd be terminated, no?"

Sarah looked out into the hall again without a response, then stepped out into the hallway and disappeared.

As Joe walked toward the door, two men dressed in suits, both Joe's height and size, reached for Joe, each grabbing one of his arms.

"Time to go," one of the men said, the two dragging Joe toward the door and down the hall. They walked him through the open glass door, into the lobby, past the woman at the front desk and shoved him out the door into the parking lot.

Joe stumbled but caught himself before hitting the pavement. "You can't just throw out an employee of the state like this," Joe said, walking to his car.

The two men stood outside the door watching him as Joe backed out of the parking space and drove away, slowly.

He looked out the passenger window toward the building as he drove for the open gate. On the other side of the plate-glass door at the entrance was a man Joe had no doubt was Nick Juliano, watching Joe drive away.

Chapter 16

BART LEANED HIS CRUTCHES against the glass table on the patio in his backyard and sat down, the umbrella overhead, across from Joe. "Can you please explain to me why the hell you'd go see Nick Juliano?" Bart shifted in the chair, using both hands to move the position of his bandaged leg.

"I was just hoping to talk to him," Joe said, "see what he'd have to say."

"You really think you'd just walk in his office, he'd start answering all your questions?" Bart reached for his bottle of beer. "And the problem you have now is that he knows who you are."

"He doesn't know my name."

Bart rolled his eyes. "But he saw your car."

Joe said, "Well, the thing is, I guess I hadn't really planned it out. I just wanted to see who this guy was, maybe get a feeling about the whole thing, see if I could figure a few things out. And, sure enough..."

"Sure enough *what?* Just because the woman from Human Resources didn't tell you anything about Craig

Peters doesn't mean the company has something to hide."

"You don't think the fact he wasn't terminated for stealing from the company says something?" Joe leaned forward on the table. "On top of that, they never contacted the police about it?"

Bart sipped his beer, shaking his head. "You're basing this all off something Dickie told you," he said. "He has no proof of any of it, and no idea whether or not Craig Peters was even involved in some so-called scheme. Juliano may know nothing about it, if it even happened." He looked down at his bottle, picking at the label on the side. "I'm still not sure I understand why you're going through all this trouble. You ask me, the only one I want to see behind bars—or six feet underground—is Craig Peters. But I'm smart enough to know I don't need to let my emotions get in the way. Woody and half the force are out looking for him." He held up his bottle. "I've decided I'm going to start to enjoy my retirement. Be grateful I've still got two legs."

"But they still believe Craig killed his wife," Joe said. "It just doesn't make sense."

"Are you serious?" Bart laughed, resting his beer on the chair's armrest. "He knows you were tapping his wife. I'd say that's enough of a motive he showed up trying to kill you. And you're going to believe whatever kind of BS he was feeding you?"

Joe leaned back in the chair and looked around Bart's backyard, beyond the fence, toward the neighbor's house. "I want to talk to the kid across from Suzanne's apartment."

"What kid?"

"The one who claims he saw Craig leaving the apartment."

Bart put the bottle on the table and rubbed both hands over his face. "Jesus, Joe. You're so goddamn thickheaded. I don't understand you sometimes."

Joe stared back at him without an answer, shrugged, and finally sipped the beer sitting on the table in front of him. "I saw the kid across the hall when I was there, the first time I met Suzanne."

"I didn't know you were there prior to—"

"I know you don't want to hear about my work with Dickie, but I went there a few days ago. I was looking for Craig."

Bart put up his hands, palms toward Joe. "You're right. I don't want to hear about it." He was quiet, looking away from Joe but turned back to him. "Okay, wait... what do you mean he's a kid? Like, how old?"

"Mid-twenties."

"Oh, okay. But, why do you need to talk to him? I'm sure Woody's already spoken to him."

Joe took another sip of beer and removed his sunglasses from his pocket, slipping them over his eyes. He stood from the table and ducked as he stepped out from under the umbrella. "Well, if he claims he saw Craig there in the middle of the night, I just want to hear it with my own two ears. And ask him what else he might've seen."

"Why don't you just ask Woody?" Bart said.

Joe shook his head. "The truth is, there might've been something going on between the two."

"What two?"

"Suzanne and the kid across the hall. He was there, came out of his apartment the same morning I was there."

"When she was dead?"

Joe shook his head. "No. I told you, I was there looking for Craig Peters, doing something for Dickie."

Bart shrugged. "You think maybe you weren't the only one she was sleeping with?"

Joe had his back to Bart, looking around the yard. "It's possible. But, either way, I'd just like to talk to him. And it's not like Woody's going to share any details with me at this point."

Bart pushed himself up from the chair. "I still don't understand why you're doing this. What's it matter at this point? And if Juliano is involved in something, then you've already blown your cover showing up at his warehouse."

"I want to know it wasn't my fault."

"That she was killed? Why would it be your fault?" Bart said. He finished what was left in his beer, grabbed his crutches, and started toward his house. "The only thing that makes sense right now is Craig Peters knew you'd slept with her, showed up and killed her."

Joe followed Bart to the back door, grabbed the handle and pulled it open so Bart could go in ahead of him.

Bart made his way to the small table in the corner of his kitchen and leaned the crutches against the counter. He rubbed underneath his armpit. "Jesus, these things hurt my arms."

Joe leaned with his back against the front of the sink, the bay window behind him. "I liked her, Bart. I know there wasn't much to it, and it was only one night. I just, I don't think it's right for me to just walk away from it, like I had nothing to do with her."

Bart cleared his throat, nodding toward the refrigerator. "Why don't you go ahead, grab a couple more beers out of there."

Joe opened the refrigerator door and pulled out a bottle, cracked the top and handed it to Bart. He didn't take one for himself. "I'm actually going to get going," he said. "You need anything before I go?"

Bart stared back at him without answering. "Joe, you're going to get yourself killed out there. Why don't you at least give me a couple days until I can walk on my own two feet without these goddamn crutches? At least someone'll have your back if you get in trouble."

Joe stared out the window into the yard. "I still think Juliano had something to do with it."

"Based on what evidence?" Bart said. "Your gut?" He laughed. "That damn thing gets you in more trouble..."

Joe shook his head. "Craig Peters was stealing from the company. His partner in crime is already dead.

Now his wife's dead. And nobody from Siskey reported it?"

"You mean that someone was stealing from them?" Bart said. "Because maybe it's all bullshit. Maybe what Dickie told you is all wrong. It wouldn't be the first time he screwed up the story."

Joe was quiet, thinking. "But that night, Craig Peters told me someone else was after him. He *warned* me. It must've been Juliano."

The two were both quiet for a few moments until Bart pushed himself up from the table and reached for his crutches. "I gotta hit the head. You staying for a couple more minutes?"

"No. I'm going to go. But I'll call you later. Or call me if you need anything." Joe walked out from the kitchen ahead of Bart and stopped in the hall, turning back as he reached for the front door. "You think you'll talk to Woody at any point?"

Bart flipped the light on in the bathroom. "He said he'd stop by for a visit, but I don't know how much he's going to tell me. He's looking for Craig Peters, and I'm not sure there's much more to it right now."

· · · · ● · ● · · · ·

It was early evening when Joe turned off Northeast Third into the parking lot of Suzanne's apartment. A hard rain was coming down as he drove to a parking space close to the stairs. He stepped out of the car and into a puddle, soaking his shoes.

He had made it to the second floor when he heard someone coming down the stairs from the third floor above him, so he ducked around the corner to avoid being seen. Leaning with his back against the wall, he waited, listening.

Whoever it was continued down the next set of stairs to the parking lot.

Once Joe knew the coast was clear, he continued up to the third floor. He turned and looked over the railing and at the parking lot and saw the man who had just left, Joe watching him with his head down, hurrying in the rain without running, making his way to an older American car with what looked to be faded blue paint. Joe was almost certain it was an old Buick Regal from the nineties. It reminded him of the one his aunt used to drive.

He turned from the railing and looked at the door to Suzanne's apartment. The police tape was gone, and there was no sign or indication anything out of the ordinary had occurred. But Joe knew that wasn't true. He wondered how soon they'd rent the place out, new tenants moving in without a clue a woman had been found dead in the closet.

He looked back at the door of the young neighbor across the way, wondering if there was really ever anything between the kid and Suzanne. Most times people moved in and out of apartment buildings in Miami without ever knowing a single neighbor's name, unless they happened to get the wrong mail. Joe found it interesting, if not a bit curious that Suzanne and her neighbor, Brad, were even on a first-name basis.

He'd since learned Brad's last name was Ridley. He was a Yale graduate who'd recently moved down to Miami for a job with one of the bigger law firms.

Joe walked up to Brad's door and knocked, looking at the other apartment doors on the same floor and down the hall toward the back of the building. He looked out through the opening over the railing. The rain had stopped with the sun already sneaking through the clouds. The humidity was thick.

He liked that his apartment wasn't the garden-style kind with the open areas exposed to the outside. *What was the purpose?*

A couple of minutes had gone by, and Brad Ridley still hadn't come to the door. Joe put his ear against it to listen for a sound on the other side but didn't hear much of anything at all. He knocked again, guessing maybe the kid wasn't home. He waited, looked at his watch, and decided he'd come back later, maybe try again in a couple of hours.

But before he turned away to leave, he thought he'd try the doorknob. He gave it a turn and was surprised when the door opened. It hadn't been locked.

Joe poked his head inside the apartment and looked down the hall before finally walking inside. "Hello?" he said.

The layout was different from Suzanne's apartment, seeming a little bigger with more space. The kitchen, where he stood, was definitely bigger. He continued down the hall with a door on the left and another door on the right. Both were closed.

But there was a light coming out from underneath the one on the right. "Hello?" Joe said.

It was quiet, other than the sound of the vents blowing cool air down from the ceiling. He thought maybe he should just get out of there before he got in any kind of trouble. Maybe Brad hadn't even gotten home from work, forgetting to lock his door before he left.

But Joe thought, with a murder across the hall, leaving your door unlocked would be foolish.

He walked to the end of the hall and looked in an open door of a bedroom, the bed made and the dresser with nothing at all on top of it. The place was clean.

He decided to get out of there. Heading down the hall toward the front door, he passed the door with the light coming from underneath it and knocked, gently, with the back of his knuckles. "Brad?" He listened, his ear turned toward the door. "You in there?"

After a moment he turned the knob and slowly opened the door.

Brad was seated on the toilet, his phone on the floor, his body slumped over with blood coming down from his head, pooling on the floor around his bare feet.

Chapter 17

"YOU DO UNDERSTAND HOW bad this looks?" Sgt. Woody Thomas said, standing face-to-face with Joe in the parking lot outside the building. He looked over his shoulder toward the officers coming down the stairway. "I'm getting heat for not arresting you, because nobody believes it's just a coincidence you found two bodies within a couple of days, in the same apartment building. I'm trying to come up with a good enough reason why they should believe you, but it's not easy."

Joe nodded, like he agreed, but had already explained to the sergeant and the detective upstairs in the apartment why he was there in the first place.

"You can't just help yourself into someone's home," Woody said, "and not expect there to be consequences."

"You're right," Joe said, looking past Woody toward the other officers staring back at him. "Does that mean you don't believe that I saw a man leaving when I got here?"

"We have officers out there looking for the car you described. But just because you saw someone leaving the apartment building, doesn't mean you saw the killer." He looked down at the wet ground for a moment before raising his eyes to Joe. "I just need you to understand my position. Even if I believe you had nothing to do with either killing, I may need to take you in just for the fact you've gotten in the way of the Suzanne Peters' investigation. And now the one witness who may've known something about what happened is dead."

"How am I getting in the way?" Joe said.

Woody gave him a look, like he wasn't sure why he'd have to ask such a foolish question. "Joe, you entered the home of two victims on two separate occasions. That's not something we in law enforcement consider a normal—"

"I don't even own a gun," Joe said. "In case you're really trying to say there's the slightest chance you think I killed either of them." He shook his head. "You know it doesn't make sense."

Woody stared back at him, his eyes narrowed. "You know how many times we've been told by a suspect he doesn't own a gun?"

Joe's eyebrows came down tight over his eyes. "So, I *am* a suspect?"

Woody looked away without answering. "Joe, as I already told you: It just doesn't look good, you being here like this. If I didn't know any better..." He paused. "I'm just not sure you're telling me every- thing I need to know."

Joe knew that was fair enough. He hadn't told Woody everything. Not even close. But that didn't make him guilty. "How many people murder someone and then call the police?"

"How many people break into two homes and find two dead bodies, all within a couple of days?" Woody started to walk away, toward the stairs, then stopped and turned to Joe. "I'm sorry, Joe. But I'm going to need you to come downtown and answer some serious questions. I'm trying to cut you a break, but—"

"I didn't even break in," Joe said. "The doors were already open. Both times. Either way, what else do you want me to tell you?" Joe thought about Nick Juliano but didn't have enough to share with Woody. For the time being, he wanted to keep it to himself until he could dig a little deeper, even if it meant Woody suspecting Joe was holding back.

Woody stared back at him. "I need to get back up there, see how my detective's making out." He looked at his watch and gave him a nod. "You can get out of here for now. But don't go far. I'd appreciate it if you'd come down to headquarters tomorrow, first thing in the morning. Don't make me come looking for you."

•••••••••••

Joe drove straight to Dickie's house from the apartment and called him on the way, but Dickie didn't pick up. When he got there, he pulled into the driveway and parked in front of the garage door on the right.

Dickie lived in a long ranch-style home with white stucco siding and brown trim. The yard was well-lit in the darkness, showing off the professional landscaping with flowering trees around the concrete water fountain in front. The lights shined on the grass, and Joe could see how green it was from all the chemicals Dickie liked to use.

Joe joked to him he'd get cancer just looking at it.

He walked up the stone steps and peeked in through the window to the right of the door, and saw Dickie slumped over on the couch in front of the TV, his chin thick, doubled up, tucked into his chest.

It made Joe nervous at first, pounding on the door and ringing the doorbell at the same time. But he was relieved to see Dickie jump to his feet, alarmed like he didn't know where he was.

The door opened, and Dickie stood staring out at him, yawning and rubbing his eyes. "Joey? What are you... What time is it?"

"Nine forty-five."

Dickie looked out toward the driveway, like he still hadn't fully woken up, then finally pushed open the door. "Come in, will ya?" He walked toward the couch, picked up the remote and turned down the volume on the TV.

"Sorry to wake you," Joe said, stepping into the house. He looked at the TV. The Miami Heat were playing the Boston Celtics.

"I must've passed out," Dickie said, scratching the top of his head. He started toward the kitchen. "So, what's the story?"

Joe followed him. "The story?"

"Yeah, I mean... what's the latest?" He pointed toward the counter with the four stools facing the other direction toward where Dickie had a new TV up on the wall over the refrigerator. "You want a drink?" He pulled a bottle of vodka down from the cabinet. "I actually picked up some cranberry juice, in case you came by."

Joe sat down on a stool and looked across the counter at Dickie on the other side. He had a crooked grin on his face, knowing the last time they saw each other the conversation was a bit uncomfortable. "A drink sounds good right now."

Dickie dropped a few ice cubes into a glass and filled it with vodka, topped it off with cranberry juice, the way Joe liked it. He slid the glass across the counter. "Sorry, no limes."

Joe reached for the glass and took a sip. "Suzanne Peters' neighbor was murdered tonight."

Dickie was making himself a martini, his eyes on the glass, but stopped and looked up at Joe. "You shittin' me?"

"No. Young kid too. I mean, he wasn't a kid but young, you know? A young man."

"How'd you hear this?"

Joe took another sip, looking at Dickie from over the rim of the glass. "I found him."

"*You* found him?" Dickie poured vermouth into the silver mixing cup with the vodka and ice. He gave it a dash of olive juice. "That can't look good for you, Joey."

"Woody was there. Maybe I made a mistake, calling them."

"The cops?" Dickie said, pouring the drink into the martini glass. "So what'd you do? After you found him?"

"What'd I do?" He shrugged. "I called the cops?"

"And what exactly did they say?"

Joe took a good drink this time, got down to at least a third of what was poured, then placed the glass down on the counter. "I don't know. Woody was doing his best to keep me out of trouble, but then he asked me to go down the station in the morning. I'm trying not to be too worried. The guy that calls the cops isn't usually the suspect, right?"

"Well, I think you need to be careful," Dickie said. "You want Stanley to go with you?"

Joe shook his head. "I don't need a lawyer for this. Not yet. But maybe give him a heads-up I'm going down there? In case I change my mind?"

Dickie leaned with his elbows on the counter, looking Joe in the eye. "Listen, Joey. I'm glad you came by. Because, I mean, I know you don't want to do this work for me anymore. I get it; you don't like it. Especially the way shit like this goes down, you get yourself all mixed up in something bad... it'll put a little scare into the best of 'em. But, I just... I hope you'll think about it a little more. Maybe once you get through this and—"

"No," Joe said. "I'm done, Dickie. I just want to make sure we can still be friends. The thing is, and I told you this already, I never intended to become this goon I've become."

"Who said you were a *goon*?"

"Come on, Dickie. You know that's where it was heading. It's just not my bag. It's the wrong side of the line."

"What *line*?"

"The line. The law. Whatever you want to call it. Good and bad. *You* know what I'm saying." Joe looked toward the floor. "And, honestly, Dickie, how much longer are you going to keep doing this? How many more years do you have in you?" He lifted his phone and pointed at the screen. "I can place a bet on my phone in two minutes."

Dickie shook his head. "I'm not worried about it. There are always going to be the schmucks who gamble, like Craig Peters, but don't have the money to put up. That's why I'm still in business. It's why I'll always be in business." He gave Joe a crooked smile. "I gotta admit, having a guy like you with brains and a little brawn to go with it... it's not easy to come by." He sipped his drink. "But I hear what you're saying."

Joe picked up his glass and finished what was left, looking at the TV on above the fridge. Dickie had the same basketball game on as he did in the other room. "Listen, though," he said. "I was hoping you could tell me what else you know about Nick Juliano? I went by his office today."

"You *what?*" Dickie's eyes popped wide open. "Why the hell would you do something like that? You like putting your nuts in a vise?"

Joe told him what had happened at the Siskey warehouse, and wondered if it had something to do with the kid Brad getting plugged. "But I don't understand why he'd kill him."

"Who?"

"The kid across the hall."

Dickie said, "Oh. Is that where he was? Across the hall?"

Joe wasn't sure Dickie was always listening to him. "I told you, he lived across the hall from Suzanne. But he was on the toilet when I walked in. Someone shot him in the head."

Dickie shook his head, rolling his eyes. "What a way to go, huh?"

Joe got up from the stool and walked to the sliding glass door. He looked into the backyard lit up so bright with floodlights, like it was in the front, that it almost looked like daytime. Dickie had a pool he hardly used, with cobblestone taking up most of the yard inside the tall wooden privacy fence, with full-grown palm trees in each corner and tall shrubs outside the fence to create plenty more privacy.

"I didn't mention anything about Nick Juliano," Joe said. "And I don't think I should, until I can dig in a little deeper." He turned from the door.

Dickie made him another drink and came around from the other side of the counter. "Maybe it'd be smart to just keep your mouth shut. I mean, I didn't think you'd go knocking on his door, show up at his office like you did."

Joe was a little confused. "But you're the one who told me. You said it yourself, you didn't think he was connected."

"I was just saying," Dickie said. "I don't know if he is or he isn't. But it doesn't mean he won't take matters into his own hands, the way his grandfather did." He held up his martini glass in front of his lips. "You know, you don't go around bragging about who you are or who you know, like they used to in the old days. Not unless you want the FBI up your ass everywhere you turn."

Joe took his drink from Dickie and placed it down on the counter without taking a sip. "So, what you're saying is there's a good chance he's not as clean as he wants people to think?"

"I'm not saying one way or the other. But you never know what a man'll do if someone steals from him."

Joe picked up the glass and took a good drink. "I guess it was pretty foolish of me to take my car over to his office."

Dickie nodded. "Of course it was foolish. That's not like you, make such a stupid move." He wagged his finger at Joe. "See, you got yourself all into helping this broad, and she's not even alive anymore." He squinted his eyes. "You sure they saw your car? I mean, I assume you didn't park it right out front, right?"

Joe felt like a chump. "I parked right next to Juliano's parking space."

Dickie rolled his eyes, shaking his head. "And you're sure nobody followed you out of there?"

"I'm fairly certain."

"*Fairly* certain?" Dickie said. "Have you been back to your apartment since you went there?"

"Since I was at Juliano's office?" Joe shook his head. "No, not yet."

Dickie pulled at his chin. "So you have no idea if he's got someone trying to track you down?"

Joe shrugged. "I can't imagine they'd—"

"You don't think they'd come looking for you? Why? Just because you used a fake name?" He nodded toward Joe. "You want the Glock?"

Joe didn't answer, thinking for a moment. "Maybe it's time I come clean with Woody, tell him everything I know."

"Who the hell's Woody?" Dickie said.

"Sergeant Woody Thomas."

Dickie smiled. "Look at you, huh? First-name basis with another cop?"

Joe didn't respond.

"As we've talked about, Joey, you start telling the cops your business—our business—all you're gonna do is open a can of worms. The best thing you can do right now is watch your ass and keep your mouth shut. Period."

Chapter 18

JOE SAT DOWN IN the small wood chair with the worn leather seat, facing Sergeant Thomas's empty metal desk. With his back to the door, he sipped a coffee from a Styrofoam cup and looked at the framed photos on the wall—the one of Woody and Bart together catching his eye. They were kids. Even though Bart was an officer with the Miami-Dade Police and Woody was with the City of Miami Police, the two had been friends for at least as long as they'd each worn the uniform. Another photo was of Woody in a military uniform with a rifle in one hand, standing in what looked like a desert.

Joe turned and looked over his shoulder when he heard someone at the door.

Woody had walked in with a folder in his hand and sipped from a mug with the Jacksonville Jaguars logo printed on it. "Thanks again for coming down, Joe." He pushed the door closed behind him with his foot and stepped around to his desk, placing the mug next to the landline phone. He sat, opened the folder, and flipped through the papers inside.

Joe had his eyes back on the photo of Woody and Bart. "How long ago was that taken?" He was curious, but also asked so he could hopefully lighten up the mood, get in some small talk before they got serious. It was something he used to do when he was a reporter, to loosen up the subject he was interviewing for a crime story.

Woody turned in his leather desk chair and looked up at the framed photos behind him on the wall. He nodded and turned to Joe with a small grin on his face. "That photo was taken thirty-one years ago. I remember it like it was yesterday. Me and Bart... we were barely old enough to buy beers." He picked up his mug and took a sip, looking down over the top of it at the papers in the folder. "All right, Joe. Let me just make it clear, before we go any further, this has nothing to do with you being a suspect at this time. So I don't want you to be too concerned. Of course, it doesn't mean there are no issues with the fact you were present for two homicides, but—"

"Can we be clear that I wasn't present when they actually occurred? I know it's a minor detail, but..."

"Right," Woody said. "What I mean is, of course, it's not something we can completely ignore. I'm sure you understand."

Joe said. "Are you telling me I'm a person of inter-est?"

Woody clasped his hands together on top of the papers. "You're someone who we believe should be able to shed some light on what the hell this is all about.

And, of course, what happened with you and Bart back at your apartment can't be overlooked, either."

Joe sat forward in his chair and nodded, licking his dry lips as he picked up the Styrofoam cup of cold coffee. He took a sip, and it didn't taste very good. He wished he'd just asked for water. "So, if I'm not exactly a suspect"—he gave a slight grin—"then is Craig Peters your *only* suspect?"

Woody picked up the papers in the folder and held them up. "We're looking into everything right now, Joe. But with Peters on the run from us, well... innocent people don't normally run."

"Innocent don't *run*?" Joe said, knowing it was not nearly enough to go into court and point a finger at a suspect because he hid from the police.

Woody gave him a look, squinting, like he didn't like being questioned. "More often than not."

Joe grinned, picked up the cup and tried another sip. "It's just... I believe there could be others out there, besides Craig Peters."

Woody said, "We have enough reason to believe Craig Peters is responsible for the killing of both his wife and her neighbor. But it doesn't mean the case is closed, Joe. We're still investigating all possible leads."

Joe thought for a moment, still not certain he should open his mouth. But he wasn't sure he had a choice. "What about Nick Juliano?"

"Nick Juliano?" Woody leaned back in his chair. "What about him?"

Joe said, "You know who he is?"

Woody seemed hesitant but nodded after a brief pause. "He's not the man his grandfather was, if that's what you're getting at. But other than having a surname most people around here recognize, he's never even stepped foot in this place. Other than as a visitor."

"A visitor?"

"Siskey Foods donates a lot of money to law enforcement in this city. He also supports plenty of charities throughout the area."

"Of course he does," Joe said, holding back from rolling his eyes. "And I assume you're already aware Craig Peters worked for Siskey?"

Woody nodded. "Of course we know that. But it was a short stint. In fact, we've already inquired about it. The fact is, he quit. Actually, he stopped showing up for work."

Joe shifted in his seat, wondering if it was smart sharing something with the sergeant he had little concrete proof of. "What if Nick Juliano had something to do with these murders? And I don't mean just the two. There's also the one up in Miami Gardens. You know the name Wendy Johnson?"

Woody shook his head. "Should I?"

"She was murdered up there."

"Well, we don't get involved up that way. Miami Gardens has their own police force." He leaned with his elbows on the desk, his hands folded in front of his mouth. "Can you explain to me what would make you think Nick Juliano, a law-abiding citizen who has always been supportive of the Miami Police, is a murderer?"

Joe said, "Well, I know this is probably going to look bad if I tell you what I'm about to tell you, but, I was there the night Wendy Johnson was murdered. I was in the parking lot."

Woody stared back at Joe and held up three fingers. "Three? You were present for three murders?" He closed his eyes, rubbing his face with both hands. "Please tell me you're not serious about this, Joe."

"I'd love to tell you that. But, I swear... I had nothing to do with that one, either."

"Let me guess. You're the one who called the police?"

"I was. But, here's the thing. This woman, Wendy Johnson, was involved with Craig Peters. Not in a romantic or any kind of a sexual way. Not that I'm aware of, at least. I mean, for his sake, I hope not."

"Are you going to tell me how Nick Juliano fits into any of this?"

Joe nodded. "I wasn't going to mention it yet because I don't have the whole story yet. But, if what I've heard is true, Craig Peters and this woman, Wendy Johnson, were involved in some kind of scheme when she was managing the National Pancake House. Craig was delivering for Siskey."

Sergeant Thomas stared back at Joe for a good few moments, like he didn't know what to say. "Okay, I'll bite," he said. "Tell me about this alleged scheme you somehow have some kind of inside knowledge about."

Joe went on and shared with Woody everything he knew. Although he knew as he told him, it wasn't nearly enough to say there was, without a doubt, any kind of wrongdoing on Nick Juliano's part. He said, "The thing is, it makes no sense any kind of crime involving Siskey Foods was never reported."

Woody held his gaze on Joe. "You mean, unless Juliano took things into his own hands."

Joe nodded. "I've already admitted to you I was looking for Craig Peters. That's how I met Suzanne. And the morning I was there, the neighbor, Brad, even showed up in the hall. I guess on his way to work."

"You didn't tell me you knew the second victim," Woody said.

Joe said, "I wouldn't say I knew him. I saw him once before. And, keep in mind, he's actually the third victim, if you include Wendy Johnson, who I have no doubt is connected."

"But I need to reach out to Miami Gardens PD before I jump to any conclusions."

Joe nodded. "Probably a good idea. And do me a favor, let them know I'm a good guy."

Woody rolled his eyes at that one.

"Can you tell me something?" Woody said. "How come, if this whole time you've been looking for Craig Peters, you never once mentioned it to me? And I'd also like to know exactly why you're looking for him. That's something I'd consider an important piece of information."

Joe hesitated. "Is it?"

Woody raised his eyebrows, nodding. "I'm afraid it *is*."

Joe cleared his throat, his cup resting on his thigh. "He owed someone money. I was just trying to find him."

Woody said, "Richard Caldwell?" He leaned even farther on the desk, folding his arms and resting them on top. "I'm not going to say I'm surprised, Joe. But... I just thought you were smarter than that. I know you've had a somewhat personal relationship with Caldwell over the years, but..."

"Okay," Joe said. "This isn't about me and Dickie. Is it? I've done nothing illegal. All I do is find the guy who has a little bit of debt. There's nothing more to it."

"Is this some kind of a regular thing for you?" Woody stared back at Joe.

Joe had to think for a second, then shook his head. "No."

Woody had a cocky look on his face. "Do you seriously believe tracking down money for a bookmaker sounds like something that's within the law?"

Joe took a deep breath and exhaled. "You're making me regret coming here, you know."

Woody seemed to ease up a bit and leaned back from the desk. He picked up his mug and took a sip, eyes over the rim on Joe. "All right," he said, easing his cup back down on the desk. "What proof do you have that this so-called crime at the pancake house even occurred? We have nothing at all on any of this. And if nothing's been reported and you don't have any solid evidence... I can't say I have much room to move. I'm sorry, but I can't just show up over there at Siskey Foods, ask about a crime nobody knows anything about."

Joe stared back at Woody with a brief pause. "So you don't believe me?"

Woody shook his head. "It's not that I don't believe you, Joe. But you haven't told me who gave you the information in the first place. Like I said, without proof or evidence, or without at least giving me some names of people I can talk to..." He held his gaze on Joe, waiting.

Joe knew he couldn't tell him it all came from Dickie. Because whoever told Dickie in the first place had to've been someone who either knew Nick Juliano directly or maybe even Craig Peters. It would almost tie Dickie to the crime, at least in a small way.

"Okay," Joe said. "Then what if I can *bring* you proof?"

"No," Woody said, without hesitation. "I can't allow a private citizen to get involved in this any more than you already are. It's not only dangerous, it would put my position as an officer—as a sergeant in this department—in jeopardy." He nodded toward Joe. "Why don't you just give me your sources?"

Joe stared back at him, pausing a moment before finally giving him an answer: "I can't. Not right now."

Woody leaned back in his chair. "All right, then. What if I said you could be charged with withholding information in a murder investigation? Would that change your mind?"

"This is bullshit," Joe said, his blood pressure creeping up into his face. "Christ. I never should've come down here. Not if I knew you'd—"

"All right, relax," Woody said, using both hands to gesture for Joe to play it cool. "But you come down here, looking to cooperate... and now you won't give me the details I need? You're tying my hands with the way you play the game, Joe."

Joe said, "It'd all be hearsay anyway. Even if I *knew* where the information came from."

Woody pulled at his chin. "You don't *know* who told you? Am I supposed to believe that?"

"Of course I know who told me. I just don't know who *initially* told the person who told *me*. Either way, you still wouldn't have the evidence you'd need. Am I right?" Joe leaned forward in his chair. "Give me another day, I'll dig something up."

Woody shook his head. "It doesn't work like that. I can't just give you the okay to go out, act like you're some kind of vigilante."

"I'm not a vigilante. And I didn't say I needed your permission. I'm just telling you—asking you—to give me some time to get you what you need."

Chapter 19

Joe turned off Second Avenue Northwest and turned left onto Northwest Sixth. He picked up the phone and called Dickie at the repair shop, telling him he'd just left Miami Police headquarters.

"You gotta be careful of their interrogation tactics over there," Dickie said. "They get you in that room..."

"I didn't do anything wrong," Joe said. "And it wasn't an interrogation. Sergeant Thomas is actually, well, he's looking for some help."

"Help?" Dickie said. "What the hell's that supposed to mean? They hiring?" He laughed.

Joe turned onto Northwest Seventh, the phone on speaker in his right hand. "I told him I could get some information about this scheme Craig Peters was involved in. He said without some kind of proof, he can't—"

"Wait a minute," Dickie said. "You told him? What the hell'd you do that for?"

Joe looked in the rearview at a dark sedan he noticed behind him ever since he'd left Miami Police headquarters. "I *had* to tell him," he said. "We're trying to solve a crime here, Dickie."

Dickie laughed. "*We* are trying to solve a crime? What do you mean, *we*? You working with the cops now? Like some kind of volunteer?"

Joe didn't respond, his eyes back in the rearview. The dark sedan—he couldn't quite make out what make or model—had fallen a couple of cars back. "Dickie, listen. Can you tell me who told you about Peters? I won't give up his name, if that makes a difference?"

"Then why do you need to know, if you're not going to use it?"

"Because, well... how about if you just get whoever it was to give me a clue where I can go to get some real details? I imagine this guy's not the only one who knows what went down. Assuming it's all true."

"Of course it's true," Dickie said.

"Then I need a way to prove it."

Dickie was quiet on the other end for a couple of moments. "You know what, Joey? I'm sorry, but I'm not sure I can help you."

Joe didn't like the way Dickie was acting. But he also understood. He knew Dickie wouldn't likely give him a name. He would *never* give someone up so easily. Although he had in the past, back when Joe was a crime journalist for the *Miami Post* and Dickie would give him tips. But it was never a tip on a friend. He'd never throw anyone he didn't want to under the bus.

That loyalty was part of what Joe couldn't help but like about Dickie.

"All right, forget it," Joe said. "But can you at least see what else you can find out? I need some kind of proof, Dickie."

"For what?"

"For *what*? To prove Nick Juliano had something to do with Suzanne's death."

Dickie sighed into the phone. "I just don't understand," he said. "This dead broad... I don't know why you've gotten yourself all wrapped up in it like, what, she's got you by the balls from the grave or something?"

The more Joe learned about Suzanne, the more he realized it would've been nothing more than a one-night stand to begin with. Even if she wasn't dead. But there was still something driving him. He couldn't help himself; he had to know what happened. It was like some kind of drive he hadn't felt in a long time, not since he was digging into crimes as a journalist, hoping he could beat the cops to the punch to find answers.

Joe said, "I'm just asking you to help me out, all right? Isn't that enough for you?"

Dickie paused on the other end. "Uh, not if what you're doing is trying to help get Peters off the hook. From where I'm sitting, that's exactly what it looks like, so if you can at least explain to me..."

"It has nothing to do with getting him off the hook. But if he didn't kill anyone... why should he fry for a crime he didn't commit?"

"Jesus, Joey. He shot your friend. You don't think he should pay?"

Joe's eyes returned to the rearview, watching the sedan two cars back. He didn't respond to Dickie, and the line went quiet. He looked at the screen on his phone. "Are you still there?"

"Yeah, I'm still here," Dickie said, quiet again for another couple of moments. "Let me ask you this: if I can get you the information you need without revealing my sources... would you be willing to do another job for me?"

"Are you serious?" Joe said. "That's the game you're going to play?"

"*What?*" Dickie said. "I'm just asking. It's one more job, that's all. This guy, he's not returning my calls at all, put eighteen grand down on an FSU game, then disappeared without paying."

"I told you I was done."

"I'm asking you for a favor, just like you're asking me. I'll even split the whole eighteen with you. Right down the middle. I'm sure you could use nine grand, no?"

Joe thought about it, knowing Dickie was trying to suck him back in. "If I say yes, you're going to have to give me some time."

"Take all the time you need, all right? I'm just... I'm happy to hear you'll help me. I was hesitant to ask, but..."

"So you'll get me a name?" Joe said. "Or at least something I can use?"

"Yeah, yeah. I'll get you something. Let me make a few calls first and I'll call you back."

Joe hung up the phone and noticed the dark sedan was still behind him. He didn't like the idea he was being followed but was fairly certain at that point that he was. It wasn't the same blue sedan, the Buick Regal, he'd seen at Suzanne's apartment before he found Brad Ridley dead on the toilet. He couldn't even get a good look at the driver behind the wheel, the way the bright sun reflected off the windshield.

He pulled down Northwest Twenty-Third and looked up in the rearview, watching the car he believed was following him continue without turning. The sun was no longer on the vehicle's windshield, and he noticed there were actually two men in the car.

He grabbed the first parking space he saw on the other side of the street from La Estrella de Plata, a pawnshop he frequented at least a couple of times a month.

His friend Juan was behind the counter, looked up, and gave Joe a big smile when he walked in. "Hey, José!" he said, coming around the display case and toward Joe with his arms out. He gave Joe a hug. "How have you been, my friend?"

Joe looked around, spotted a framed picture of Johnny Cash on the wall and without a second of hesitation pointed at it. "I'll take that."

Juan smiled. "I thought of you when a customer brought it in. I almost called you..." He stepped over and pulled the framed poster down from the wall, leaning it against the glass display case beneath the register. "Are you looking for something, my friend?"

"I'm not sure," Joe said, although that wasn't exactly true.

He turned toward the door, looked out through the plate glass with the black iron bars over it and into the street. He watched as a black sedan—the one that was behind him—drove slowly past Juan's shop.

Joe said, "I'll be right back," and ran out the front door and into the street. He watched the black car pull into a parking space half a block away. He was almost certain, after catching a better glimpse of it from behind, the car was an older Chevy Malibu.

He walked back inside the shop and went right for the guns inside the glass display case. "Can you hook me up with a gun?" he said.

Juan nodded, looking past Joe toward the front of the store. "What I don't understand," he said, "is why you don't keep the ones you purchased from me before? You buy them, then bring them back. And you don't even ask me for money in return."

Joe shrugged. "I don't really like them."

Juan looked confused. "Then why do you buy them?"

"Well"—Joe looked over his shoulder—"sometimes I need them. And right now, I have an *immediate* need."

Juan's eyes opened wide. "Uh-oh, amigo. Is everything all right?"

Joe had his eyes on the pistols behind the glass, leaning in with his hands on his knees. "I'm not sure," he said. "But I'd like something I can use right now." He looked up at Juan. "I'll need bullets."

Juan shook his head. "I'm sorry, José. But you know I can't do that."

Joe pointed with his thumb, over his shoulder. "Juan, I have two men outside waiting for me."

"Friends of yours"

Joe shook his head. "I don't think so. I don't even know who they are or what they want. But if I walk out of here unarmed, they're likely going to kill me."

Juan swallowed, walked to the door and tried to look back and forth along the street, his face practically pushed up against the glass. "They followed you here?"

"I only came here because they were following me. I thought you'd help... with a gun. I was hoping you'd help me out."

Juan sighed, nodding, as he stepped around the other side of the display case. He pulled a set of keys from his pocket and unlocked the back of the case, sliding the steel panel open. He reached inside and grabbed a .38. "I just got this one in."

Joe liked the look of the other bigger handguns, and pointed at one that caught his eye. "What's that one?"

Juan reached in and lifted a 9mm from the case. "Smith & Wesson. Nice piece." He placed it on top of the counter.

Joe picked it up and looked it over, feeling the weight of it in his hand. He tucked it in the front of his pants to see how it felt, then pulled it out and turned, pointing it toward the wall to his right. "I'll take it." He pulled cash from his pocket—he always had cash from working with Dickie—and started to count out the bills. "How much?" he said, then pointed at the Johnny Cash poster. "Oh, and don't forget to ring me up for this."

Juan said, "Three fifty, my friend."

Joe was shocked and surprised. "Three fifty? Three *hundred* fifty? Are you serious?"

Juan nodded. "The thirty-eight I showed you, I'd sell for one-twenty-five. This one cost more."

Joe swallowed, looking at the 9mm in his hand. He liked the way it felt, thought about it, then pulled out three hundred and fifty dollars from the wad of bills in his pocket. He counted them out on the display case.

Juan picked up the cash without counting it and tucked it in his pocket. "You're not going to change your mind again, bring this one back... are you?"

Joe looked the gun over. "Nah, I think I'll keep this one. Maybe learn how to use it the right way." He tucked it in the front of his pants and reached for the framed poster, stepping toward the door.

Juan said, "José, wait." Joe turned, and Juan ducked down behind the counter, coming up with a box of bullets. "There are only a few left in here. They're on the house, if you want them?"

Joe thought about it, shaking his head. "Hold on to them for me. I'll get them next time I come in." He continued toward the door and walked outside onto the sidewalk. The sun was bright, and felt like it had gotten warmer since he'd gone into the shop, although Juan never cranked the air-conditioner the way Joe liked to at his apartment.

He looked down the block and saw where the Malibu was parked. But before he walked to it, he stopped off at his car and stuck the framed Johnny Cash poster in his trunk. He kept his eyes on the Malibu as he closed the lid and started toward the parked car, keeping his hand on the 9mm tucked in the front of his pants.

He walked on the edge of the sidewalk by the road, balancing himself without falling against the cars as he walked. He wanted to stay out of view from the two men, at least as much as possible. As he got closer, he stopped when he didn't see the man in the passenger seat.

Joe removed the gun from his pants, ducked down low and practically crawled up to the passenger window where he straightened up, tapped on the glass with the Smith & Wesson's muzzle and pointed it toward the man behind the wheel. "Put down the window," he said.

But the man, heavyset with grayish hair slicked back on his head, gave Joe a broad smile without putting the window down.

Joe knocked again with the muzzle of his gun. But when he did, he felt something hard poke into his skull. He didn't have to turn around to know what it was.

He raised his hands, still holding the 9mm he bought from Juan. As he tried to get a quick glance over his shoulder at whoever was behind him, he felt a crack against the back of his head.

Joe dropped to the ground, holding the back of his head. His new gun fell from his hand, and as he turned to look up, the muzzle was five inches from his face.

"Get up," the man said, grabbing Joe by the back of his shirt. "Get in the car."

Chapter 20

Joe recognized the man next to him in the back seat with the gun pointed at him. He was the same one who had tossed him out of Siskey Foods when Joe went looking for Nick Juliano.

The one in front, bigger and older looking compared to the one next to Joe, looked into the rearview. "You want to tell us who you're working for? And why you were at Siskey Foods asking questions about a former employee?"

Joe picked up on the man's accent right away and placed him up north somewhere, most likely New York. The hard G he used at the end of the word "asking," came across like Long Island. Not that it mattered. But these two men were no doubt a couple of Italian goons like you'd see in a movie. And if Juliano wasn't connected, as some had believed, it certainly didn't appear that way with the two taking Joe for a ride.

Joe said, "I have no idea what you're talking about."

He wasn't planning to answer their questions. But he realized there could come a point the two might decide to make it a little harder on him not to talk, no matter how much he wanted to hold out.

The driver laughed, his eyes still in the rearview on Joe. "Do we look that stupid?"

Joe looked at the gun's muzzle, pointed at him, and shifted his glance to the man with the double chin holding it. "Do you really want me to answer that?"

The driver put his arm up on the back of the passenger seat and turned, almost all the way around, and glared at Joe. "Don't be a wiseass, buddy."

Joe looked toward the windshield as the car swerved into oncoming traffic. He yelled, "Hey! Watch the road!"

The driver yanked the wheel at the last second, tires squealing, and straightened out in the lane, nearly sideswiping a minivan next to them.

Facing forward again, his eyes on the road now, the driver said to Joe, "Listen, we don't want to have to do something you're not going to like just to get you to talk. So the best thing you can do, if you want to be able to chew your own food again, is to answer our questions. Because, the thing is, we know you were there. And you seem to be sticking your nose where it don't belong."

Joe glanced at the 9mm he got from Juan, but the man next to him had it tucked in the storage pouch behind the passenger seat, along with Joe's phone.

"Don't try anything stupid," the man said.

The driver looked back, "Hey, Bobby, he pulls anything back there, go ahead and whack him if you gotta."

"Yeah, yeah, you don't have to tell me twice," the man said, a crooked smile on his face as he stared back at Joe.

"So where are you taking me?" Joe said, looking at his watch. "I have somewhere I need to be."

The driver looked at Joe through the rearview. "You tell us what we're asking, and there's a good chance you'll make it home for dinner. It's as simple as that."

Joe moved his face away from the gun, leaning as far to his left toward the door as he could. He looked ahead toward the windshield and watched as the driver turned off 95 before the attorney sign he recognized that said, *INJURED?* with 1-800-GET-PAID underneath.

They turned off Exit Nine toward Gratigny Parkway, then onto Seventh toward Northwest 125th. Joe could see the sign for Siskey Foods up ahead and wondered what was about to happen. It couldn't be good.

The driver picked up his phone and had it up to his ear, Joe watching as they continued on the street and went right past Siskey Foods. The driver said into the phone, "Yeah, tell him we're on our way. We'll bring him inside."

Joe looked past Bobby and out the window as they passed the long white building with rows of tractor-trailer trucks backed up to the loading docks. "We're not going to see your boss?" he said.

The driver said, "How about you just shut your mouth now. You had your chance." He turned right down Northwest Fifth and took a quick left onto 122nd.

Joe looked through a chain-link fence enclosing the parking lot of another commercial building, but it looked old and run-down with a brick exterior. There weren't any cars in the parking lot with grass growing up from the cracks in the asphalt. The building appeared to be abandoned, the only sign was the one on the fence that said, PRIVATE PROPERTY. DO NOT ENTER.

They stopped at a gate that was closed with a lock and chain. The driver put the car in park and stepped out, stuck a key in the lock and removed the chain. He pushed open the gate.

Joe glanced at Bobby watching his friend and thought about ripping the gun from the man's hand.

But before he could make a move, Bobby turned back to Joe. "I told you, don't try anything foolish."

Joe stared back at him, doing his best not to look intimidated.

The driver got back in the car, pulled forward through the gate, and stepped out again once they were on the other side. He got out and closed the gate, wrapped the chain around it and locked the lock. He got back in the car and looked in the rearview at Joe, but didn't say a word.

The driver turned the car to the right and drove around the side of the brick building toward the back.

Joe noticed the windows on the building were old and dirty enough he couldn't even see inside. Some were cracked or broken.

As soon as they turned the corner to the back parking lot, Joe spotted the same white BMW that was parked outside Siskey Foods.

He knew it was Nick Juliano's.

Joe eyeballed the pouch behind the passenger seat once again, thinking about reaching for the gun. But the fact it wasn't loaded kept him from taking the chance trying to grab it.

He thought maybe it was time he stopped using weapons that weren't loaded. It never really worked out.

Bobby reached for the gun from the pouch and dropped it over onto the front seat. "Tony, hold on to this, will you?"

The driver said, "Jesus Christ, Bobby. How many times do I gotta tell you not to use my name?"

"But you used *my* name," Bobby said, that dumb look on his face staring at his buddy in front.

"Tony, huh?" Joe said, shaking his head with a laugh. "I would've never guessed, with those New York accents. Are there many guys named Tony in New York? I heard there might be."

The driver, Tony, stepped out of the car and opened Joe's door. "I told you to knock off the smart-ass act." He reached for Joe's arm. "Now, let's go."

Joe got out from the car on the driver's side, and Bobby stepped out from the other, walking around to where Joe stood, and poked the gun into his back. "Go on, up the stairs."

Joe looked the building over. "You mind telling me what we're doing here?"

Neither man answered as Tony, the driver, had to jam his shoulder into the door to open it. The door made a loud cracking noise when it opened, and Tony walked in ahead of the other two.

There weren't any lights on inside, and the hall they walked down was mostly dark. There was dirt all over what looked like hardwood floors, but they were pretty worn down.

Joe still had the gun at his back, following Tony as he turned the corner and stepped into a room fairly well-lit from the sun coming in through the dirty, cracked windows. It was the size of a basketball court or an average-sized church. There was even a stage, and he wondered if the place might've been a school of some sort at one time or another.

There were old dust-covered desks and dried-leather chairs scattered all around the room. The ceilings were at least twenty feet high with large fans hanging down that weren't turned on.

It was quiet and Joe wondered what was about to happen. He felt, if they were going to kill him, they could have done it already. *Why would they have gone through all the trouble, bringing him to a random abandoned building just to kill him?*

"Sit down," Tony said, grabbing a regular chair he slid in front of a desk that appeared to be the only piece of furniture not covered in dust. Even the leather chair behind it looked fairly new compared to all the others.

Joe sat down as he was told and faced the empty desk in front of him. He turned around and looked at Tony and Bobby. "What's with the theatrics?"

The two looked at him, confused. Neither answered.

A door opened on the far side of the room and in walked the man Joe recognized right away as Nick Juliano. It was the first and only time he'd seen him in person.

The first thing Joe thought of was how much he looked like his grandfather. "It's like I'm looking at a ghost," he said, his eyes on Nick walking toward him. "You look just like your grandfather."

Nick gave a slight nod, fixing his tie and giving the front of his suit jacket a tug. As he approached Joe, he extended his hand. "Nick Juliano."

Joe stared at his hand and, after a pause, reached out and shook it. He didn't say his name, assuming the man already knew what it was.

Nick stepped around to the desk and sat in the big leather chair across from Joe. He extended his hands, held them out wide with his palms up. "You like the new digs?"

Joe gave a quick glance around, shaking his head. "Not really."

Nick leaned on the desk and folded his hands. "I'll fix it up eventually. But it does the job, for what we use it for."

"And what would that be?" Joe said.

Nick again straightened his tie, leaning back in his chair. "Dealing with people who don't know how to keep out of other people's business." He held his gaze on Joe, his chin down a bit.

Joe pointed to himself. "Are you referring to me? Because, I don't know anything about your business. Why would I?"

Nick laughed. "I deal with people like you all the time. You think you're smarter than everyone else. Am I right?"

Joe didn't answer.

Nick said, "Okay, well... you showed up at my place of business asking questions about a certain employee who no longer works for my organization. You didn't fool anyone, with whoever you tried to say you were. So, here we are. I'd like you to tell me what it is you want to know."

Joe turned and glanced over his shoulder at the two goons behind him, both with their hands folded together in front of them. He thought he was past the point of trying to bullshit Nick Juliano.

So he went with the truth.

Mostly.

"I'm looking for Craig Peters because he owes me money. I thought, perhaps, you or someone at your office would know where I could find him."

Nick leaned on the desk again. "You're looking for Craig Peters?" He looked past Joe at the two goons. He pointed with his finger in his own chest. "And you think *I* know where he is?"

Joe shrugged. "Well, he worked for you. Didn't he?"

Nick stared back at Joe, taking a moment before he answered. "He was a short-term employee. But as I believe you were already informed, he left the company on his own terms."

"Yes, that's what I was told."

Nick got up from the desk and stepped around to the other side where Joe was. He leaned against it, looking Joe in the eye. "So, you mind telling me what it is you're after?"

Joe shifted in his seat, not comfortable with how close Juliano stood in front of him. "I told you. He owes me money."

Nick laughed. "Oh yeah?"

"Is that funny?" Joe said.

Juliano's smile dropped from his face. "Not really. No. It's just, well..." He straightened out from the desk and stepped back to the other side, but this time leaning on the back of the chair, his arms folded on top of it. "I understand you used to work for the *Miami Post*. And you knew my grandfather?"

Joe nodded. "I interviewed him from prison for an article. Talked to him more than once." Joe cracked a slight grin. "For someone who killed as many people as he did, he didn't seem like a bad guy."

Nick smiled, nodding. "My grandfather was the best."

Joe wanted to roll his eyes but kept his thoughts to himself.

Nick continued. "And now, what do you do? Is it true you're pretty good at finding people?"

Joe wasn't sure how to answer. Or where Nick had even heard anything about the work he did for Dickie. He never did the same for anyone else, not in the same capacity. He thought maybe the man who told Dickie how Craig Peters ripped off Nick Juliano could've been passing information both ways, to Dickie and Juliano.

Joe didn't respond and felt a shove from behind him.

"Mr. Juliano asked you a question."

Joe glanced back at him over his shoulder at Tony, giving him a look. He turned back to Nick and nodded. "Yes, I've done a few jobs for a friend."

"Dickey Caldwell," Nick said, making sure Joe understood he knew more about him than he realized.

Joe said, "You know Dickie?"

Nick shook his head. "Not personally. But we do have a mutual friend."

Joe realized he was right. Whoever it was that told Dickie about the scheme must have been talking out of both sides of his mouth. Although he wished Dickie had told him who the guy was.

Nick straightened up from the chair behind the desk and walked toward one of the windows, standing with his back to the room. "I would like you to find Craig

Peters and bring him to me. Alive." He turned from the window, his hands clasped together behind his back, slowly walking toward Joe. "What is your fee?"

Joe was caught off guard for a moment, unable to answer. He didn't really have a fee, just took whatever Dickie would share with him. It was usually more than enough. He paused, thinking. "I have no idea where Craig Peters is. If I did, I'd—"

"I didn't *ask* if you know where he is. What I said was I'd like you to find Craig Peters for me. It's not exactly a request. But you will be fairly compensated." He tugged at the front of his suit coat again. "I'll give you ten thousand dollars. And you'll have five days."

Joe did not want to work for Juliano, although he didn't have much of a choice. At the very least, he could get close enough to him over the next five days to dig in a little deeper.

It was a game he felt he could play. But he wasn't quite ready to give in so easily. "What if I say no?" he said.

Nick stepped back to the front of the desk, leaned on it again right in front of Joe and pulled a phone from his pocket. He tapped the screen and turned it to Joe. "She sure is a beautiful woman."

It was a picture of Lauren.

Joe popped up from the chair like he was going to grab Juliano, but the two goons were there behind him, each with a hand on his shoulder.

They pushed him back down into the seat.

He felt pressure in his chest, the way his heart was pounding. He stared Nick in the eye. "I swear, you do anything to hurt her..."

"Bring me Craig Peters. And you won't have to worry about a thing." He gave Joe a sly smile. "But don't you dare do anything stupid. You decide you want to go to the police? Let's just say I hope you have fond memories of the last time you saw your girlfriend up there in Daytona. Because that's all that'll be left of her."

Chapter 21

JOE WALKED DOWN NORTHWEST Sixth in Little Havana, looking up and down the street at the parked cars. It wasn't usually hard to pick out his '86 convertible Mercedes with the green paint, but this time he was having trouble. He walked past La Estrella de Plata, his friend Juan's pawnshop, and looked well past it toward Northwest Second, for the car. But on top of being in a rush when he first went in looking for a gun, he couldn't think clearly enough to remember where he'd parked.

He fixed the gun tucked in his pants, surprised Juliano had his dogs give it back to him in the first place, and walked back inside the shop.

Juan was behind the counter helping another customer but looked past her toward Joe, giving him a nod with his chin. He continued ringing up the woman and didn't say a word until she walked past Joe and went out the door.

"Back so soon, my friend?" Juan said, a smile on his face but a look like he knew something was wrong. "Is everything all right?"

Joe didn't shake his head or nod. He stepped to the counter. "Can I get that box of bullets you had for me?"

•••••••••••

Joe stepped off the elevator on the twenty-third floor, turned down the hall for his apartment, and started to slide the key in the door. But before he'd stuck it all the way in, the door opened without Joe having to even turn the knob. He realized the lock was busted.

He leaned the framed Johnny Cash poster against the wall outside and removed the 9mm from his pants. Doing his best to keep quiet, he stepped inside. He took light, slow steps, looking around his apartment. At first glance, everything appeared to be in its place. He walked into the living room, and the first thing he did was check his albums. His record collection seemed to be untouched.

Joe went through the rest of the apartment, checking the bedroom, under the bed, the two bathrooms, in the showers, and in the closets. He looked everywhere and was certain nobody was inside. That much was clear.

And as far as he could tell, nothing had been stolen. The apartment looked as clean as he'd left it. He wondered if it was Nick's goons, might've broken in looking for him, perhaps before they tracked him down and followed him into Little Havana. And if it was, the way the lock was busted looked to be the same way it was done to both Suzanne's apartment and the kid across the hall.

He never even asked Nick or his two goons about Suzanne. He knew if he had, and they realized his real plan was to prove they were the ones who shot Suzanne, he may not have left that warehouse on his own two feet. If at all.

His phone rang, and he pulled it from his pocket to look at the screen.

It was Lauren, returning his call. But just as he was about to answer, he heard a creak he was sure had come from the door to his apartment. He tapped the button and ignored Lauren's call, tucking the phone back in his pocket. He lifted the 9mm and stepped around the corner toward the door.

Bart was in the doorway leaning on a cane, examining the busted lock. He looked up at Joe, saw the gun in his hand and put up his hands, holding the cane up in the air.

Joe let out a sigh of relief and cracked a grin, tucking the gun back in the waistband of his pants. "I thought you weren't supposed to be driving?" he said.

Bart shrugged, pushed the door closed as much as he could, and nodded. "I've done a lot of things in my life I was told not to do. Why start listening now?" He pointed over his shoulder with his thumb toward the door. "I guess you're all right?"

Joe nodded and glanced at Bart's leg and the cane he was leaning on with his straightened arm. "How's it feel?"

"I don't know. I guess the way it's supposed to." He walked with a limp into the living room and leaned back on the side of the couch, looking around. "I just gotta sit a minute." He nodded at Joe. "So what happened? They take anything?"

"Not that I know of. Someone must've come here looking for me."

"Any idea who?"

Joe paused, looking over at Bart. "Actually, I think I do."

"Peters?"

Joe shook his head. "Nope." He looked away, his eyes toward the glass doors in front of his balcony, quiet for a moment.

"Are you going to tell me what's going on?" His eyes went to the gun sticking out from Joe's pants, the hem of his shirt caught on it. "When did you get another gun?"

Joe pulled the 9mm from his pants and put it down on the coffee table in front of Bart. "Picked it up earlier when I was being followed by the two goons I'm fairly certain broke in here looking for me."

Bart picked up the gun and looked it over, placed it back down. "What two goons?"

"Nick Juliano's guys."

Bart straightened up, his eyebrows raised. "Are you serious?" He shook his head. "I told you it was a mistake going over to that warehouse like you did."

Joe went ahead and told him how it all went down, how he got the gun from Juan when he was being followed but only hoping to use it to find out who the two men were. He then went into how his plan backfired when the one in the passenger seat, Bobby, had stepped out of the car to go get a coffee.

But he stopped short of telling him about the arrangement he made with Juliano. He wasn't sure how Bart would like it.

Bart said, "So, looks like he's not just the squeaky-clean grandson of Michael Juliano? Is that what you're telling me?"

"I mean, he had two goons. Even had his office set up in this dirty old warehouse. The whole setup was strange. Almost like he's got his own thing going, not necessarily connected to the actual Mafia, but acting like he is, keeping whatever else he's up to separate from Siskey Foods. It was only a block away from the warehouse."

Bart narrowed his eyes. "So are you gonna tell me what happened? You got out of there on your own two feet, so I guess nobody broke your legs or anything."

Joe didn't answer, walking toward the front door and into the hall where he'd left his Johnny Cash poster outside. He took it in and leaned it with Johnny's mug facing the wall. "Juliano offered to pay me to find Craig Peters."

Bart stared back at Joe, a blank look on his face but with a slight grin like he couldn't believe what Joe had just said. "He offered you money? And what'd he say when you told him *no*?"

Joe cleared his throat but looked toward the kitchen without answering.

"Oh no," Bart said. "Please don't tell me you accepted his offer? Joe, you can't—"

"I didn't have a choice," Joe said. "He brought up Lauren's name and her picture. He already knew all about me. He knows Lauren lives up in Daytona. He knows where she works."

"Jesus, Joe. You gotta call Woody."

"No!" Joe snapped. "He said if I call the cops… that's when he brought up Lauren's name. Like I said, I don't have a choice. He wants me to find Peters, bring him to him."

Bart used his cane and pushed himself up from the arm of the couch, walking with a limp as he leaned on the cane toward the sliding glass door. "Okay, well, this is kind of funny," he said, looking through the glass toward downtown Miami. "I was coming here to see if you'd be ready to help *me* find Peters. I know Woody wouldn't approve of it. But it doesn't appear they've made much progress. I just want to get the son of a bitch. I'll bring him in myself."

"Can you do that?" Joe said.

Bart shrugged, shaking his head. "Legally, I'm no different than you or any other citizen now. But, I don't know. Maybe I should just shoot him, get him back for what he did." He cracked a small grin. "You know there's a chance I might be stuck with this goddamn limp?" He lifted his cane. "Using this for the rest of my life?"

Joe knew Bart was serious about the limp, but he wasn't sure he was kidding or not about shooting Craig Peters. "I'm really sorry about what happened to you, Bart. We both know if I hadn't—"

"Oh, shut the hell up, will you? Wasn't for you, I would've lost the whole damn leg. So let's just start looking ahead." He looked down at the 9mm on the coffee table. "What is it with you and guns? It's like you want to use them, but then you change your mind. Haven't you returned a couple of them already?"

Joe shrugged. "I'm just not comfortable with the idea of shooting at someone. I think it certainly gives you a bit of power, just the threat of pointing it at someone. But, I do realize there'll come a time I might need it for something more."

Bart picked up the 9mm and looked it over. "You got this from your friend, over at the pawnshop?"

Joe nodded, knowing Bart sometimes liked to think he was still a cop.

Bart said, "You're supposed to be able to demonstrate competency with a gun before he sells you one. Does he know that? I hope he's following the law over there."

Joe pulled the gun from Bart's hands. "I've known Juan for a long time. But, yeah, he follows the rules. At least for the most part. He'll help me out when I need it."

Bart huffed out a laugh. "I've seen you fire a weapon. And it's not a pretty sight." He looked at the 9mm in Joe's hand. "Look at you. You don't even know how to hold the goddamn thing." He stepped over, took the gun back out of Joe's hands. "Second rule is keep your goddamn finger out of the trigger area."

"Oh, sorry." He looked down at the gun. "What's the first rule?"

"Rule number one is you always treat a firearm as if it were loaded."

"But it's not loaded." Joe said. "The bullets are in a box, on the table. I'm actually not even sure there's a right way to load it."

Bart rolled his eyes. "See, this is what I mean. You're not even competent enough to use a gun." He eject- ed the magazine, looked it over, and placed it down on the table. He worked the slide backward, and a round popped out from the chamber and landed on the hardwoods. "Jesus Christ, Joe. See what I mean? The goddamn thing's loaded."

Joe swallowed, his face flushed red with his eyes wide open. "Shit, I'm sorry, Bart. I just—"

"Don't be sorry," he said. "But this is why you don't just go in a place that sells used records to buy a gun. It's also why you need to know what the hell you're doing, you're going to carry—legally or not." He picked up the magazine and looked the gun over once again. He pulled the slide back and pulled it close to his eye, looking inside the chamber. "What do you say we take a ride to the shooting range? Got a friend of mine, owns one down by Three Lakes. I can at least show you a thing or two, make sure you don't shoot your own dick off."

Joe pulled out his phone. "First I gotta call a lock-smith, get the door fixed."

· · · ● · ● · ● · · ·

Joe took the ramp for 395 from Northeast First, heading south, quiet for the first few miles of the ride until he finally turned to Bart in the passenger seat. "So, what do you think? We both want to find Peters, but we're going to have to agree to what we do when we find him. I'm supposed to deliver him to Juliano."

Bart glanced at Joe and shook his head. "You really think that's the smart thing to do? You understand you'd be an accomplice, right?"

Joe glanced at Bart but didn't respond, even though he knew Bart was right. He hadn't thought everything through yet, and wanted to hold off telling Bart more than he had to until he had a few more things lined up. Either way, he knew he'd want Bart's help.

"What if we can't find him?" he said. "I mean, isn't there a chance he's long gone by now? Could be across the country, for all I know."

Bart nodded, his eyes straight ahead. "Didn't you say there could be a third person involved with him and that woman up there, the one who owned the bar?"

"Wendy Johnson," Joe said, nodding. "Yeah, al-legedly there was someone else they were working with. But I don't know if it's even an option trying to find the guy, whoever it is."

"What I'm saying," Bart said, "is if this third person has the money they stole, don't you think Peters is likely trying to find *him*?"

Joe glanced at Bart. "I should've been straight with Juliano, told him I know why he wants me to find him."

"You'd be dead right now if you told him what you know," he said. "That's never a good move, letting the man know what's in your head."

Joe turned the wheel, heading toward Southwest 114. "I wish I'd at least asked him why he was after him, let him tell me."

"But you already know why he's after him. Why would you ask? Just to cause trouble?"

Joe thought for a moment. "What if the story I have is wrong? What if Dickie didn't get the story straight?"

Bart was quiet, looking out the passenger side. "What else did he say?"

"What else?" Joe said. "That's about it."

Bart picked up his phone and looked at the screen. "Did he give you a specific amount of time?"

"I thought I already told you. He said I have five days."

Bart snapped a look at Joe. "What? Are you kidding me? Five days? No, you didn't say a word about it. You don't even know where to begin. How the hell are you supposed to find him in five days?"

Joe looked up in the rearview. "That's what I've been wondering."

Chapter 22

DICKIE WAS OUTSIDE WITH the hose, watering the flowers planted along the front of the house when Joe and Bart pulled in the driveway. He said, "Hey, Joey," with a quick smile that dropped from his face when he saw Bart step out from the passenger side of Joe's Mercedes. "You brought the cops?"

Bart shook his head. "Dickie, if I were still a cop I'd have the cuffs on you already."

Dickie laughed at that one.

The two had some history together over the years, although nothing like the friendly one Joe and Dickie had. Bart and Dickie weren't what you'd consider friends but got along better than they had in the past, once Bart retired and Dickie just got older.

"Can we go somewhere and talk?" Joe said, giving Dickie one of his more serious looks.

"Uh-oh," Dickie said. "Am I in some kind of trouble?" He stepped over the flowers and reached for the spigot behind a tall flowering shrub under the window, then yanked at the hose and rolled it up, hanging it on the holder attached to the exterior. He stepped out onto the driveway and looked down at Bart's leg. "I were you, I'd look for that prick, Craig Peters; give him exactly what he deserves." He nodded at Joe. "I bet you wish you could find him now, huh?"

Joe nodded, giving Bart a quick glance. "That's what we're here to talk about."

Dickie walked ahead of him and opened the front door, holding it for Bart and Joe to go in ahead of him. "I'd say we sit out back, but it's a little too warm today."

Bart walked past him into the house. "What's the matter, you still have that New York blood in you?"

"I don't know if it's New York. But it gets warm like this, it's like you got a mask over your face, trying to breathe." He pulled the door closed behind him and turned the lock.

The three walked into the kitchen, and Dickie pulled three beers from the refrigerator, using an opener to pop off the tops. He slid two across the counter toward Bart and Joe and said, "So, what's the story?"

Joe picked up the beer and took a sip. "I met with Nick Juliano."

"You what?" Dickie's eyes opened wide, his thin white eyebrows high on his head. "What the hell'd you do that for? I told you not to say anything about what I told you."

"I didn't say a word," Joe said. "He actually sent his two goons out to get me, brought me to see him."

"Yeah?" Dickie stepped around the counter and sat down in one of the four stools on the other side next to where Joe and Bart were standing. "What'd he want?"

"The same thing as everyone else," Joe said. "He wants Craig Peters."

Dickie scratched the top of his head. "And, what, he thinks you know where he is?"

"I don't think so. He wants me to find him. And I'm not sure your friend, whoever it was that told you about Peters working that scheme, isn't the same person who told Juliano I could help him. He knows I'm the guy who showed up at his office, but then went out of his way to have me tracked down. So, I'm just wondering..."

"I don't know why she'd give him your name," Dickie said.

"She?" Bart said. "Your friend, the one who knows about this Peters ripping off Siskey Foods... it's a female?"

Dickie didn't answer, instead mumbling, "I didn't mean to say that."

"What? I couldn't hear that," Joe said, even though he had. "You need to tell me who she is, Dickie. I want to talk to her, because she—whoever she is—obviously knows what's going on."

Dickie shrugged. "I told you, I can't tell you who she is. I'm sorry, but it would cause a whole lotta trouble if I did."

Joe was quiet for a moment, thinking. He narrowed his eyes, waiting for Dickie to look up at him. "Are you going to tell me?"

Dickie cleared his throat. "Scarlett."

Joe closed his eyes, shaking his head as he held a finger up in the air. "Wait a minute. Please, tell me I heard you wrong, Dickie. You didn't just say it was Scarlett, did you?"

Dickie looked up, his eyes right on Joe's, but he didn't respond. At least not right away.

But Joe still couldn't believe it. "Scarlett? Really?" He looked at Bart. "You know who Scarlett is, don't you?"

Bart nodded. "Dickie's ex-girlfriend? The young, pretty one who conned him out of nearly half a million?" He smiled. "How could I forget?" He turned to Dickie. "Are you nuts? Talking to her, after—"

"She got out of jail a couple of months ago," Dickie said. "Came by to see me. But she apologized. For everything."

Joe covered his face with his hands, shaking his head. "Dickie, come on. This is crazy." He pulled up a stool and sat next to Dickie, turned to him, his elbow on the counter. "How does she know about Craig Peters? And this whole scheme?"

Dickie rubbed the back of his neck. "Guy my age, you don't turn down a good-looking broad like Scarlett."

"You slept with her?" Joe said, surprised.

"Me?" Dickie shook his head. "I wish. But, no. We've just been, you know, having conversations. We've been talking."

He thought for a moment. "What you're telling me is that she knows both Craig Peters *and* Nick Juliano? So, is she the one who told Juliano about me?"

Dickie paused a moment before he nodded. "Maybe she was trying to do you a favor?"

"Jesus Christ," Joe said. "I don't need any favors. Certainly not from her."

Bart said, "I'm surprised she made parole so soon." A grin took over his face. "What'd she... uh, take care of someone high up?"

Joe gave Bart a look, like he didn't think he was funny. He turned to Dickie. "So where is she now?"

"Scarlett?" Dickie said, like he was playing dumb.

"Who the hell *else* would I be asking about?" Joe took a deep breath and tried to get as much air as he could into his lungs, exhaling it all with a heavy sigh. "I want to talk to her, Dickie. Get her on the phone right now. I'm serious."

Dickie moved his hands up and down, palms down. "Take it easy, now, Joe. I *know* you're serious. But I just want you to understand..."

"Understand, what?" Joe said, his eyes in a squint, staring at the side of Dickie's head. "That Scarlett's up to something again? But the problem now is that, this time, it's me holding the shitty end of the stick."

"What'd she do?" he said. "You're getting yourself all worked up, but she hasn't done anything wrong."

Joe glanced at Bart, who gave him little response aside from a shrug.

"I'm not sure what you're getting all worked up about, either," Bart said.

Joe's shoulders dropped. He got up from the stool and walked to the sliding glass door, looking out into Dickie's backyard. With his back to Bart and Dickie, he said, "I want to know how she knows Craig Peters. And what her relationship is with Juliano. Something doesn't smell right."

Dickie stood up from the stool. "Where's my phone?"

Joe turned from the door and looked around the kitchen. "I have no idea. Are you going to call her?"

Dickie nodded. "Yeah, why not? I don't think she's done anything wrong. But if you want to talk to her, be my guest. I'm sure she'd love to hear from you."

Joe laughed, not that he found it funny, and was still having a hard time understanding why Dickie would let this woman back into his life. "She practically got us both killed, Dickie, on top of draining your bank account." Joe didn't deny she was attractive. And being half Dickie's age, he could understand it from Dickie's perspective. But he still didn't like the idea she had the nerve to show her face after she and her two sisters landed in Lowell Correctional.

"She did me right, in the end," Dickie said.

Maybe that was true, Joe thought. But it wasn't like she did nothing wrong. "How much time did she end up doing?"

Dickie sipped his beer, wiping his chin with the back of his hand. "Eighteen months. The two sisters got five on top of the eighteen. She said they'll both be up for parole next year." He walked into the living room, came back a moment later with his phone in his hand, his reading glasses on his face. He tapped the screen and put the phone up to his ear.

Joe stood, watching him as he sipped his beer and gave Bart a quick glance, shaking his head.

A smile filled Dickie's face. "Hey, beautiful." He nodded. "It's me. Yeah. Dickie." The smile left his face for a moment, but then he smiled again. "Oh, okay. Well, maybe you oughta put my number in your phone, then. I have yours in mine, so..." He nodded again, listening. "Yeah, okay. Sure. But, Scarlett... listen. Joey's here." He paused, his eyes squinted, shaking his head. "No, I didn't. Yeah. Okay. But he wants to talk to you." Quiet again, he nodded. "Well, maybe you can come over here? Or, we can come to wherever you are?" Dickie paused, listening. "Okay, I'll tell him. Okay." He tapped the phone's screen and placed it down on the kitchen counter. "She can't meet you today," he said. "She's got something else she has to do."

Joe couldn't believe what he'd just heard, the way Dickie was acting like a little kid on the phone with her. *Where did his balls go?* He pointed at Dickie's phone on the counter. "Call her back. I don't give a shit if she's busy. Either she's going to help us find Peters, or she's going to tell me what her deal is with Juliano. I'm not going to wait until she's ready to talk to me."

Dickie pulled at his chin. "All right. She just... I'm not sure she was expecting me to tell her you knew she was around. She sounded kind of upset."

"What the hell did she expect?"

Dickie shrugged. "I don't know. I guess maybe I should have kept quiet about it for now."

Joe glanced at Bart drinking what was left of his beer.

"You want another one?" Dickie said, taking Bart's empty bottle from his hand.

"That'd be good," Bart said. "I'm kind of enjoying the entertainment here. I'm not exactly sure what the hell is going on, but..."

"I'll tell you what's going on," Joe said. "Dickie's old girlfriend Scarlett is up to something again. She's *always* up to something. That's just how she rolls."

Dickie was on the other side of the counter with a bottle in his hand he'd pulled from the refrigerator. He popped the cap off and handed Bart the beer, then turned to Joe, shaking his head. "That's not how Scarlett rolls. Not anymore, Joey. She just happens to know people." He pulled off his reading glasses and tucked them into his shirt pocket. "You know, I'm just thinking, if she can help find Peters, then—"

"If she knew where Peters was," Joe said, "then why would Juliano have come looking for me?" He glanced from Dickie to Bart, both nodding their heads like they agreed.

"Good point," Dickie said. He picked up the phone. "Anyway... she said she'd call you."

"She's going to call me?" he said. "When?"

Dickie shrugged. "I don't know. Later, I guess."

"She still has my number?"

Dickie stared back at Joe for a moment, like he was thinking. "I'll have to assume she does."

Chapter 23

Joe dropped Bart off at his car on the street in front of his apartment and turned into the parking garage, holding his phone in his hand. He wondered why Lauren hadn't returned his calls and had started to worry, calling her at least a half-dozen times. Although he only left a message the one time, he couldn't figure out why she wouldn't call him back.

But as soon as he stepped out of his car, he heard a voice he recognized, without a doubt, echoing off the concrete walls surrounding the parking lot below his building.

He turned and couldn't hold back his smile, staring as Lauren walked toward him from her car parked in the visitors' spaces across the garage from where he stood.

"I was wondering when you'd get home," she said, walking toward him. She reached out and hugged him with a tight squeeze.

He held her and loved the way she felt in his arms. But when he tried to kiss her, she turned her cheek.

Joe eased up on the hug. "Oh, uh..." he said, trying to make light of it, but he knew it wasn't good.

Lauren had a small grin on her face, her eyes shifting to the concrete floor of the garage. "I'm sorry," she said, putting her hand flat on his face. "It's nice to see you, Joe. You look good."

Joe looked Lauren over, thinking to himself she looked even better than the last time he saw her. Or maybe he'd simply forgotten how much she'd changed and become an almost completely different person from who she was way back when they worked together at the *Miami Post*. It had actually occurred to him, more than once, that perhaps he was out of her league, with the way she looked. And he started to wonder if maybe she knew it.

"I forgot how beautiful you were," he said, even though he somewhat wished he hadn't as soon as the words left his mouth. He felt like a high school kid, like he was trying too hard.

"Are you serious?" she said.

He didn't know if she meant she didn't believe what he'd said, or if it was something else.

"Of *course* I'm serious. Why would you... I can't—"

"Just because you told me about that woman you slept with doesn't mean you have to try and butter me up." She smirked, giving him a look like she was waiting to see how he'd react.

He didn't bother trying to explain himself, pointing toward the elevator. "You want to go up to my apartment? Or are we just going to hang down here in the garage?"

"Actually, I'm starving. I was thinking maybe we could go out and grab a bite to eat?"

Joe nodded. "Yeah, sure. Me too. But can we just go up to my apartment for a minute? So I can powder my nose?"

She let out a small laugh, nodding, and they both walked together toward the elevator.

Joe said, "So how come you didn't answer my calls? I left you a message."

"I'm sorry," she said. "I was on conference calls the whole ride down. Then I just thought I'd show up and surprise you." She looked over at his car. "I'm just glad I didn't get here, see you with some woman I wouldn't approve of."

Joe didn't bother to respond. He didn't know what to say anyway.

The elevator bell dinged and the door slid open. Lauren walked in ahead of Joe, and he stepped in after her, pushing the button for the twenty-third floor. He stood next to her at the back of the elevator and could smell her perfume, the same kind she had on the last time he saw her.

"Did you really come down here just to surprise me?" he said.

Lauren took a moment before she answered. "We need to talk."

Joe held his gaze on her for a moment, wondering what it was she had in mind. "Must be important, making the drive down to tell me?"

She nodded, with a small grin on her face, but didn't say much else.

The door opened, and the two walked down the hall toward Joe's apartment. The locks had been fixed, but the damage done could be seen on the edge of the door. He slid the key in and unlocked it, with Lauren standing behind him.

"Is that a gun?" she said.

Joe reached around the back of his pants and pulled the Smith & Wesson from his waistband, holding open the door with his other hand. He was surprised she hadn't felt it when they hugged.

"I thought you said you didn't want a gun?" She went into the apartment ahead of him and turned once she was inside.

Joe stepped around her and into the kitchen, placing the 9mm on the table. "I haven't told you much of what's happened since we last talked."

Her eyebrows were raised, shaking her head. "No, I guess not."

"Well, you know how I had you dig up what you could on Nick Juliano?"

She nodded, waiting.

"Well, he sent his two lapdogs after me. They were following me, and I took a detour over to Juan's shop. They were outside waiting for me." He picked up the gun. "So I bought this and went out to surprise them, see what they wanted. But it turned out they were a step ahead of me, threw me in the back and took me for a ride to see Nick Juliano."

Lauren hadn't said a word, her mouth slightly open.

Joe said, "And now he wants me to find Craig Peters."

"Craig Peters? He's the husband of the woman you..." She paused, looked over into the living room. "The woman who was killed?"

"Yes."

"And you agreed to it?"

Joe nodded, but was trying to think about how he could tell Lauren that they know who she is, without scaring her. "I believe Juliano killed Suzanne Peters."

"Suzanne? She's the woman you slept with?"

Joe hesitated, chewing the inside of his lip. After a moment, he nodded. "I'm really sorry, Lauren. I just thought—"

"I told you, you don't have to be sorry," she said. "This is what we agreed to, Joe. It still bothers me a little. I'm not going to lie. But I'm also not leaving my job. And you're not leaving Miami. So, it's just fair to both of us that this is the way it is. Nature calls, I don't think either one of us should have to worry the other will be bothered by it."

Joe grinned, his lips tight. He didn't exactly like the arrangement but she was right. It was what it was.

Of course, if it were up to him, and Lauren wasn't living in another city, he'd want to be with her.

But it wasn't his choice.

"So, then, what's your plan?" she said. "You believe Nick Juliano had something to do with your friend being killed, but now you're going to help him find her husband? I guess I don't get it."

Joe leaned back against the counter. "He didn't go into details, and I didn't ask a lot of questions. I don't want him to know what I know."

Lauren was quiet, her eyes on Joe. "But you *don't* know. You said you *think* he killed her. Sounds like it's nothing more than a hunch?"

"Well, of course it's a hunch. I don't have any proof yet. But when I find Craig Peters, he'll be the one person who can help me nail Juliano."

Lauren put her hand up, her palm toward Joe. "Wait a minute," she said. "You've agreed to help find this guy only so you can get him to help you prove Nick Juliano's a killer?"

Joe paused a moment, thinking, before he finally nodded. "Bart's going to help me, but he wants to find him for a different reason."

Lauren said, "Because he shot him, right? So he's going to help you, but it sounds like you're both hoping for different outcomes?"

Joe nodded. "Bart wants to find him so he can bring him in."

"Bring him in? Did he forget he's not a cop anymore?" she said.

"I'm not sure. But I don't care if he's thrown behind bars, as long as I can get him to talk. So Bart and I will just have to agree what to do, once we find him. But that also means he'll have to come clean."

"Come clean about *what?*"

"Ripping off Juliano's company. The only way I can pin the murder on Juliano is if he—"

There was a knock at the door, and Joe reached for his gun, holding it by his side as he walked past Lauren. He turned to her and put his finger straight up in front of his mouth in a *sssshhh*.

He stood at the door and looked through the peephole, and under his breath said, "Oh shit." He glanced back at Lauren watching him and had to think for a moment before he finally unlocked the door and pulled it open.

Scarlett was on the other side, standing in the hall with a weak smile on her face. "Hi, Joey."

He stood staring at her, almost unable to speak, he was so surprised to see her. Her blonde hair was no longer blonde. More of a light brown and much shorter than the last time he saw her, before she went to prison.

"Aren't you going to let me in?" she said, stepping over the threshold before he answered or even said a word.

She walked toward the kitchen and stopped mid-step, when she saw Lauren standing there, quiet, looking back at her. "Oh, hello," she said. "Lauren, right?"

Lauren looked at Scarlett, then at Joe walking up behind her.

"You remember Scarlett?" Joe said.

Lauren gave a slight tilt to her head, her eyebrows tight over her eyes. "Aren't you supposed to be behind bars?"

"She's on parole," Joe said.

Lauren had her eyes on Joe and held her gaze for a couple of seconds. "So, what's this all about?" Her eyes opened wide, like a thought had just entered her mind. "Oh, no. Please don't tell me you two are—"

"No, no, no!" Joe said, almost laughing but shaking his head like he was trying to knock something loose inside his skull. "God, no." He stepped around Scarlett and stood next to Lauren. "I didn't think you'd just show up at my door," he said, looking at Scarlett. She was just as pretty as the last time he saw her. But it was only skin deep.

Joe turned to Lauren. "Scarlett knows Nick Juliano."

"How so?" she said, folding her arms in front of her chest as she looked Scarlett over. "Are you friends with Mr. Juliano? Or, is there something more to it?"

Scarlett smiled, stepping away from the two and into the living room. She walked over to Joe's record collection and pulled an album off the shelf. "It's so quiet in here. I don't think I've ever been here when you weren't playing your records," she said, almost like she was trying to let Lauren know she'd been in Joe's apartment more than once.

"Well, we were actually just on our way out," Lauren said. "For dinner."

Joe sensed the tension between the two. In a way, he didn't mind it. Not that they were fighting over him in any way, but there was no doubt something in the air, and he liked the way Lauren appeared to be acting jealous.

Scarlett said to Joe, "Well, Dickie said you wanted to talk to me. So..." She started to walk toward the front door.

Joe stepped in front of her. "Wait, no. I do." He looked at Lauren. "We're not in a hurry, are we?"

Lauren rolled her eyes. "I'm starved." She went and opened the refrigerator. "Do you at least have any white wine?" She held the door open, leaned over, showing off her physique from the back side so Joe could see it.

He, of course, took notice. "I have a bottle in the pantry. But it's warm." He turned and looked over at Scarlett. "You want a glass of wine, Scarlett?"

She smiled, nodding. "I could use a drink. Wine sounds nice."

Lauren gave Joe a look that said she was clearly not enjoying the whole scene.

Joe opened the pantry, grabbed a new bottle he'd had on hand, but he never really drank white wine. He pulled two glasses down from the cabinet. "You want ice?" he said, looking from Lauren to Scarlett.

They both nodded, and he dropped a few cubes in each, then poured the wine over the top. "I used to have some snobby friends who got mad at people who put ice in their wine." He handed Lauren her glass and walked over to Scarlett with hers.

"Aren't you having a drink?" Scarlett said, looking Joe in the eye with a look Lauren wouldn't appreciate if she saw it.

"Not right now." He nodded toward the couch. "Why don't you have a seat?"

Scarlett walked past him with her catwalk strut and sat on the couch, crossing her long, bare legs. With the wine glass resting on her thigh, she looked at Joe as he sat in the chair on the other side of the room in the corner by the balcony. She said, "So, where would you like me to start?"

Joe glanced at Lauren. "Why don't you have a seat," he said, nodding toward the couch.

She shook her head. "No, I'm good."

The two looked at Scarlett and Joe said, "Start by telling me how you know about this scheme Craig Peters was involved in."

"Craig and Wendy," Scarlett said, as if correcting Joe.

"You knew Wendy?"

"Not personally. She'd been around the block, to say the least."

Joe had a slight smirk on his face. "What exactly do you mean by that?"

Scarlett shrugged and sipped her wine, looking back at Joe over the rim. She took her time answering. "I don't mean in a sexual way. Although, I guess I don't know much about her deal in that department. I mean, she's the type of person who always had something going on, putting something over on someone or running some kind of scheme, just like the racket she and Craig Peters had going."

"Sounds like someone else I know," Joe said, staring back at her.

Scarlett rolled her eyes. "Come on, Joe. I paid my dues. I'm a changed woman."

Lauren let out a laugh, then cleared her throat. "Sorry."

Joe said, "Okay, but I thought you knew Nick Juliano. Isn't that really how you found out?"

"I know Nick's cousin, Carl. We kind of dated way back, a long time ago."

"Not anymore?" Joe said.

Scarlett shrugged. "We get together once in a while, but…"

Joe and Lauren exchanged a glance.

"So you're sleeping with Nick's cousin?" Joe said. "And, what, this guy has a big mouth? Sounds to me like he told you something he maybe shouldn't have?"

Scarlett placed her glass on the coffee table in front of her, shifting in her seat and leaning forward on the edge of the couch. She sat with her legs together, her elbows on her knees and hands folded out in front of her. "All he told me was that Nick was looking for Craig Peters because he ripped him off. He didn't really come right out and say it, but it sounds to me like Nick might've killed a few people, or at least had something to do with it."

Joe nodded, listening, but Scarlett hadn't given him anything groundbreaking. "Okay, but... did Nick kill Craig Peters' wife?"

Scarlett was quiet for a good few seconds, like she was thinking it through. "Carl never got into any specifics about who Nick killed." Scarlett gave a slight tilt to her head. "Why do you care who killed his wife?"

Joe didn't look at Lauren but could feel her looking his way, like she was waiting to hear the answer. "Listen," he said, knowing he wasn't going to answer her question. "Does this guy Carl know anything about me?"

Scarlett shrugged. "I've never mentioned you, if that's what you're asking?"

Joe nodded. "Good. Okay. Just do me a favor, and don't mention my name. Don't tell him, or anyone else, you came here to see me. All right?"

"Oh, you don't have to worry, Joe." She gave him one of her looks, like she'd seduce him if Lauren weren't standing right there. "My lips are sealed." She made a motion like she was zipping her lips and flipped her hand, as if tossing away the key.

Joe looked over at Lauren rolling her eyes.

He said to Scarlett, "So this guy's name is Carl?" Joe said. "Carl *what*, Juliano?"

She shook her head. "No, his last name's Murphy. I have no idea how he's even related to Nick, because Carl's *very* Irish." She cracked a grin. "You ever hear of the Irish Curse?"

Chapter 24

Joe and Lauren were seated outside on the sidewalk patio at Ristorante Casio, off Southeast First Street. Joe sipped his vodka cranberry and watched Lauren drink from her glass of red wine without saying much at all.

It was uncomfortable for Joe. "How come you're not talking?" he said.

She finished her wine and placed the glass down, running her fingers up the stem. "I don't understand why you're doing this," she said.

"Doing *what*?"

"This hero crap." She stared into his eyes. "You still haven't told me why you won't go to the police and tell them everything you know. Why can't you just tell them Juliano's paying you to find Craig Peters before *they* do."

Joe hesitated, looking at the ice in his glass. "There's a risk to opening my mouth like that," he said, trying to figure out exactly how to tell her the real deal without freaking her out.

"Do you really think Nick Juliano is even that powerful?" she said. "I told you, from everything I could find, he doesn't appear to be this mob guy you've made him out to be. I found nothing. Zero. As far as I can tell, he's just a businessman."

Joe was somewhat annoyed, wondering why she didn't seem to believe him. "Well, as good as you are at digging deep into people... this time I'm afraid you're wrong," he said. "But I have a feeling he's worked hard to hold up his reputation all these years. The thing is, an honest businessman doesn't hire someone to track someone else down."

Lauren sighed, looking out toward the cars driving by on the street. "You do tend to have an imagination," she said.

"People are dead. And you think it's my imagination?"

She looked down into her glass without a response.

Joe pushed his drink aside and leaned forward on the table. He took a deep breath and looked around, making sure nobody was close enough to hear what he needed to tell her. He looked down at the piece of bread on the plate in front of him. "Okay, I don't want you to panic," he said. "Can you promise me you won't? That you'll trust me? There's something you need to know, that'll pretty much answer your question."

"Which one?" she said, staring back at him.

"Why I can't go to the cops." Joe stayed quiet for a moment, making sure in his head that he needed to tell her.

"Will you just spit it out?" Lauren said.

He ran his hand over his eyes and squeezed his face, like he was going to pull the skin right off. He kept his voice to a whisper, looking at the people around them who were decidedly not paying Lauren and him any attention. "Juliano knows who you are. He knows there's something between us. Not that I'm even sure myself what it is between us, but"—he cleared his throat—"if I go to the police, and if I don't do what he's asked, I'm putting your life in danger."

Lauren's eyes opened wide.

Joe reached for her hand. "I didn't want to tell you. It's just—"

She pulled her hand from Joe and pushed her chair back, standing without a word. She looked confused for a moment, like she was unsure which way to go, then started for the glass door into the restaurant but stopped. She turned and walked through the opening between the planters leading out from the enclosed sidewalk dining patio.

"Wait," Joe said, running after her. He turned to the waitress, already walking toward him.

"Is everything all right?" she said.

Joe reached in his pocket and pulled out a couple of twenty-dollar bills. They hadn't ordered but had gone through a few drinks. "Here," he said. "I'm sorry, I have to..." He handed the woman the cash. "Keep the change." He hurried after Lauren, already walking ahead of him along the sidewalk.

She continued in a hurry away from the restaurant and right past Joe's parked Mercedes.

"Lauren," he said, jogging up behind her. He reached for her arm. "Lauren, wait. Please. Listen."

She stopped and turned to him. Tears were coming down her face. "You did this, Joe. I thought I could help you." Her voice cracked. "And all you've done is put my life in danger!"

He tried to wrap his arms around her, but she pushed him away. "I didn't mean to get you involved," he said. "Not like this. But, they knew... Juliano knows you mean something to me. I don't know how. But he knows."

Lauren turned from him and continued down the sidewalk "Just leave me alone. I want to get away from you, Joe." She stopped, looking him in the eye. "You're not the same person I..." Closing her eyes, she turned and continued walking.

"Where are you going?" he said, still following after her. "We already passed my car."

She picked up her pace. "I came down here to tell you I was thinking of moving back to Miami." She looked him in the eye, shaking her head. "I have a job offer on the table from a new start-up media company down here. But, if I knew you'd become this... this... if I knew you'd turned into someone completely different from who you used to be, I would have never even entertained the idea." She continued ahead of him.

Joe had stopped, watching her for a moment, thinking about what she'd just told him. But then he hurried to catch up to her. "Lauren. I'll make this right. I promise." He reached for her arm again, trying to stop her. "I won't let anything happen to you. I swear to you."

She yanked her arm from his grasp and kept walking. "I don't know you," she said.

"I'm still the same person," he said. "I'm going to be done with all of this crazy business with Dickie, and everything else. But I can't... I can't just walk away from it all until—" He stopped when his phone rang. He knew he should ignore it but pulled it from his pocket anyway. "I'm sorry," he said to her as he looked at the screen. "It's Bart. Can you wait? Just let me..." He tapped the screen and answered. "Bart, hey, I'm—"

"Hey, I just got some news you might need to hear. You know that broad, Scarlett? Dickie's lady friend?"

"Of course. Yeah. She was just at my apartment a little while ago."

"She what? Oh Jesus, Joe. What do you *mean* she was just at your apartment?"

"I mean, how else do you want me to say it? She showed up, gave me some information. I'm not sure it was useful, but she knows both Craig Peters and Nick Juliano through Juliano's cousin. I guess she was sleeping with the guy. But, listen, I'm out with Lauren now. I was going to call you later. Can I call you back?"

"Uh, yeah. You can call me back. But you're going to want to hear this before you hang up."

Joe glanced at Lauren watching him and nodded. "Hear *what* before I hang up?"

"Scarlett. They just fished her body out of Biscayne Bay."

· · · · ·●·●· · · ·

Bart was parked on Southwest 162nd Street in front of Dickie's house, flashing his headlights as Joe drove toward him from the other direction before turning into the driveway.

Joe glanced at Lauren and turned off the engine, not feeling too good at all, knowing he was most likely going to be the first person to break the news to Dickie that Scarlett was dead. He looked toward the street as Bart limped toward him, leaning on the cane.

Lauren stepped out from the car and walked down the driveway to meet Bart. She opened her arms and gave him a hug. "I hope you're doing all right," she said, backing away as she looked at his leg.

"First time I've worn pants since it happened," he said. "But it's getting better, I think." He lifted the cane in the air. "Feel like a ninety-five-year-old, walking around with this goddamn thing."

Joe stood at the front of his car, waiting for Lauren and Bart.

The front door to the house opened, and Dickie stood in the doorway looking out at them with the glow of the light coming out onto the porch. He turned on the exterior lights, and the yard and driveway lit up like a football field.

"Joey?" he said. "What are you doing out there?" He looked at Bart, then smiled as his eyes shifted to Lauren. "Hey, look who's here! How you doing, beautiful?"

Lauren had a forced grin on her face. "I'm all right, Dickie."

Bart gave him a nod, and Dickie held the door open. "Come on in, before the cool air gets out."

Joe held the door for Lauren and Bart and gestured for Dickie to go back in ahead of him.

"So what's with the surprise visit?" Dickie said, walking to the coffee table in front of his white leather couch. He reached for the remote and lowered the sound on the TV. He looked at his watch.

Joe, Bart, and Lauren stood next to each other, not far from the door. No one answered Dickie's question.

He looked from one to the other. "Hello? What the hell's the matter with you people? Cat got all your tongues?" He laughed.

Joe stepped forward, put his hand on Dickie's shoulder, trying to lead him toward the couch. "Uh, well, there's been a... I have some news." He nodded toward the couch. "Maybe you should sit down."

Dickie gave him a funny look, like he thought Joe might be acting a little crazy. "What's the matter? Why're you acting so... Is everything all right?"

Joe took a second before he nodded, sticking his hands in his pockets like he didn't know what to do with them.

Lauren and Bart hadn't said a word and hadn't moved, the two watching Joe and Dickie from just inside the front door in front of the credenza.

Dickie sat on the couch, and Joe sat next to him with one big cushion between them.

"Scarlett's dead," Joe said, getting right to the point without beating around the bush.

Dickie cocked his head back, eyes raised, staring at Joe. He started to smile, like maybe he thought Joe made a joke. But then his expression quickly changed, and he stood from the couch. Dickie looked from Joe to Lauren, then to Bart, then pointed to his chest. "*My* Scarlett? She's... what the hell do you mean she's *dead*?"

Joe swallowed hard, nodding his head but not sure what else to say. "They found her body in the bay."

Dickie's face looked like it had drained of all color. His mouth hung open until he swallowed, turning his face away with his eyes toward the TV. "You friggin' kidding me? She drowned?" He shifted his gaze back to Joe. "You sure?"

Bart and Lauren finally walked over to Dickie, and Lauren wrapped her arms around him. "I'm so sorry, Dickie."

Dickie's arms hung by his side. He looked at Joe over Lauren's shoulder. "What do you know about this? Does it... she told me she was going to go see you earlier. I was going to go, but she didn't want me to. Did she... she never showed up?"

"She did," Joe said, nodding. "She came to my apartment."

Dickie looked at his watch, shaking his head. He didn't cry, in fact, didn't appear like he knew what to say or how to act. "Jesus Christ."

"You all right?" Joe said, standing from the couch.

Dickie said, "It's not like, well... you know how it was with me and her. I mean, I don't know, maybe I'm just in shock or... the truth is... I don't know..." He cleared his throat, rubbing the back of his neck. "What the hell am I supposed to say?"

Joe put his hand on Dickie's shoulder. "Are you all right?"

Dickie took a deep breath and let it out in a sigh, nodding. "I guess so. Yeah. I just can't believe she's dead." He looked at the TV. "You guys know what happened?"

Bart shook his head. "I spoke to Woody. He's certain foul play was involved, but it's still early."

Dickie said to Joe, "So, what, it musta happened after she left your apartment?"

"Well, yes. Of *course* it happened after she left. What are you asking?"

"Yeah, no. I'm just..." Dickie was quiet for a moment. "You think maybe someone saw her go in your apartment? Maybe... I don't know. I mean, she made it clear I wasn't the only man in her life, you know, so...."

Joe said, "Did you know she was screwing around with Nick Juliano's cousin, Carl?"

"Carl? No shit? I know Carl. She was screwing *him*?" Dickie made a face, like he'd bitten into a sour apple.

"She didn't use those exact words," Joe said. "It didn't sound like they had anything serious going on, but I bet this guy knows plenty more about what's going on. Maybe Juliano found out Carl told her some things he shouldn't have."

Dickie said, "So Murphy's the one who told Scarlett about Craig Peters? And he must've known about that skank who was shot up there in Miami Gardens, too, huh?"

"She never mentioned his name?" Joe said. "Or where she got her information?"

Dickie shrugged. "She told me not to ask, 'cause she wasn't going to tell me. But, yeah, I know Murphy. Younger than me and you. Maybe he's Scarlett's age, or older by a couple years. He's a wormy little prick. Friends used to call him The Weasel."

Joe and Bart exchanged a look, and Joe said to Dickie, "You know where he lives?"

Dickie said, "Used to live with his mother out in Pinewood. I heard she died. Rumor was he killed her so he could get her house."

Joe wished he'd asked Scarlett more about Carl Murphy when he'd had the chance. But he didn't expect she'd turn up dead an hour after she left his apartment, after her visit got to a point it was just time for her to go.

He turned to Lauren. "You need to go somewhere, get away from here." He looked at Dickie. "Can you take care of her? Get her somewhere safe?"

Lauren scoffed at what he'd said. "Take care of me? Are you serious? You think I need—"

"Lauren, please," Joe said. "I just want you to be safe. You *and* Dickie. Just get away from here, go somewhere nobody will find you."

"Like where?" Dickie said, like he was trying to hold back a smile, eyeballing Lauren. "Maybe we can get a nice hotel? They got that new five-star down on—"

"I don't even know if a hotel room is safe right now," Joe said. "We don't know what kind of connections Juliano has."

Dickie said, "You don't think we're safe staying here?"

"If we're going to bring Juliano down..." He shook his head. "No, neither of you are safe until we do." Joe thought for a moment and said to Dickie, "What about that berry farm down in Homestead? Does your friend still own it, the one with the guesthouse on the property?"

Dickie nodded. "Yeah, he still owns it. Although last I talked to him, he was looking to get a license to grow cannabis."

Joe glanced at Lauren and the annoyed look on her face. He turned back to Dickie. "Can you call him? See if he has room for a couple of guests?"

Chapter 25

Joe parked in front of the yellow house on Little River Drive in Pinewood. It was dark outside, the only light coming from the streetlamp and the dim glow through the windows from inside the house. He walked ahead of Bart toward a maroon Crown Victoria parked at the side of the house under a palm tree. He looked inside but it was empty. An air-conditioner hanging out of one of the windows clanked and ticked as it ran.

Joe stepped around two garbage cans placed outside the front door in the driveway. Looking at a piece of paper he pulled from his pocket, then at the number on the door, he confirmed he was at the right house: number 151. He felt around for the Smith & Wesson he had tucked in the waistband in back of his pants. He hoped he wouldn't have to use it, but he wasn't going to take any chances without it.

Joe looked back at Bart, a couple of paces behind him, limping with every step. Without the cane in his hand, Bart said, "What are you waiting for?"

Joe sniffed the air when they got close to the front door, then turned to Bart. "You smell that?"

"Marijuana?" Bart nodded. "Of course I do. Smelled it as soon as I stepped out of the car." He walked toward the air-conditioner hanging from the window. "Blowing out right here."

They both looked over at the neighbor's house across the street when an engine started. A car with its headlights on was parked and running in the driveway. It was hard to see who it was in the dark, but a man walked out the front door and got in the passenger side right before the car backed out and took off down the street.

Joe turned back to the door and listened for a moment. He heard a sound inside—*a TV*, he thought—and finally knocked.

The two waited at least a minute, but nobody came to the door.

Joe knocked again, this time a little harder and feeling it in his knuckles. He said to Bart, "You think he's asleep?"

"Or he's sitting right there, not answering since he just smoked a joint." Bart took a step and seemed to wince, grabbing his leg as he started toward the side of the house. "I'll look around back."

Joe knocked again, this time wondering if he needed to be careful instead of standing right there like nothing could happen. He didn't know much about Carl "The Weasel" Murphy, other than it was obvious he didn't live the same kind of rich life as his cousin, Nick. At least based on the kind of place he lived in. He again felt around back for the 9mm and pulled his shirttail down, making sure the pistol was covered.

Bart yelled for Joe from the backyard, and Joe took off and ran around the side of the house, into the backyard. Bart lay in the grass with lawn chairs tipped over around him, like he'd fallen into them.

"Bart!" Joe said, reaching down to help pull him up to his feet.

"Don't worry about me!" Bart yelled, pointing toward the yard behind them. "It's him! Don't let him get away!"

Joe saw the man running but stayed and tried to help Bart to his feet. But Bart pulled his arm away. "Go get the son of a bitch!" Bart said. "Leave me your keys!"

Joe reached in his pocket for his keys and tossed them to Bart, turned, and started to run toward the chain-link fence between the yards. He climbed over it and was in the neighbor's yard, running as fast as he could, tripping on a plastic bucket he didn't see in the overgrown grass. But he kept his balance and stayed up, kept running until he got to the other side of the neighbor's yard and climbed with one quick jump over another fence.

As soon as he landed on the other side, he realized his 9mm had dropped out of the back of his pants as he'd gone over. So he climbed over the same fence to the other side, grabbed the gun from the ground and made it back over to see Carl run across what looked to be a fairly busy street for the middle of the night.

Carl had some distance, well ahead of Joe, and turned left onto Northwest Twelfth, drivers' horns blowing as he tried to dodge the oncoming traffic.

Joe tried to keep up, cut in front of an oncoming car with brakes screeching as he hurried across. His breathing was heavy, doing all he could not to lose Carl Murphy already running between two houses.

Carl tried to climb another fence but this time caught his foot on top and dropped on his back, screaming in pain. But he was back up on his feet and headed toward another street.

Joe was gaining ground when he stopped, watching Carl run out in front of a Volkswagen Bug. It hit Carl, knocking him into the air and clear across the street into a collection of trash cans on the sidewalk.

The car kept going without stopping.

Joe ran across the street with his gun in his hand, breathing hard, pointing it at Carl before he could get up.

Carl moaned in pain, rolling on the ground holding his leg.

Headlights came around the corner and stopped, shining on Joe and Carl. The driver's side door opened and Bart stepped out, the cane in his hand this time, walking toward the two.

Carl got up on one knee, wiping blood from his mouth with the back of his hand. He looked at Joe, as if just noticing the gun pointed at him, and raised his hands up over his head. "Please! Don't shoot!"

Joe shook his head. "We just want to talk." He reached down to help Carl to his feet.

Carl rubbed the back of his head, looking around the ground. "Where the hell's my gun?"

Bart walked onto the lawn of the house the three were standing in front of and bent over. He picked up a small .38 revolver. "Play nice, and I'll let you have it back."

Carl touched his mouth, looked at his fingers with blood on the ends. "You guys cops?"

Joe and Bart both exchanged a glance, neither giving him an answer.

"I haven't done anything," Carl said. "So I don't know what the hell this is all about."

"Then why'd you run?" Bart said.

He looked at Bart but didn't answer, easing his hands down by his side.

An older woman with a robe on and curlers in her hair came out from the house. "Hey! *What's going on out here?*"

Bart pulled out his wallet, flashed it at the woman even though he didn't have a badge. "Miami-Dade Police. Please go back inside your home, ma'am. And keep your door closed."

The woman was already halfway down her steps but turned right back around and went inside, closing her door without another word.

Carl looked from Joe to Bart. "Who the hell *are* you guys?"

Joe tucked the gun in the back of his pants, grabbed Carl by the arm and pulled him toward the Mercedes. He gave Bart a nod. "You all right driving?"

Bart didn't answer but got back in the front seat behind the wheel.

Joe walked Carl around to the passenger side, opened the door, and slid the seat forward, pushing him into the back seat. Joe got in behind him, pulled the door closed, and pulled the front seat back against his knees. He had his gun out again, pointing it at Carl.

"So if you ain't cops," Carl said, "then who the hell are you? Did Nick send you over?"

Joe gave Bart a quick glance and said to Carl, "Why would Nick send someone over?"

Carl shook his head. "Oh, uh, no... nothing. I was just... I was just asking." He shifted his eyes from Joe to the gun. "Are you gonna kill me?"

"It depends," Joe said. "How about you go ahead and tell me what you know, and we'll see where we end up?"

Bart pulled the Mercedes away from the curb and started toward Northwest Ninetieth.

"Tell you what I know about *what*?" Carl said. "I don't have any idea what this is about?"

Joe gave him a crooked grin. "You don't, huh? How about we start with Scarlett. You know her, don't you?"

Carl froze for a moment, and Joe lifted the gun, pointing it at Carl's face. "Don't tell me you don't know who she is. Or that you had nothing to do with her being killed."

Carl held his gaze on Joe, then finally shook his head. "I had nothing to do with it. I swear. I really liked Scarlett."

"You liked her, huh?" Joe said. "But that didn't seem to make a difference, did it."

Carl cleared his throat, looking forward at Bart behind the wheel. "I don't know nothing."

"That's a double negative," Joe said. "So what you're really saying is you *do* know something."

Carl's mouth hung open, staring back at Joe like he didn't know how to respond.

Joe said, "Do you want to explain why you asked if your own cousin sent someone after you? Is there a reason you're worried he'll come after you? Does it, by chance, have anything to do with Craig Peters?"

Carl swallowed again, Joe starting to see why the guy was called The Weasel.

Carl said, "How do you know Craig Peters?"

Bart took a quick glance into the back seat.

Joe said, "How about *I* ask the questions, since I'm the one holding the gun."

Carl nodded. "Sure, yeah. Okay. Sorry."

Joe shifted in the seat, getting comfortable so he could face Carl without having to turn his neck. "Is Scarlett dead because you told her some things maybe you shouldn't have? Does it have anything to do with this scheme Craig Peters was wrapped up in?"

"How'd you know about that?" Carl said, although the look on his face said he hadn't meant to let it slip out that he knew exactly what Joe was referring to.

Joe grinned. "I'm glad we're almost on the same page. Now, why don't you tell me exactly what your involvement was. Did your cousin get you to kill Suzanne Peters?"

Carl shook his head. "No. No way. Nick doesn't have me do stuff like that. I swear. He said I have a big mouth, so he doesn't really trust me."

"I think I'd have to say I can't blame him," Joe said, huffing out a slight laugh. He glanced at Bart's eyes, watching them in the rearview.

Carl turned away from Joe, shaking his head as he looked out the driver's side. "I liked Suzanne," he said. "She didn't deserve to die the way she did."

Joe slapped Carl's arm with the back of his hand. "Why don't you turn this way, look at me, and tell me what you know."

Carl turned to him. "I told you, I don't know nothing."

Joe lifted the gun and poked Carl right in the face. "Again with the double negative. Do you even know what that is?"

"What *what* is?" Carl said.

Joe rolled his eyes. "What's Nick's story? Did he have Suzanne killed?"

Carl shrugged. "I barely talk to him anymore."

Joe said, "You barely talk to him, but you asked if Nick sent us after you? There must be a reason for that, no?" He pressed the muzzle into Carl's cheek.

"I don't know what Nick knows," Carl said.

"What Nick knows about *what*?"

Carl tried to shake his head. "No. Nothing."

Joe moved the gun up toward Carl's temple and pushed it into his skull with a little more pressure. "Nothing? Are you *sure*?"

Carl didn't respond, the sweat dripping down his face, his breathing getting heavy.

"You obviously know whatever it was Craig did to your cousin. So either you were involved, or..." He thought for a moment. "Did you know Wendy Johnson?"

"Wendy?" He said it like he knew exactly who she was but then tried to take it back. "Who? Uh, no. Never heard the name."

Joe smiled and looked up at Bart. "What do you think? Sounds to me like Carl might've been involved in ripping off his cousin."

Carl shook his head. "No way! It wasn't me. I swear. I had nothing to do with it."

"But you just happen to know exactly what I'm talking about, and the other two people involved? And I'd say I'm almost certain that big mouth of yours is what got Scarlett killed." Joe reached for Carl's throat and squeezed it with his free hand, pressing the gun into the middle of his forehead. "Start talking now, or your brains'll be splattered all over Miami."

Bart looked into the back seat once more. "Hey, maybe you should take it easy, Joe."

But Joe kept his eyes on Carl, holding him by the throat. "I *said* you'd better start talking. I'll give you ten seconds, or this isn't going to end well."

"Okay! Okay!" Carl cried. "I'll talk. But, you have to promise me you won't go back to my cousin. He finds out I was involved, I'm..."

"Involved in *what*?" Joe said. "Start talking."

Carl took a deep breath. "Okay, so... it was me. *I* was the one, me and Wendy, I mean. We put the whole plan together to rip off Siskey Foods."

Joe stared back at him, somewhat but not completely surprised at the revelation. "I thought so," he said. "So it was you. The other person involved with Craig and Wendy."

"Well, like I said. It was really me and Wendy. At least at first. The thing about Craig is he wasn't even supposed to be involved. He only came in, almost by accident, when my friend Lionel got cold feet and bailed on us."

"Lionel?" Joe said.

Carl looked up at the gun over his eyes. "You mind moving that? It's hard to talk with a muzzle pressed into your skull."

Joe let up on the pressure, and eased the gun down, but kept it pointed at Carl. He repeated, "Who's Lionel?"

Carl rubbed the area on his head where the gun had been pressed. "Lionel was a friend. He used to run the route to the National Pancake House. It was the three of us when we first started. I was in the warehouse, Lionel doing deliveries, and Wendy, she was the manager at the restaurant."

"The National Pancake House?"

"Yeah," Carl said. "At least until she left to run that bar. She didn't have a choice. And she was afraid someone had figured out what we were doing."

"Nick?" Joe said.

Carl shook his head. "I don't think so. But, of course, it got back to him."

"And what was your role in all this? You worked at Siskey Foods too?"

"Yeah, in the warehouse, getting the trucks loaded. That's where I came up with the idea to start a little wholesale business on the side."

"What's that mean?" Joe said. "What'd you do, steal food from the truck, sell it to your own customers on the cheap?"

Carl shrugged. "Something like that."

"So, your cousin puts you in the warehouse, you load up the trucks and, what, deliver half to the customer who paid for it?"

"Not half. They'd notice if it was too much. So, National Pancake House'd get their delivery, but we'd hold back a portion of it that I'd sell to my own customers."

"And you did this all working from the warehouse? Your own cousin couldn't even give you a desk job?"

Carl laughed. "You kidding? Lucky Nick the Prick even gave me a job in the first place. You know that business was started by our family? Nick took over when our uncle died, kicked all the relatives out of the business and took it over for himself."

Bart looked over his shoulder. "No shit, huh?"

Carl said, "So, you know what? I took what I deserved. I don't even consider it stealing."

"So, what happened to Lionel?"

"I wish I knew. He disappeared. He might be dead, like the rest of 'em. I went into work one day, he wasn't there. Had the truck already loaded the way we'd been doing it. Then I find out Craig was taking over that route. He'd only been working there a few weeks, and at that point, I had no choice but to clue him in. I could only hope he'd be on board with putting a few extra bills in his pocket."

"Guess he was," Joe said, looking at Bart watching them in the rearview. "Your cousin really has no idea you were involved?"

Carl shook his head. "I don't work there anymore. And we haven't talked much since. But I'm afraid his goons are going to show up at my door any minute now. I was sure that's who you were."

Bart looked at Carl in the rearview. "So why haven't you gotten out of here? Disappear, before your cousin figures out you ripped him off?"

Carl shrugged. "That's a good question."

Chapter 26

JOE GOT LESS THAN a couple hours of sleep and woke up early, sending Lauren a text to make sure everything was all right for her and Dickie out at the farm where they were staying. He made himself a coffee waiting for her to reply.

He poured himself a mugful once it was ready, and his phone rang as he was about to take his first sip. He hurried over to pick it up off the counter, expecting it to be Lauren.

But it wasn't. It was Bart.

He answered, "Bart?"

"We've got a problem," Bart said, before Joe had said another word. "Officers from Miami-Dade PD were called to Carl Murphy's house last night, not long after we dropped him off. Neighbor called after hearing gunshots. The man's dead, Joe."

Joe placed his coffee down on the kitchen table. "Murphy? He's dead? Are you serious?"

Bart was quiet. "Dead serious. But that's not the problem," he said. "Somebody reported an older model, green Mercedes in the area late last night. They saw your car, Joe."

Joe stood silent and closed his eyes, shaking his head. "That's not good, Bart. You think they're looking for me?"

"Well, don't forget about me, Joe. I was with you. I was planning to make a call in, see if there's someone there I can talk to. But I thought about it, and we may want to meet with Woody as soon as we can."

"But you said it's Miami-*Dade* Police."

"You think just because he's City of Miami PD, he can't help us? He's in the middle of multiple murder investigations right here in the city. The sooner we let him know what we know, the faster he can coordinate with Miami-Dade and keep our asses out of the fire."

"Don't you know someone over there?" Joe said.

"Of course. But I don't think that's the best avenue right now. This is Woody's case."

Joe thought for a moment, finally taking a sip of coffee. "Here's the problem: Nick Juliano gets wind I went to the police... he gave me his warning, and he's the reason Lauren's out at that farm. I can't take the chance."

"You think it's better you sit around, wait for them to figure out it was your car? It could be today. It could be next week. But they'll show up at your door, Joe. I promise you that."

"They have my plate?" Joe said.

"I don't know. It doesn't sound like it. But, you know, a 1986 Mercedes, painted forest green, isn't a vehicle you see every day. That's why I'm telling you, it's only a matter of time they track you down. *Then* what? You lie to them? Tell them you weren't there? Nobody's gonna buy it."

Joe was about to take another sip of coffee but paused, holding it in front of his chin before placing the mug on the table again. The way his stomach felt, all tied up in knots, he wasn't sure he needed to drink it anyway. "Bart, what the hell are we supposed to do?"

"I just *told* you what to do. We go see Woody. Tell him what we know."

"I can't take that chance," Joe said, pulling the phone from his ear to look at the screen. "I've been trying to get in touch with Lauren, but she hasn't responded."

"You called her?"

"I sent a text."

"When was the last time you heard from her? Or Caldwell?"

"Not since they left. I would've called her if we hadn't spent the evening with our friend."

"Our *dead* friend," Bart said, the line going quiet.

Joe was thinking. "Christ, you know, I didn't really want to panic Dickie and Lauren, but I wish I'd mentioned for them to pay attention, make sure nobody followed them.

"I think you're being a little paranoid," Bart said.

Joe shook his head. "No, Bart. This guy Nick... look at the people he's killed."

"The people you think he's killed. We have no proof of anything, and until we do, nobody knows for sure it's him. That's why I'm saying you need to get law enforcement involved. This is beyond anything either of us are capable of dealing with. It'd be different if I still wore the badge."

Joe walked into the living room with his coffee and sat on the couch. He placed his mug on the table in front of him. He said, "I didn't actually tell you this yet, but last time I spoke to Woody, I told him I believed Juliano had something to do with Suzanne's death."

"You *told* him that?" Bart said. "Without any proof to back it up?"

Joe said, "Well, he didn't believe it then. And I'm not sure he's going to buy it now."

"It's not like Woody to just blow something off like that, not get a detective or two to at least look into it."

Joe looked out the glass door toward the Miami skyline beyond his balcony. "Woody defended Juliano, said he donates a lot of money to the city and the police department."

"Have you talked to him since?"

"Who, Woody?" Joe shook his head. "I told him I'd find a way to get him the proof he'd need. but I don't think he expected much from me."

"I hate to tell you this, Joe, but I'm not sure Woody's ready to look at you as anything more than a former journalist who can't keep himself out of situations you may not be qualified for. It's nothing personal, but he just feels you're overstepping your bounds, putting people in danger."

"Oh, believe me, I know how he feels," Joe said.

The line went quiet for a moment.

Bart said, "If you can hang tight, I'll see what I can find out."

"So what am I supposed to do now?" Joe said. "You expect me to just sit around and wait for you to call me back?"

"Well, you know, I was thinking." Bart paused on the other end. "Have you spoken to Juliano?"

"Not since our little meeting at that abandoned building."

Bart was quiet, then said, "What if I can get Woody to send you in to meet with Juliano."

"Get Woody to send me in to meet Juliano? I'm not following. Why would he—"

"How do you feel about wearing a wire?"

"A wire? Are you crazy? I'm not going to go meet Juliano wearing a wire. Besides, he's not going to say much. He didn't the first time. He never even told me why he was looking for Peters, and I don't think he planned to. On top of it, he has no idea what I know."

"I wouldn't be so sure," he said. "You think it's just a coincidence that bodies have shown up soon after you've been around the victims? Come on, Joe. You're not thinking with your head. Think about it; even the one-night stand with Peters' wife. She was killed within hours of being at your place. Same thing with Dickie's friend. She leaves your apartment... dead. Nick's own cousin is killed not more than a handful of hours after we left his house. You really want to believe this is all just a coincidence that has nothing to do with you?"

Joe thought about it, trying to work it through in his mind. "I didn't think about it like that. But then why would he hire me to find Peters?"

"I wish I had an answer, Joe. But he might know more about you than you'd like to admit. Maybe there's something more to this whole thing. Did you ever think of *that*?"

Joe thought about it some more, rubbing the back of his neck. "So, what would I do? I mean, wearing a wire. If he feels I'm up to something or suspects I'm trying to wrap him up in these murders, then there's no way he's going to talk."

"It could be worth a shot. Bringing him down alone, if that's your goal, isn't going to be as easy as it seems." Bart paused. "You know, I wish we'd recorded his cousin last night. I never thought he was going to sing the way he did. And now, we don't really have much proof of anything. It'll be a matter of getting someone to believe us."

Joe stood up from the couch. "You don't think Woody'll believe you?"

"Woody will," Bart said. "But I'm not sure about anyone else. That's why I still think Woody's our best chance, if he agrees to send you in there. So, are you good if I call him?"

"Call Woody?" Joe had to think about it. "Yeah, I guess so. But I'm not sure about wearing a wire, Bart. That's a little bit too much of a risk I'm not sure I can—"

"It's not like the old days," Bart said. "You can hide a recording device in your damn cufflink."

"I don't wear cufflinks," Joe said.

"Yeah, I know. I'm just saying…" The line went quiet again. "Let me feel Woody out. If I don't call you back, I'll come by your place within the hour."

· · · ● · ● ● · · ·

Joe stepped out of the shower when he heard his phone start ringing. He grabbed the towel and wiped his hands as dry as he could, water dripping off his body and hair as he stepped across the bathroom floor. He almost slipped, reaching for the phone next to the sink, checking the screen.

It was Lauren.

"Lauren?" he said. "How's it going out there? Is everything all right?"

"I guess so. I just woke up. I didn't sleep much at all, expecting you to call me when you got back from whoever it was you said you were going to see."

"I'm sorry," Joe said. "I was with Bart. Didn't you see my text?"

"Not until a little while ago. I had my ringer turned down."

"How's the house? Everything okay so far?"

Lauren took a moment before she answered. "Joe, how long do we have to be here? This place isn't exactly a five-star hotel. It's old. And it's kind of dirty here. There's not even any WiFi, and the mattress I slept on's probably thirty years old. I almost went and slept in Dickie's car."

"You have your own room at least? I hope?"

"No, Dickie and I slept in the same bed."

"Are you kidding?"

Lauren let out a small laugh. "Of course I'm kidding. Be serious, Joe. You really think I'd sleep in a bed with Dickie?"

"I'm sorry," he said, rubbing his head of wet hair with the towel in his free hand. "Where *is* he?"

"Out talking to his friend. He snores so loud, Joe. I don't think I can do this for another night."

"Dickie snores, huh?" He huffed out a slight laugh. "Well, hopefully it'll be over soon. It's just best that you stay where you are for now."

Lauren was quiet on the other end. "Are you ever going to be straight with me... and tell me why you're involved in all of this, Joe? I still... I just don't get why you couldn't have just stayed out of it."

Joe knew she was right but wasn't going to admit it. Not right then. "It's too late for that." He went on and told her about Carl Murphy, and the fact he was killed hours after they dropped him off. "Bart seems to think there's more of a connection to me than I realize. But I'm not sure that's the case, although there's no doubt Nick Juliano's behind all of it. Now all we have to do is find a way to prove it."

"You need to be careful," Lauren said. "Actually, what I'd like you to do is... Can you do me a favor? Can you promise me this is it with whatever it is you think you're doing? Maybe you could just get back to your writing... finish the book for once, and leave all this tough-guy, heroic crap for someone else?"

Joe pressed the phone against his ear, wrapping the towel around his waist. "I think that sounds like a good idea." He walked into his bedroom and pulled out a pair of pants, sitting on the bed and trying to pull them on with one hand. He looked toward the hallway when there was a knock at his door. "Someone's at my door," he said, looking at the time on his phone. "It's not even six thirty."

"You want to call me back?"

"Yeah, give me a few minutes." He ended the call and put the phone down on the bed, standing up to button his pants and slip on a T-shirt. He walked down the hall and wondered where he'd left his gun.

Whoever was on the other side of the door knocked again.

Joe looked out through the peephole at two police officers, he knew from their uniforms were with Miami-Dade. He thought maybe he shouldn't open the door but knew there was a chance they'd likely wait for him, knowing he was home.

He decided not to play games and removed the chain, turning the locks on the door. He cleared his throat as he pulled it open. "Hello, Officers? Is everything all right?"

The taller and older of the two spoke first. "Joe Sheldon?"

Joe forced a grin. "That's me."

"Would you mind if we came in?"

"Would I mind?" He thought about his gun, and remembered he'd left it out on the table. It was legal and registered at that point, but he still didn't like the idea of two officers walking in seeing it out in the open. "Forgive me for asking, but, uh, do you happen to have a warrant?"

The older of the two shifted his stance, his hand on his belt near a holstered gun. "We'd like to ask you some questions about an incident that occurred early this morning, a couple of hours ago out in Pinewood."

Joe said, "It sounds to me you're saying you don't have a warrant?"

The cop said, "There is no need for a warrant at this time. Again, we are simply here to ask a couple of questions."

"Okay, maybe we can do it like this, right here in the doorway, if that works for you?"

The two officers exchanged a look, and the older one said, "We were down in the parking garage below your building looking your car over. A vehicle very similar to yours—a 1986 Mercedes 560, convertible, with forest-green exterior—was spotted by a witness who said it was parked in front of a home at 151 Little River Drive, in Pinewood."

Joe tried to hide his swallow. "Uh, okay. What's that mean? I'm sure there are plenty of forest-green Mercedes 560s in the area. No?"

The officer shook his head. "Actually, there is only one other forest-green Mercedes in Florida. It belongs to a retired judge up in Jacksonville."

Joe pulled at his chin. "Um, well"—he shrugged—"you know, on second thought, I think I'm going to pass on answering any questions. In fact, how about I come down in a couple of hours? I could do that, but I'd like to consult my attorney before I say anything else."

"Sir, there's a chance we'll return with a warrant before that time, so it may be—"

"A warrant for what? My arrest?"

The younger of the two officers, who hadn't said a word, finally spoke up. "Mr. Sheldon, we may have the right to search your car, downstairs in your garage. I hope you understand."

Joe wasn't sure what to say. He didn't want them in the apartment. But he didn't think there was anything in the car they could use against him, either. Sure, Carl Murphy had been in the back seat. But Joe didn't kill him. "Why don't you go ahead down there. I'll even give you the key as long as you bring it back. In the meantime, I guess I'll call my attorney."

Chapter 27

JOE STEPPED FROM THE sidewalk into Bart's car, brushing his hand through the air as he slid onto the passenger seat, clearing the smoke from Bart's cigarette. "I thought you quit?"

Bart took his foot off the brake and hit the gas, heading west toward First. "Not this week," he said. He flicked the cigarette out the window. "Woody's waiting," he said. "Miami-Dade's agreed to back off, but only for twenty-four hours. So we won't have much time." He looked ahead, turning right onto Fifth. "I know Officer Barker."

"Barker? Who's he, the older one?"

Bart nodded. "He's two months from retiring, and said you were cooperative and respectful, other than refusing to answer any questions." He gave Joe a quick glance. "He said you handed him your keys, let 'em take the Mercedes?"

Joe shook his head. "I didn't think they'd tow it."

Bart had his eyes on the street. "All they're going to do is run the fingerprints, which obviously isn't a good thing for me. I didn't tell him the whole story yet, for obvious reasons." He turned down Second and into the visitor parking lot across the street from the station. "The thing is, if we can't get Woody to buy into this plan, we're both going to be in deep shit." He turned off the engine and stepped out from the car. "But don't worry. I won't send you down the river by yourself."

Joe looked at Bart across the roof. "I appreciate what you're saying. But I'm not sure it makes any sense for you to admit you were with me over at Murphy's, does it?"

Bart leaned on his cane. "My prints are all over your car. I drove it. They're on your steering wheel."

Joe crossed the street ahead of Bart. "They have your fingerprints?"

"Of course. They're in a database. Everyone has them: the FBI, State Bureau of Investigations, Miami-Dade PD... who knows where else. So, yeah, even if I wanted to leave you to deal with this mess yourself, I couldn't."

They walked into the station through the main entrance, across the brick-colored tile floor, and stopped at the desk. The officer behind it looked so young, Joe wondered how he could be old enough to wear the uniform.

Bart stepped up to the young man. "Good morning. We're here for Sgt. Woody Thomas."

The officer picked up the phone but held it in his hand before pressing any buttons. "Is he expecting you?"

"Of course. Yes. Just tell him it's Bart. Bart Holden."

The young officer looked up from the phone at Bart. "Bart Holden? Are you related to Officer Bart Holden, with Miami-Dade PD?"

"Related?" Bart nodded. "Yeah, that's me."

The young officer smiled. "My dad was an officer with Miami-Dade."

"Yeah?" Bart had a crooked grin on his face. "Who's your dad?"

"Officer Carlson. Retired."

"Eddie Carlson? He's your dad?" Bart had an excited look on his face.

The young man nodded, looking at Bart like he'd met a celebrity. "He used to talk about you all the time." He dialed the phone and put it up to his ear. He said into the phone, "Please tell Sergeant Thomas that Officer Bart Holden is down here in the lobby." He paused, nodding as he listened to whoever was on the other end. "Yes, sir. Will do. I'll send him right up." He pointed toward the elevators as he hung up the phone. "He'll meet on the fourth floor, so you can go ahead and head up?"

Bart reached out and shook the kid's hand. "Tell your dad I said hello. Maybe I'll give him a call sometime; we can grab a beer." He started for the elevator and looked back at the young officer, then leaned toward Joe with his voice low. "What a real prick his old man was."

• • • • • • • • • • •

The door slid open as Joe leaned against the rail across the back of the elevator, waiting for Bart to step off ahead of him. Bart's limp seemed to be more pronounced than it was the day before, and Joe wondered if it would ever get better, or if the damage had been done.

He stepped off and followed as Bart turned right and continued down a short hall ahead of him. They were about to turn when Woody came around the corner in front of them.

He had a folder in his hand and his eyes went to Bart's leg. "How's it doing?"

Bart shrugged. "It doesn't get better, I think I might just take a chainsaw to it myself."

Woody huffed out a small laugh. "I'm sure it's better than it was, no?" He continued ahead and pointed in the direction he was headed. "This way." They walked past the elevator and down another hall until Woody stopped outside an open door. "We thought we had a lead on Craig Peters, but it turned out to be a dead end." He gestured for Joe and Bart to walk through the doorway. "Have a seat in there. I'll go get Officer Harper."

Joe glanced at Bart, wondering if he knew who Officer Harper was, but didn't ask. The room was bigger than an office but not by much, with wood paneling on the walls and white vinyl tiles on the floor. There was a bookshelf against the back wall and a round table in the middle of the room with four chairs around it. A laptop sat on the table with devices around it that looked like thumb drives, to Joe, but he wasn't sure if that's what they were.

Joe said to Bart, "You didn't mention to Woody about me wearing a wire, did you?"

Bart sat down in one of the chairs, hanging the hook of his cane on the edge of the table. He got himself comfortable, then looked up at Joe. "I might've mentioned it to him."

"I didn't say I'd do it," Joe said.

"Relax, Sunshine, will you? We're just going to talk. Your other option is to go talk with the boys over at Miami-Dade. I can promise you they won't be as accommodating as Sergeant Thomas."

Joe turned to the door as Woody walked into the room with another uniformed officer behind him.

Woody said, "Joe, Bart, this is Officer Gary Harper. He's recently taken over a new program in the department. He manages covert surveillance for us." Woody introduced Joe as someone who'd been in and out of the station over the years as a crime reporter for the *Miami Post*. "And Bart's a retired officer with Miami-Dade."

Joe sat down next to Bart and looked over the items on the table. He looked up at Woody. "I don't know what Bart told you I was willing to do, but I'm not sure I'm comfortable with this."

"With *what?*" Woody said.

"Wearing a wire."

Woody sat down at the table, across from Joe and Bart. "The truth is, I don't know how long I can hold off Miami-Dade. I'm actually surprised I even got the go-ahead to pursue Nick Juliano this way, simply based on everything Bart told me." He looked Joe right in the eye. "The fact is, we need your cooperation. Otherwise, I can't make you any promises. Those Miami-Dade officers are foaming at the mouth right now, with no other suspects they can link to Carl Murphy's murder." He shifted his eyes to Bart. "As I told you, you're in the same position. So unless the two of you want to wait this out, see how out of hand it can get, I'm willing to put my neck on the line for you. But you'll have to do your part to help me."

Joe looked up at Officer Harper, standing over the table, thought for a moment, then finally nodded in agreement.

Woody looked at the devices on the table. "How about we let Officer Harper explain how some of these things work."

Harper opened the lid on the laptop, walked across the room, and turned to the three at the table. He held up what looked to be nothing more than a silver metal pen. "Click the top, like this." He clicked the button and placed it on the floor in the corner. "Now, take a look at that laptop. You can see the frequency levels. I just want to show you how sensitive this is."

"That's a recording device?" Joe said, looking at the so-called pen a good ten feet away from where they were sitting.

Officer Harper nodded. "It's one of many options. We don't use wires anymore. That pen, as you'll see, looking at the screen, can pick up voices from forty-five feet away."

Joe and Bart both looked at the screen, the bars jumping up and down as the officer spoke.

"If you have it in your pocket, I'm comfortable with twenty feet of space. Any more, and you may not pick up the entire conversation.

"So I'm going to have a pen in my pocket? What if they search me and take it?"

The officer nodded, walked to the table, and opened a small black box. Inside was a brown button, like the one he had on his uniform. He removed it from the box and handed it to Joe. "Your max distance is going to be ten feet with this one. The risk is, you may not be close enough, especially if someone paces back and forth, or has his back to you."

Joe looked over the device. "What would I do, sew this on my shirt?"

Officer Harper smiled, shaking his head as he looked at Woody, then Joe. "We'll take care of that part. We'd like you to have both devices on you at the same time, in case one fails for some reason."

"Why would one fail?" Joe said, although he knew, of course, there could be a number of reasons.

Harper said, "Well, let's say, for instance, the button gets wet."

"Oh," Joe said, handing the button back to Harper. He looked from Woody to Bart, and back at Woody. "What if I can't get anything out of Juliano?"

"It would be a good idea you do all you can to make sure he talks. We'll discuss some ways to do that," Woody said.

"I'm pretty good at getting people to talk. It's how I've made my living for the last twenty-something years."

Woody nodded with a small grin. "I'm heading over to Miami-Dade headquarters within the hour, bringing the files, and making sure we can all get on the same page. They pulled Bart's fingerprints from your car, so now they want to talk to him. But I'm doing what I can to hold them off, trying to assure them we have a strong lead here. Besides, a cracked-out neighbor seeing a vehicle outside a home isn't exactly what anyone would consider solid evidence. But the fact is, Joe, we'd really like your help."

Joe looked down toward the floor, thinking. After a moment, he looked over at Woody. "But you didn't believe me Juliano was involved the first time I told you. Why now?"

Woody shrugged. "Don't take this personally, Joe. But I only know you from the trouble you somchow get yourself wrapped up in. I've known Bart for almost thirty years. His word is as good as anyone's."

Joe turned to Bart, who was staring back at him. He sat quiet for a good half minute and looked over the high-tech devices in front of him. There was something about it he didn't like. But, on the other hand, he saw it as a unique chance to play around like he was

James Bond, maybe even bring down a man nobody suspected could be guilty of murder.

Chapter 28

Joe drove past the Siskey Foods building and continued down Northwest 125th. He passed the cargo van parked on the street with South Beach Cleaning Services painted on the side, knowing there were four officers inside with the Miami Police. The only windows on the van were on the driver's and passenger side doors, although the glass was tinted enough it was hard to see inside. He looked in the rearview at the windshield as soon as he'd passed it and could see Officer Harper behind the wheel. The other officer, one Joe had met only briefly, was in the passenger seat to Harper's right.

Woody wasn't supposed to be inside the surveillance van, but Joe also didn't know where he'd be. And although Woody made Bart promise he'd stay clear of the entire area, Joe had a feeling he was around somewhere. He just didn't know where.

Joe glanced down at the listening device in the shape of a button, attached to his shirt. He played with it, adjusting it with his fingers, and trying to remember the last time he wore a button-down shirt with long sleeves. It made him somewhat uncomfortable, like he was going to work at the office. As he continued toward the building, he thought about Lauren, wishing he could've told her what he was about to do. But he didn't want to hear it, listen to her freak out and tell him he was putting his life on the line for a crime she believed was none of his business.

He could hear her voice. And he knew she was right. *Too late to turn back now.*

Joe cut the wheel and turned toward the closed gate, facing the parking lot of the abandoned building where he'd first met Nick Juliano face-to-face, just a couple of days earlier.

A thick chain hung from the gate and wrapped around the posts with a heavy lock keeping it closed. A sign Joe hadn't noticed the first time he was there hung on the gate: Private, Do Not Enter. He looked through the chain-link fencing toward the building as he picked up his phone and dialed the number he was told to call when he arrived.

Joe knew it was Tony—the older of Nick's two goons—who answered the phone on the first ring.

"Yeah?" Tony said.

"I'm out front."

"Yeah, no shit. I see you. Wait there." Tony hung up.

Joe watched the building, looking around toward the sides and into the back lot as far as he could see. He studied the front entrance, the large door at the top of the stone-faced steps. There was a sign on the door, but Joe couldn't quite make out what it said.

The sky had darkened in just a few short minutes since he'd arrived, the sun covered over by thickening clouds. In a matter of seconds, rain started to spit on the windshield, then quickly picked up as heavy drops pounded against the surface. The hard rain tapped on the roof, slowly at first, then to a point where it was coming down so fast and loud, it made it hard for Joe to hear himself think.

He looked up toward the building, expecting Tony to come out. But it was Bobby, the younger and dumber sidekick, with a jacket draped over his shoulders, his back hunched to keep it from falling off.

Bobby hurried toward Joe's car, walking with long steps through the pouring rain. He didn't look at Joe through the fencing but removed the lock from the chain and swung the gate in toward the parking lot. He gave Joe a nod, gesturing for him to drive forward.

Joe kept his window up and grinned at Bobby as he drove slowly past him, continuing along the side and around to the back behind the building. He pulled into a space with faded white lines and parked next to the black Chevy Malibu. Nick Juliano's white BMW was parked a few spaces away, on the other side of the Malibu.

The door on the back of the building opened, and Tony stood holding it open, exposing his arm to the rain. "Hurry up, will ya?"

Joe stepped out of the Mercedes and ran toward the back door. He was soaked in the two seconds it took him to get to Tony. He stepped past him and started inside.

But Tony grabbed him by the arm and stopped him. "Slow down, Cowboy. Arms up."

Joe raised his arms, and Tony patted him down, feeling his pockets, then crouching down, moving his hands up from around Joe's ankles and around his calves, then up and inside Joe's thighs.

"You like touching me like that?" Joe said.

Tony straightened out and looked Joe in the eye, getting right up in his face. He pointed with his finger an inch from Joe's nose. "Watch yourself." He reached into Joe's pockets and pulled out the pen with the tiny microphone. "Nice pen," he said, looking it over. He twisted the top and the tip of the ink poked out the bottom, then twisted the top again to close it. "I think I'll keep it," he said, dropping it in his suit jacket's pocket.

Joe's heart started to race, but he didn't say a word about asking for it back. He thought maybe it wouldn't be so bad, having it in Tony's pocket... as long as Tony didn't figure out what it was.

Tony made a motion with his fingers, palm up. "Come on, lift up your shirt."

Joe untucked his shirt and lifted it up as far as it would go, then turned around to show that he wasn't wearing a wire.

Tony stepped around him, looking him over, and nodded for Joe to let it down. "This way." He walked down the hall ahead of Joe, turning through the doorway into the big open space with the high ceiling.

Nick was seated behind the big desk in the oversized leather chair with a glass and a bottle of liquor in front of him.

Tony said, "He's clean."

Joe stepped toward the desk and stood across from Nick.

Neither man extended a hand.

"Have a seat," Nick said, pouring a glass of what Joe saw was a brand of Scotch he'd never heard of before.

"I love what you've done with the place," Joe said, sitting in one of the two chairs, looking around the room. It was still dirty, and Joe couldn't figure out why the guy was using the place as his personal office space, other than to maybe keep the shady side of his business away from Siskey Foods, less than a block away.

A door slammed from down the hall, and Bobby walked in a moment later, soaked from head to toe from the downpour.

"Jesus Christ," Nick said, looking him over. "How many times I gotta tell you not to slam that goddamn door?"

Bobby nodded, running his hand over his face in an effort to wipe away the water. "Sorry, Nick. I just—"

"Shut your mouth," Nick snapped. "Look at the water you're getting all over the floor!" He shook his head, turning to Joe. "Can't find decent help nowadays, you know what I'm saying?" He picked up his glass and shot back what was inside. "You want a drink?" he said. He turned to Tony and Bobby at the doorway. "One of you get him a glass, will you?"

Tony turned with a nod and disappeared down the hall without a word.

Nick pushed his glass to one side and the bottle of Scotch to the other, leaning forward with his hands folded together in front of him. "So," he said. "What's so important you needed to discuss with me?"

Joe looked over at Bobby, soaking wet and watching him from the doorway, then glanced down at the button on his shirt. There was water all over it, and all he could remember was Officer Harper telling him not to get it wet.

And now the backup, the pen, was somewhere else in the building inside Tony's pocket.

Joe said, "Well, the truth is, you haven't given me enough time to find Peters. And, to be honest, I'm not sure it's even enough money at this point."

Nick raised his eyebrows and cocked his head back. "Are you telling me you can't do the job?" He looked over toward the doorway. "Bobby, you believe this guy?"

"The truth is," Joe said, "I feel like you haven't been honest with me."

"I haven't been honest with you?" Nick leaned back in his chair. "What the hell is *that* supposed to mean?"

"Well," Joe said, adjusting his shirt. "You didn't tell me why you were after Craig. And, I guess I'd like to know why?"

Nick stared back at Joe, his eyes narrowed. "I thought this was your thing. You track people down. No? And now, you come in here because you need to know why I hired you to do a job?" He laughed, looking at Bobby. "Bobby, you ever in your life ask me why I needed you to do something?"

Bobby shook his head. "No, Nick. Never."

Nick turned to Joe, pointing toward Bobby with his thumb. "You see? Bobby doesn't ask me any questions. Tony never asks. I tell them 'Hey, I need you to do this or that.' Nobody asks me *why*." He poured another shot of Scotch into his glass. "So, if you want to know why... then I gotta ask you why it would matter. Will it help you find him?" He shook his head. "I don't think it makes a difference."

Joe cleared his throat, shaking his head. "Actually, it might've made things a little easier if you'd been straight with me."

Nick said, "You don't think I've been straight with you, eh? Well, let me tell you something about—"

Tony walked into the room with a glass in his hand, but Joe noticed he was no longer wearing the suit jacket. He had the sleeves rolled up on his white buttoned shirt as he placed the glass on the desk.

Nick grabbed it and poured a drink, pushing it across the desk toward Joe. "I think you need a drink." He looked at Joe, like he was studying him. "Everything all right with you? You look to me like you're a little nervous." He looked over at Tony and Bobby. "He look nervous to you?" He leaned back in his chair. "I thought you were supposed to be Joe Cool, no? What's the matter? Too much pressure for you?" He poured himself another drink, took a sip and rested the glass on the desk.

Joe said, "Why won't you just tell me what happened to Craig?"

Nick didn't answer.

Joe had hoped it would've been easier to get him to start talking, but he wasn't having much luck. He shifted in his seat, thinking. "All right, you don't want to tell me? Then how about I tell you what *I* know?"

Nick just stared back at him, waiting.

"I know the whole story," Joe said. "I know you're afraid word gets out Craig and your cousin ripped you off, it's all going to come out you took the law into your own hands, killing everyone who either crossed you or got in the way. I know you killed Craig's wife. I know you killed Scarlet... *and* your own cousin. The only one you haven't gotten yet is Craig. And, for some reason, you want me to find him."

Nick had a grin on his face and started to laugh. "You're a joke," he said. "You think you're a tough guy? You think, what, like you're some kind of Miami detective?" He looked over at Tony and Bobby. "You believe this guy? Sleeps with Craigs' wife, doesn't even think for a second he's the reason she's dead?"

Joe wouldn't believe it. He watched Nick, following him as he got up and walked around to the front of the desk and leaned back right in front of Joe, facing him.

He nodded toward Tony and Bobby. "Go tell him he can come out now. We'll all have a good laugh."

Tony elbowed Bobby who turned into the hallway.

Joe looked from Nick to Tony, both with big grins on their faces.

"You're a fool," Nick said.

Joe tried to get up from the chair, but Nick glanced over at Tony and gave him a nod.

Tony pulled a gun from inside his pants and walked toward Joe, sticking the gun in his face.

"You want to know why you couldn't find Craig?" Nick said.

Joe's eyes went from the gun's muzzle to Nick, trying to piece together what was about to happen. He had a feeling between the wet button and Tony's jacket somewhere else in the building, there was a chance he'd lost communication with the officers outside.

Nick walked over to the doorway, past Tony, and disappeared around the corner. Ten seconds later he walked back into the room. But he stopped, smiling at Joe, and looked through the doorway behind him.

Craig Peters stepped out from around the corner behind Nick, looking back at Joe with a smirk. "Found me!" He laughed, along with Nick and the two goons standing next to them.

Joe swallowed hard, wondering if anything had been said that was enough to get the police waiting outside to make a move. "What the hell's going on here?" He looked at Craig. "What are you doing here?"

Nick put his hand on Craig's shoulder. "Well, we've come to an agreement."

Joe looked from one to the other but didn't respond. "He doesn't have any idea where your money is, if that's what he's promised you."

Nick gave Craig a nod. "You want to tell him the rest of our deal?"

Craig nodded and said to Joe, "I get to kill you myself. Right here. Today." He laughed, removing a gun from his pants.

He turned to Nick. "He doesn't know where the money is. He's lying to you."

Nick looked at Craig and held his gaze, turning back to Joe. "You had no idea Craig and I go back a long ways?"

Joe was confused. Nothing was making sense. "What do you mean you go back a long way?"

"I don't know how long it's been. Maybe twenty years? When he came to me, told me Wendy and Lionel and my own cousin were ripping off my company and one of my best customers, well, I have to say... most people would take the money and run."

"What?" Joe said. "Then... you mean he's been involved with you this whole time?"

Nick grinned. "Took you long enough," he said.

Joe looked past the men and into the hall, wondering how much longer until someone was going to come through the door, although if the police weren't able to hear anything, he knew he'd be in trouble.

He said to Nick, "Why did you want to hire me to find Craig? I don't get it."

"That was kind of a last-minute thing when I had Tony and Bobby bring you in. I knew you'd never find him. Not unless you looked for him at my house, where he's been staying."

"But, then..."

"I knew it'd keep you busy until I figured out what to do with you. And it seemed to work for a short time. I mean, I was hoping I could avoid having to kill you. I know you're friends with that retired cop with the bum leg."

"But you had no problem killing everyone else?" Joe played with the button on his shirt, hoping it worked.

Nick smiled. "Sometimes you just have to clean up the mess." He pointed with his thumb at Craig. "But his wife, and the kid across the hall..." Nick put his hands up. "Out of my hands. And, well, Craig can be a bit of the jealous type."

Joe tried to adjust the button, wondering if the rain had stopped it from working. Or if Nick and Craig were even close enough to transmit what was being said.

"Everything all right?" Nick said, stepping toward him. His hand was behind his back but he brought it around, holding a gun. "What's up with your button, Joe? You keep playing with it, like you're a little nervous about something." He stepped up to him and reached out and pulled open Joe's shirt. He yanked at the button. "Jesus Christ," he said, finally ripping it from Joe's shirt, studying it, holding it close to his eyes. "He's wearing a goddamn wire!"

There was a loud explosion-like bang and the sound of a door being busted open. Dozens of footsteps and yelling followed.

Nick grabbed Joe, wrapping his arm around his neck with the gun up to his head, dragging him across to the other side of the room away from the doorway.

Craig and the other two started to run in the other direction out of the room, but Craig slipped in the puddle from where Bobby had stood, dripping from the rain. His feet came out from under him, and he smacked his head on the edge of the doorway on the way down to the floor. His body was still, his eyes closed.

Another crash sounded, and yelling could be heard from somewhere toward the front of the building. A cop yelled, "Drop your weapons!"

Gunshots followed and stopped after three or four were fired.

Nick had Joe in his grasp and whispered in his ear, "Make any stupid moves, and I'll put a bullet right through that thick skull of yours."

Police officers in tactical gear turned the corner, guns raised toward Nick and Joe. "Drop your weapon!" one of them yelled.

Nick shook his head. "You drop *your* weapon, unless you want this fool's blood on your hands. You're the clowns who sent your amateur guinea pig in here in the first place. It'll be on your hands if he has to die because of your stupidity." He dragged Joe toward another door not far behind them, taking his gun away from Joe's head to turn the knob and open it.

But that split second gave Joe his chance, and he used his feet to thrust himself backward, sending Nick into the door, slamming it closed.

The gun in Nick's hand fired, and Joe ducked, dropping down to the floor out of the way to give the police a clean shot at Nick. He covered his head with his hands and stayed down.

Two shots fired, and Joe took a peek up at Nick holding out his gun, firing back at the cops. He got off two more shots before he was hit, stumbling back as he shot again, but this time into the air toward the ceiling. His body collapsed on the floor next to Joe, clutching the gun in his hand.

Joe wanted to grab it but thought it'd be better he lie still, not wanting the officers to be confused or too jacked up to think straight if Joe got up with a gun in his hand. He kept his hands where the cops would see he wasn't armed and slowly got up to his feet.

The officers charged toward him, grabbing Joe by the arm and pulling him away from Nick's bloodied body.

Joe looked over and saw Craig facedown, out cold, but still being handcuffed. The officers lifted him to his feet, and someone else grabbed his arm, pulling him toward the door.

It was Woody, pushing him toward another officer. "Get him out of here."

Chapter 29

The sun had started to break through the clouds, reflecting off the wet asphalt as Joe stood by his car, watching Bart walk toward him without his cane, although the limp was still there.

"Sorry I wasn't there," Bart said. "Woody said he'd have to arrest me if I interfered." He pointed over his shoulder. "I was right over there, had the Mossberg in the trunk just in case."

The two looked at the officers leading Nick and his gang out of the building and into the backs of cars. "You know, I didn't get to hear a whole lot about what was going on in there, but it looks to me you pulled it off." He waved over at Craig Peters being put in the back of one of the Miami Police cruisers. "I still would've liked to've gotten the son of a bitch back. At least shoot him in the leg."

Joe laughed. "Well, now we don't have to worry about either one of us spending any time in jail."

Bart nodded, looking across the parking lot toward the front of the building. "You want to grab a drink?"

Joe took a deep breath and let out a sigh. "I think I could use one. Although there's a bottle of Scotch inside, maybe we can grab."

"Scotch, huh?" He shook his head. "Nah, not my thing."

Joe looked at his watch. "I need to call Lauren, let her and Dickie know it's over."

"Then what are you waiting for?"

Joe thought for a second, then opened his car door and grabbed his phone. He said to Bart, "Would you take it personally if I said I'd rather go get Lauren?"

Bart laughed, shaking his head. "I'd call you an idiot if you *didn't* go get her." He turned and started around the building. "Call me when you want to grab that drink. I just hope it's not six months from now."

Joe grinned, watching Bart walk away toward Woody and the other officers parked along the side of the building. He dialed his phone, and Lauren answered on the first ring.

"Joe?"

"Yeah, everything's good," he said. "It's all over."

• • • ● • ● • ● • •

Joe was at his kitchen table, had Jimmy McGriff's "The Worm" playing on his turntable, up louder than he normally played his music, as his fingers moved fast on his laptop, trying to keep up with the story coming out of his head. He stopped, mid-sentence, when his

297

phone rang. It broke his train of thought, but Lauren had told him to expect an important call.

He grabbed his phone and hurried over to the turntable and lowered the volume before he answered. He took a quick glance at the number on the phone but didn't recognize it. "Hello?"

The voice on the other end was a woman's. "Is this Joe Sheldon?"

"It is. Who's this?"

"My name's Maureen. Maureen Carter. Lauren Reed gave me your name and number, although I'm already familiar with your work."

"My work?" Joe said, wondering why Lauren didn't want to tell him who the woman was that would be calling.

"Well, your work for the *Post*. But, I've also read your fiction. At least what you have so far."

"Oh," Joe said, completely caught off guard. "Lauren gave it to you?"

"She did. And I'd like to meet with you to discuss it."

Joe smiled but wasn't going to get too excited yet. He'd been down this road before.

"Are you a publisher?"

"I'm an agent," she said. "But I already have a publisher lined up, if you're interested."

"Interested?" he said, walking back to the table to grab his drink. He took a sip to kill the dryness in his throat. He still wasn't sure it was a good idea to drink booze while he wrote, but it seemed to work all right. "Of course, yeah, I'm interested. Can you tell me anything else?"

"I'd like to meet to get into the details, maybe discuss a series. I have a publisher who may be willing to go with three, to get started."

"Three what—books?" Joe said, walking toward the balcony with the phone in on hand, his drink in the other. He opened the glass door and stepped out onto the balcony, where it had to be at least ninety degrees, but Joe didn't mind it.

"They'd give you an advance on a three-book contract. Like I said, if we can meet..."

Joe looked at his watch. "Yeah, I can meet. Tell me when and where and I'll be there."

· · ● ●· ● ● ● · ·

It was a little before nine when Joe heard the knock at the door. He got up from the couch, still dressed nice in a shirt and tie after his meeting with Maureen Carter, his new agent.

He looked through the peephole at Lauren waiting out in the hall, then turned the lock and let her in.

Lauren stepped inside and handed him a bottle of champagne. "Congratulations," she said, leaning into him with a kiss.

"I'm still in shock," he said. "I don't know how to thank you." He took the bottle from her and placed it on a small table near the door, then reached for her with a hug. "Thank you."

"You don't have to thank me," she said. "I'm just happy; maybe I won't have to worry about you as much."

They held each other for another moment, then he let go. "What's that supposed to mean?"

"Well, you have a book deal. Now all you have to do is *finish* the books, and you won't have to do any more of this extracurricular activity you keep getting yourself wrapped up in."

Joe looked at her, nodding, then turned and grabbed the bottle, taking it into the kitchen. He pulled down two regular glasses—he'd broken the only two champagne glasses he owned—and popped the cork on the bottle. He poured the champagne into the glasses and handed one to Lauren, raising the other in a toast.

He sipped from the glass, being quiet.

"What's wrong?" she said.

Joe knew it wasn't going to go over well, what he was about to tell her. But he knew he had to tell her the truth. "Well," he said, "the only reason I was able to write that story is because of the work I'd been doing with Dickie. I mean, all this stuff, everything I've been involved in... it's the only reason I was able to write again. I can't just sit here, waiting for an idea. I need to feed it. Does that make sense?"

Lauren held the glass up in front of her and took a sip, staring back at him over the glass. She placed it down on the counter. "Are you trying to tell me you're going to continue working with Dickie?"

Joe shrugged. "I don't know yet. Maybe not with Dickie, but... me and Bart were talking..."

"Oh, Joe. Please tell me you're not serious. You can't—"

"Like I said, I can't sit around and just write all day. I need to be out there, doing what helps me come up with fresh stuff. If the well runs dry..."

Lauren shook her head, like she was trying to shake something loose. She put her hand on her forehead. "Joe, I put my neck on the line for you. Maureen's a friend, but—"

"I'm going to write the books. Don't worry about that part. But... I don't know. I like the action too. I think I *need* it. Like I said, it helps me."

Lauren rolled her eyes, and Joe put his glass down on the table next to hers and reached out, pulling her toward him. He said, "Can't we just celebrate tonight? And have a good time?"

She took a moment before she finally put her arms up around him, resting her head against his shoulder. "I don't like it, Joe. I thought you would have—"

Joe's phone, on the counter behind them, started buzzing. He glanced down at the screen and saw it was Bart calling. He paused, about to answer, but reached out and flipped it over and ended the call.

· · · · ● · ● · ● · · ·

Thank you for reading *Play It Down*. If you have a minute, an honest review on the store where you made your purchase makes a real difference for an author. Even a line or two helps other readers find the series.

Stay up to date on all the latest releases by joining my newsletter at <u>GregoryPayette.com</u>. You'll receive three free stories just for signing up.

Ready for a new thrilling adventure? *Shake the Trees* is the first book in the new U.S. Marshal Charlie Harlow series.

Visit GregoryPayette.com to find out more.

Visit GregoryPayette.com for all books, stories, and art

We're Not Down (July 2026)
The Hard Ground (Fall 2026)

JAKE HORN MYSTERIES
A Ring and a Prayer (Series prequel)
A Good Time for Goodbye
The Silence of the Sand
When the Smoke Clears

U.S. MARSHAL CHARLIE HARLOW
Shake the Trees
Trackdown
Half Moon Rising

HENRY WALSH MYSTERIES
Dead at Third
The Last Ride
The Crystal Pelican
The Night the Music Died
Dead Men Don't Smile
Dead in the Creek
Dropped Dead
Dead Luck
A Shot in the Dark
Dead or a Lie

JOE SHELDON MIAMI CRIME SERIES
Play It Cool
Play It Again
Play It Down

STANDALONES
Bicayne Boogie

GREGORY PAYETTE

Drag the Man Down
Half Cocked
Danny's Womack's .38

www.ingramcontent.com/pod-product-compliance
Lightning Source LLC
Chambersburg PA
CBHW021234310726
48971CB00006B/1811